W9-CTO-527

ELENA

a novel

By Keith Adams

Copyright © 2016 Keith Adams
Printed in the United States of America by CreateSpace
ISBN-13:978-1535555586
ISBN-10:1535555580
Cover Design and Formatting by Heather Desuta

For my mother, may she dance in heaven.

CHAPTER ONE

The ache for home lives in all of us.
–Maya Angelou

Elena Shaughnessy blew a kiss at her mother's photo and opened the kitchen door. A pair of mourning doves darted skyward from the deck railing, their whistling wings accompanying their melancholy song. The screen door yawned and clapped shut.

She started toward the stairs, hoping that a walk through town would clear her mind after a long day of delivering babies. At the top of the steps, white tulips sprayed out of a copper planter that had been weathered to beauty by the patina of time. Their petals seemed to breathe as she passed.

The scent of lilacs greeted her between the garage and the house. She hurried down the driveway, trying but failing to ignore the Coldwell Banker sign planted on her lawn. A mixture of nostalgia and nausea stirred in her stomach. She stopped at the sidewalk, bent to tighten a shoelace that wasn't loose, and stole a glance across the street. Neither Martha Morrison nor her poodle was perched at the window.

Elena stood and faced her house. Young leaves fluttered in the wind. The afternoon sun peeked through the trees, casting a mottled pattern of light and shadow on the white brick colonial that had stood on the knoll since 1835 in Beaver, Pennsylvania, thirty miles north of Pittsburgh.

"Seventeen years," she whispered under her breath. "Where did they go? ..."

Make a home movie. Just for you.

She wandered past the For Sale sign to a spot where the house was framed between two oaks and slipped her phone from her pocket. After converting it into a video camera and convincing herself that it was socially acceptable to talk out loud while filming, she stretched her arm out in front of her and pressed the red dot.

"Jack's room looks so much cleaner out here," she said in the hushed but enthusiastic tone of a golf sportscaster. "I'll never forget the night I caught the Simpson twins tossing Skittles at his window. They were *so* embarrassed." She closed her eyes and pictured her twenty-one-year-old son, who would finish his junior year at Penn State next week, as a boy grinning in his Little League uniform. It pained her to think that this would be the final summer they'd live under the same roof. "When did my little Jackster become a man?"

Opening her eyes, she pivoted to her left. "Look at my bedroom sheers flapping like Casper the Friendly Ghost. ... I wonder whatever happened to him."

She lowered her arm and zoomed the lens on the living room windows. "The upper left pane is the one Emma broke with a baseball when she was ten or eleven. She's still a wild pitcher. Still boy crazy." Elena's thoughts turned back to the day last August when she had helped Emma move into her dorm room at Case Western Reserve University in Cleveland, a two hour drive from their home. It seemed like a month ago.

My arm won't stop shaking.

She pulled the phone toward her face, counted eighteen black shutters two at a time, and swallowed the lump in her throat. "This is where I raised my babies. Where I changed diapers, read bedtime stories, and pretended to be the Easter Bunny, Mrs. Claus, and the Tooth Fairy. ... But now—" Her voice caught. "—Jack and Emma are all grown up. Young adults. ... Flying the coop."

She stopped the camera and gazed longingly at the house. *It's twice as big as I need or want. I won't be able to afford it when my alimony ends. ... At least I convinced James to wait until Emma's freshman year to put it on the market.* Her jaw clenched at the thought of her ex-husband, who, at her urging, had moved out three years ago. *If it sells before the wedding, should I live with Dad or move in with Michael? What will everyone think? … Quit worrying about what people think. You don't even know when the wedding will be.* She sighed. *I hope it takes a year to sell.*

Elena strode up the lawn and around the garage to the high point of her two acres. She aimed and zoomed the lens beyond the grassy portion of the backyard. Her garden's palette of colors and aromas was a balm to her nerves. Birds and butterflies cavorted among her flowers, which she had long referred to as "her girls."

She resumed filming, panning the camera from left to right. "There's my oasis, my healthy obsession. … I'll miss my girls twice as much as I'll miss the house. They need me more than Jack and Emma do."

Her arm reversed course. "And I need them."

My walk can wait.

She stopped the camera, dropped the phone into her pocket, and stepped toward the side door of the garage.

When the left stall's door screeched open a minute later, Elena emerged pulling her tool-laden garden cart. She chuckled at her appearance, knowing that with her Georgetown T-shirt and black running skirt accessorized by a straw hat, yellow gloves, and lavender clogs, she looked as if she were headed to a neighbor's costume party dressed as a marathon runner with a green thumb.

Rolling the cart through the backyard, she reflected on

how fortunate she was that her three passions—gardening, motherhood, and nursing—dovetailed into a seamless whole dedicated to nurturing life. Each of the three required and cultivated its own blend of love and patience. Being a gardener and the director of the local hospital's maternity unit helped her to be a better mother. And being a mother made her a better gardener and nurse.

The gate clicked shut. *Good afternoon girls!*

Elena strolled along the roundabout path, touching and smelling her flowers and surveying what needed to be done. Her girls released their best scents and welcomed her in subtle, catlike ways. Purple sage leaves fondled her fingers instead of prickling them. Orange snapdragons reached toward her more than the breeze seemed to warrant.

Five weeks ago, the day after the sign had appeared in her yard, she decided to continue to care for her flowers as if they would always be hers. Since then, she'd doted on them like infants in an incubator. The two scarecrows she had dressed and planted Wednesday evening surpassed all of their predecessors. She didn't care if her next water bill rivaled the one she'd paid after last July's drought. Transplanting was the only task she intended to forgo. Too risky. Elena hoped her girls wouldn't feel abandoned when she was gone and wondered if the eventual owners would mind if she visited occasionally. A true gardener would understand her sense of loss.

She parked the cart in front of the garden's centerpiece, an oval-shaped, pool-sized bed where many of her mother's bearded irises and their offspring lived.

"Hello Mom," she whispered with a smile. "Happy Friday before Mother's Day."

Out of long habit, she grabbed a hand trowel and kneeling cushion from the cart, loosened a circle of soil, and buried her hands in it. Closing her eyes, she pictured the photograph that hung beside her kitchen door. She was fourteen when her father had taken the candid shot of her mom and her working side by side in a patch of irises. A few months later her mother learned that her breast cancer had spread to her brain.

Thank God for family, friends, and flowers.

Elena's knees creaked as she rose to her feet. After unloading the tools, she wheeled the cart to a compost pile tucked behind a clump of maiden grass and stabbed her pitchfork into the fertilizer. The earthy aroma opened a cedar chest of memories. Images flitted across her mind's eye from the three-month anniversary of her mother's death—the first Saturday after her sophomore year of high school—when she ventured into the neglected garden, a jungle of pain, and attacked it with fury from dawn to dark. The more tears she'd shed on the flowers that summer, the more they flourished, shifted from being her mother's girls to being hers, and reconnected her to her mom.

She tugged on the overloaded cart's bar handle and rewound her mental slideshow a month to the Friday night she had smoked her first cigarette, drunk her first beer, and lost her virginity to Michael Marino.

Elena parked the cart in front of the iris bed, wiped the sweat from her chin with the back of her glove, and lifted the pitchfork. Her spine tingled at the thought of Michael's recent hints about proposing to her next month on the second anniversary of their reunion. The prospect of marrying him filled her with anticipation. Anticipation and dread.

She felt a flutter of panic at the memory of breaking off their relationship thirty years ago. *Stay calm and breathe.* She thrust the pitchfork into the ground, leaned against the handle, and took a long, slow breath. Then another. And a third. Her anxiety subsided, but it scared her that this was the closest she'd come to having a panic attack in years. Decades.

She heaved four or five forkfuls of compost and succeeded in not thinking about anything. Then, as if a radio inside her head was tuned between AM stations, two inner voices talked over one another, repeating the debate they had been waging for weeks. As always, the high-pitched voice commanded her attention first:

Everyone will be thrilled when you and Michael get engaged next month. He'll buy you a beautiful diamond and let you redecorate his home. It'll become your home. You'll transform the backyard into a garden showplace. You won't have to worry anymore about losing your job or growing old alone. ... So what if he golfs a lot and has a high opinion of himself? No man is perfect. You'll wear the pant—

Stop listening to such nonsense, the resonant other voice interrupted. *You love the security of marriage more than you love Michael. You knew thirty years ago that he wasn't the right man for you. He still isn't. ... You need a man who nurtures your heart and stimulates your mind. Don't settle for less than you deserve. Buy a townhouse, join a garden club, and thrive as a single woman. The right man will come along when you least expect it.*

Elena attempted to settle the dispute by asking herself whether her mother, who had never met Michael, would be in favor of her marrying him. As in past deliberations, she wavered.

He may not be my knight in shining armor, but he's better than being alone. I'll be fifty in October. I can't afford to be too picky.

Or not picky enough, the other voice asserted. *Admit your mistake in getting back with him and move on. Trust your intuition and embrace change. Your confusion and fear will pass.*

№ № №

Early that evening Michael tapped the brakes of his Audi, rousing Elena from her reverie. She turned her gaze from

Pittsburgh's three rivers to him. His flaring nostril told her that a traffic tantrum was imminent. She stifled a sigh. As the region's Assistant District Engineer for Maintenance of the Pennsylvania Department of Transportation, he had a disdain for traffic that went far beyond the ordinary—it bruised his professional ego.

They coasted up the ramp and joined the parade of vehicles inching across the Fort Duquesne Bridge. The opening notes of Fleetwood Mac's "Go Your Own Way" played on the radio. He drifted over the dotted white line and screeched to a stop. Her upper body recoiled, pressing back against the seat as he flung an expletive and a finger at a man in a pickup truck.

She winced. *Men acting like boys. Testosterone. ... Don't provoke him.*

She leaned forward, flipped the sun visor down, and opened the vanity mirror. Fading sunburn rouged her cheeks. *Is that a freckle?* She brushed a speck of something from her nose and checked her teeth for lipstick. *Ugh! That laugh line wasn't there yesterday.* She backed away from the mirror, tightened an earring, and inspected her short, wavy bob. After the birth of her children, Elena's hair had mellowed a few shades to a coppery auburn that, thanks to her stylist's magic wand, continued to garner rave reviews. She finger-styled it and was relieved to not find any gray roots.

She closed the mirror and visor and sneaked a peek at Michael before settling back in her seat. The allure of his dark hair, almond eyes, and chiseled Italian features was tainted by his scowl. He bullied his way in front of a minivan. She looked away, bit her tongue, and tried to distract herself with Point State Park's fountain and flowering trees. A half-minute later he veered into the far left lane and lurched forward.

A ramp funneled them into downtown. The radio segued from a Geico commercial to the Doobie Brothers' "What a Fool Believes." While Michael navigated the urban maze, Elena tried again to solve the mystery of where he was taking her. In the three days since Tuesday, when he had announced their special date, all he would tell her was to wear her teal blue dress.

They crossed Liberty Avenue, leaving the Cultural District and dashing her hopes of going to a play after dinner. Her thoughts drifted to how much she looked forward to having Jack and Emma home for the summer. They passed the William Penn Hotel's rear entrance and turned down Fifth Avenue. Elena stared at Macy's storefront windows, naked and dark, and tried to envision the Kaufmann's Department Store of her youth, with its dazzling Christmas window displays. Michael lowered the volume, mumbled something about parking, and swerved toward the curb.

"Surprise!" he said, shifting into park.

"The Capital Grille! Well-done, Michael."

He shook his head and grinned. "Medium-rare."

Their laughter died when the valet attendant tugged on Elena's door handle. He greeted her, waited as she tamed her dress, and helped her onto the sidewalk. She thanked him and glanced at her reflection in the restaurant window. *My legs would look better in heels*, she thought, wishing for the hundredth time that she and Michael weren't both five-eight. He took her arm and whisked her past the twin copper lions guarding the entrance.

They spent the next half-hour ordering, reveling in the atmosphere, and savoring the wine, bread, and salad.

Elena thanked the waiter for replenishing her wine and chased a crouton with her fork. "Why won't colleges let mothers schedule final exams?"

"Is this a joke?" Michael asked, perplexed.

She shook her head, her frown deepening. "I'm upset that Jack and Emma won't be home on Mother's Day. It's the first year I'll be alone."

He squeezed her arm. "I'll be with you, honey."

She gave him a half smile, blocked the crouton with her knife, and lifted her last bite of salad to her mouth.

"I wish your kids were ours," he added wistfully.

Elena chewed faster and told herself to change the subject before he got started about the children they could have had together. "As of yesterday," she said, swallowing, "your birthday is less than a month away."

"Don't remind me."

He reached for a roll and slid the butter dish closer. She sipped her wine and recalled the Sunday afternoon in March when the two of them and his mother had planned his fiftieth birthday party. From the invitations to the menu, cake, and music, he'd made his preferences known as if he were a bride arranging her wedding.

"Your party may not be a surprise, Michael, but your mom and I have a few tricks up our sleeves."

"Be careful or I'll pay you back in October."

The waiter cleared their salad plates. Elena wondered for the second time that day when her first hot flash would strike. "Where did my forties go?" she asked, not expecting an answer.

Michael's eyes fell to the V-neck of her dress. "Most forty-year-old women—and *all* forty-year-old men—would love to have your body."

"You flatter me." She looked away and pictured Sara, her only sibling and best friend, proclaiming in a toast to her that forty-nine was the worst age in a woman's life. "Fifty sounds so old."

"You'll be a grandmother before you know it."

"Not till I'm sixty, I hope."

"You'll still turn heads then."

"So will you," she said, matching his grin. The toe of her shoe grazed the heel of his. "And not just because you wear Italian shoes."

He tucked his feet under his chair. "I can't believe you think I spend more on shoes than you."

"I know you do." She tapped her foot twice against the leg of his chair, daring him to a game of cat and mouse.

His eyes darted away. "I wouldn't want to scuff your shoes."

"*My* shoes?" She tapped his chair again.

He nodded to his left. "Listen."

The sizzle and aroma of steak wafted toward them, casting a sensual spell.

Their waiter arrived tableside with a server in tow. "Please be careful, your dishes are very hot." After serving her filet and Michael's porterhouse, he turned toward the server who, one by one, passed him heaping dishes of roasted wild mushrooms, mashed potatoes, and grilled asparagus with lemon mosto.

Silence reigned in the wake of the waiter and server's departure. Elena sprinkled mushrooms on her steak. A moan escaped Michael's lips. She planted her fork in the meat and flirted with the idea of reenacting Meg Ryan's restaurant scene from *When Harry Met Sally.*

Come on, she coaxed herself. *You'll finally be able to cross Culinary Climax off your bucket list.* Her eyes swept across the room. *You don't know anyone. Do it now or you'll chicken out. You'll know when to stop.*

She slipped a morsel of steak into her mouth and talked herself out of making a scene. The satiated look on Michael's face prompted her to wonder whether he'd prefer a Capital Grille steak or a round of sex with her. It didn't take her long to conclude that he'd take the steak and try to wangle his way into getting both.

The next twenty minutes passed with idle conversation filling the gaps between their bites of food. Elena spent most of the time people watching and thinking about the two desserts she'd eaten here in the past—crème brûlée and a flourless chocolate espresso cake with berries and whipped cream.

After deciding to order the cake, she contemplated women's obsession with chocolate and guessed that half of American women over forty, if given the choice, would select a slice of restaurant chocolate cake over fifteen minutes of passion with their mate. She asked herself the same question and didn't hesitate to choose the cake.

Seconds later she changed her mind. *Chocolate can soothe me and make me tingle, but it can't hold me or make me laugh. It can't love me.*

Shortly after Michael finished his steak, Elena surrendered the uneaten half of hers to a take-home box. The waiter arrived with dessert menus and hurried away.

"Want to split something?" Michael asked.

"Order crème brûlée. It won't go to waste."

"What about your waist?" he asked, smiling at his wit.

"I'll walk or garden the calories off tomorrow."

He reached under the tablecloth and found her knee. "I'd be glad to help you burn them off tonight."

"I bet you would," she said with a teasing smirk, shooing his hand away.

Moments later, when the waiter shuffled off with their dessert order, Michael pushed his chair back and said, "Excuse me while I use the restroom."

He stood and hesitated as if he had more to say. His hand shook. He dropped his napkin on the table, knelt on one knee beside her, and took her left hand in both of his.

Is he going to ask me to mar—

"Elena," he said, searching her eyes, "I've loved you since we were sixteen and want us to spend the rest of our lives together. Will you marry me?"

"But all your hints," she said just above a whisper. "Our anniversary?"

"I couldn't wait."

She looked at his hands, smiling, expecting him to reach into his pocket and pull out a ring.

"I want you to pick out your diamond, sweetheart."

He glanced to either side of him and inched closer. "Now I'll ask you again. Elena Shaughnessy, will you marry me?"

CHAPTER TWO

It's so great to find that one special person
you want to annoy for the rest of your life.
–Rita Rudner

Michael surprised Elena in bed that night by not needing a pill to perform. She raced to catch up with his passion and came up short. He cried out in ecstasy. Her moans disguised sighs. He collapsed onto her, sweaty, satiated.

Together but alone, she thought. *This must be how a mare feels after being mounted by a stallion.*

His manhood wilted, his panting slowed. Her breathing and wordless movements asked him to get off of her.

He rolled onto his side. "I should propose to you more often."

"Maybe you should."

She wondered if he'd heard the disappointment in her

voice. He snuggled closer and rested his arm under her breasts. "Honey?"

"Yes?"

"You know how we talked on the way home about spending tomorrow morning together?"

"Yes?"

"Well ..."

Her hand slipped from his thigh to hers.

"Well?"

"I've been invited to golf with Congressman Jenkins and two county commissioners at Allegheny Country Club."

Elena pulled the sheet to her chin and rolled onto her side, her back to him.

The nerve of him to wait until now to tell me. After he got what he wanted.

Michael scooted closer. She wiggled toward the edge of the bed until he got the hint. Only his hand touched her now. It clung to her hipbone like a rope tethering a boat to a dock.

I bet he's known about this all week. If he had mentioned it in the car, I would've been excited for him. She pressed her thighs together to stem the tide of wetness. *I can't let him get away with disrespecting me like this. What should I do?*

His breath fogged the back of her neck as she weighed her options.

The stakes are too high for me to force him to back out now. It could hurt his career.

She curled into a sitting position and asked over her shoulder, "Why didn't you say anything about this on the way home?"

He looked away. "I'm sorry."

"Sorry and selfish."

Elena stormed into the bathroom, wiped tissues between her legs, and slipped into her robe. While washing her hands, she saw a silver lining in Michael's rudeness. She'd use it as leverage in convincing him to delay announcing their engagement. Since their desserts had arrived at the Capital Grille, doubts had been gnawing in the back of her mind. Seller's remorse. She also feared that the news of their engagement would divert attention away from her niece, who had recently gotten engaged.

She tightened the sash of her robe, flipped on the bathroom light, and started toward the bed. Michael lay on his back with the sheet up to his waist, his silence announcing his fear. She sat sideways, their hips almost touching, and took a deep breath. The scowl drained from her face as she exhaled. A forgiving smile rose with her chest.

"It's not every day you get invited to golf with VIPs, Michael. Go play and have fun."

He kissed the sleeve of her robe. His expression swung from surprise to relief to gratitude.

"Thanks for understanding, honey. I promise I won't be late for your father's party."

Elena shifted her weight and covered her thigh with the robe. "Who knows that you planned to propose to me tonight?"

"No one. Not even my mother. I want us to surprise her on Mother's Day." He propped himself up on one elbow and gave her a questioning look. "Why do you ask?"

"We need to keep our engagement a secret for now."

His eyes bulged. "Why?"

"Tomorrow it'll be two weeks since Catherine got engaged. It would be rude of us to draw attention away from her, Jonathon, and Sara. Let's give—"

"Can't we share the spotlight?"

She caught the nearer of his waving hands and guided it to her lap. "If you had sisters or children, Michael, you'd understand that weddings are a much bigger deal to women." She stroked his forearm. "Catherine isn't only my niece, she's my Goddaughter. And her wedding will be Sara's first as a mother. Let's give them their fifteen minutes of fame."

"For what, a week?"

Elena smiled, hoping to soften the blow. "Let's break the news to my family next month at Hilton Head. With all your hints since Christmas about proposing to me there on our anniversary, I got it into my head that that's how it would be."

"I dropped the hints to throw you off. I wanted to surprise you tonight."

"Why tonight?"

He sat up and touched her shoulder. "To make your Mother's Day weekend happier."

"That's sweet of you." She kissed his cheek. "But we need to wait."

"But I've already waited. Thirty years."

"What's a month compared to thirty years?" She held her bare left hand up to him. "It'll give us time to pick out my ring."

He smiled his most charming smile. "What if we tell just my family and three or four of our closest friends?"

"Sara knows your brothers and their wives. And she's too plugged in to our network of friends. She'd strangle me if she heard it through the grapevine."

Elena cocked her head at an angle that told him she wouldn't budge.

He tugged on the sash of her robe. "Will you make it worth my wait?"

She stifled a laugh, knowing that another round of sex wasn't an option. Not for him. "It's late. What time do you need to get up in the morning?"

"Five-thirty."

"Come on then." She stood up and pulled on his hand. "You golf better when you sleep in your own bed."

He gathered his clothes off the hardwood floor. "Can we at least tell my mom at brunch on Sunday? It would be a Mother's Day gift she'd never forget."

"I'll think about it."

"She's dreamed of this for as long as I have." He slid his briefs up his legs and lifted his shirt off the bed. "Remember, she's Sicilian. She won't tell a soul."

"Let me sleep on it."

Elena fixed a leg of his inside-out pants. It dawned on her that the timing of Michael's marriage proposal had more to do with pleasing his mother than pleasing her.

Her stomach twisted into a knot.

🐿 🐿 🐿

After a restless night, Elena lay curled up under the covers imagining a future without Michael. A lightness filled her heart. The ceiling fan whirred and clicked and circulated air that smelled of earth and rain and new beginnings. Outside her windows, baby robins chirped hungrily as their mother delivered a fresh batch of breakfast.

A wave of fear washed over her. She rolled onto her other side, imagined herself married to Michael, and tried again to forget her doubts.

"Elena Marino," she muttered under her breath. "Mrs. Michael Marino. … Elena Shaughnessy Marino." *That one's a mouthful.* She counted nine syllables in her head. Her bladder begged for relief.

She scrambled to the bathroom and distracted herself by reviewing her mental to-do list. Her father's birthday party started at noon. She had to wrap his gift, buy a card, and pick up the cake at the bakery. Jack and Emma's beds needed fresh linens. She debated whether to clean the house for the two home showings scheduled that afternoon. The floors glistened and the grout gleamed in her mind's eye. She'd crank up the music and escape. The morning would fly. But the cleaner the house was, the sooner it might sell.

My girls need me. I'll work in the garden. She glanced at the clock on the shelf. *It's early. Try to sleep.*

Elena dried her hands, pulled a pair of earplugs from the medicine cabinet, and walked back to bed. She pinched the bridge of her nose and counted to a hundred twice before the ceiling fan lulled her to sleep.

When the sun broke through the clouds and awakened her, she looked at the clock radio and did a double take.

11:28

"Shit! Dad's party starts in half an hour."

CHAPTER THREE

Let's face it, a nice creamy chocolate cake
does a lot for a lot of people; it does for me.
—Audrey Hepburn

Moments later Elena shook her hair and planted her other
girls, still damp, into a black bra. *No time for panties or panty
lines.* She ran to the closet and tangoed into an orange
sundress. *No time for hair.* She reached for a hat, slipped into
a pair of dressy black sandals, and clopped downstairs. After
squeezing her dad's birthday sweater into a recycled gift bag,
she slung her handbag over her shoulder, blew a kiss at the
photo of her mother, and wrestled with wrapping tissue on
her way to the garage.

Elena drifted through four or five stop signs and stopped
at a red light. She leaned toward the rearview mirror, applied
lipstick, and inspected the MR. John Jr. black straw hat she

had fallen in love with last summer at a vintage clothing shop in Shadyside. With its narrow turned-up brim overlaid in ivory-colored fabric and a banded bow of black silk, the hat reminded her of something Jackie Kennedy would have worn in the 1960s. *It's about time I wear it.* She tipped it at a jaunty angle and turned onto 3rd Street.

She thanked the parking gods and angled her silver Explorer into a space. Exiting the Hostess Gift Shoppe a few minutes later, she hoped her father wouldn't notice that she had purchased the second card she touched and hurried down the block. Wafted by the breeze, the aroma of Kretchmar's Bakery lured her forward.

The door jingled. Her eyes grew wide. As always, Elena marveled at how little the bakery had changed since she was in grade school. It seemed as if only the clerks behind the counter were different. She scanned the crowded pantry-sized customer area, didn't recognize anyone, and winked at an elderly gentleman, a habit she'd cultivated in her early forties. He winked back and matched her smile. The twinkle in his eyes told her that she had made his day.

She pulled ticket 192 from the slot, frowned at the red 184 flashing above the bread case, and searched in vain for tickets 185 and 186. The looks of longing on customers' faces convinced her to abandon any hope of arranging a ticket exchange.

"One eighty-five," a clerk called out above the din.

"That's *me*," a very pregnant woman said, waddling toward the cupcake display case.

Elena reached into her handbag and fished for her phone. After typing a text to her sister Sara, she pressed Send and read what she had written:

Today 11:53 AM
Kretchmar's is a zoo! Running late. Sorry.

She scrolled through her texts.

Kathleen Riggs. The sight of her realtor's name triggered a picture in Elena's mind of her panties, nightshirt, and towel strewn across her bedroom floor. *Shit! Nice welcoming committee for the people coming to look at the house. Maybe Kathleen can bail me out.* She tapped the screen and typed.

"One eighty-six is next," a clerk announced.

"Excuse me, miss," a man standing behind Elena said. She turned sideways to let him pass, but he didn't move.

What man wears a navy blue suit and an orange silk tie on a Saturday?

Her eyes crawled up his tie, paused at his neck, and slid over his dimpled chin and full lips and up the slant of his strong nose. Their green eyes met, their smiles widened.

"The hat looks stunning on you."

She touched the side of the brim and wondered whose cheeks were redder. "Thanks."

"It looks like something Audrey Hepburn would have worn in *Breakfast at Tiffany's*."

"Audrey is one of my heroes," she said without thinking.

"Mine too."

Elena remembered to breathe. "Really?"

He has perfect teeth. I bet he's six two.

He blushed a deeper shade and ran his fingers through the salt-and-pepper hair above his ear. "I realize that's unusual for a man who … who's attracted to women."

A tightening around his eyes told her he wasn't finished. Her nod of interest seemed to bolster him. He continued, "Audrey's legacy as an actress and a humanitarian is unmatched. It's rare to find a woman who's beautiful, elegant, *and* courageous."

"Yes, but it's impossible to find a single man"—Elena scratched her neck as if it would stem the flow of blood rising to her cheeks—"or a married one, who possesses all three qualities. He'd need a legion of bodyguards if he did."

His grin applauded her quick wit. A boy begged his mother for a donut.

"Now serving number one eighty-seven," a clerk called out.

The crowd swirled like a school of fish. Elena and the man in the blue suit swam together. She studied a tray of pies and searched for something clever to say, something Audrey would have said to Cary Grant.

Wait, wrong movie!

He stepped back to let a woman pass. "The supermarket bakeries haven't hurt Kretchmar's business," he said, reclaiming his spot beside her.

"I'm going to be late for my father's birthday party." *Why did I just say that?*

A clerk announced, "One eighty-eight."

"Here." He touched Elena's ticket with his. "I'll trade my one eighty-nine for your one ninety-two. You're in a hurry and I'm not."

He's not wearing a wedding ring.

"That's so kind of you." She exchanged tickets with him.

"It's my pleasure. Would you like to—"

"One eighty-nine is next."

She waved her hand at the clerk and turned to the mystery man and smiled. "Thank you."

He nodded. "Have fun at your dad's party."

"Thanks." She stepped to the display case. "I'm here to pick up a birthday cake under the name of Shaughnessy. Elena Shaughnessy."

"Let me find it." The clerk turned to the shelves loaded with orders for pickup.

I wonder if he'll introduce himself. She felt his eyes on her back. *Should I turn and face him? What was he about to ask me?*

He inched his way into her peripheral vision, moving like a dancer uncertain of his steps. His awkward smoothness stoked the fire of her anticipation. He touched her elbow lightly.

"Hello Elena. My name is Patrick Jameson."

"Hi Patrick. My intuition tells me you're not from around here."

"I grew up across the river in New Brighton, but I live in Sewickley now. I'm in town for a wedding." He tugged on his tie. "We match."

"We do."

"Do you live here in Beaver?"

"My whole life, except college." She wished she sounded more like Audrey and fought the urge to mention that she was a Georgetown girl.

"Your cake must be in the back," Elena's clerk said, starting toward the baking area.

Patrick pointed at a tray of cupcakes. "You'll win one of these if you can name a town in Western Pennsylvania that has more of a Norman Rockwell feel to it than either Beaver or Sewickley."

"Hmm." She thought for a moment. "Oakmont comes close. But it doesn't surpass either of them."

"I admire Beaver's spunk. How it resurrected itself after the steel industry died. Can you imagine a restaurant like Biba on 3rd Street twenty-five years ago?"

"No. It's one of my favorites." Her eyes fell to his hands. She wondered how old he was and what he did for a living.

"Now serving number one ninety-one," a clerk announced.

"Elena, I'd hate for our conversation to end here. Would you like to have coffee or lunch sometime?"

Her pulse raced, her mind froze.

"I'm flattered by your invitation, Patrick, but I have a—" she hesitated, looking away and then back at him, "—a boyfriend."

"I understand." His smile failed to mask his disappointment.

Elena's clerk, cake box in hand, stood beside a co-worker, waiting for her to finish ringing up a customer.

Patrick pulled a business card from his wallet and handed it to Elena. "Please let me be the first to know if your boyfriend moves out of state. Or you discover an identical twin who's single."

"I will. Have fun at your wedding."

"My wedding?"

Her eyes narrowed, matching his. "Didn't you say you're in town for a wedding?"

An embarrassed grin spread across his face. "I forgot."

Chapter Four

A family with an old person
has a living treasure of gold.
    –*Chinese Proverb*

The cake box on the passenger seat convinced Patrick that he wasn't dreaming. He slipped his sunglasses on, turned right at the Beaver County Courthouse, and decided to stop at his mother's house. His mind skipped back to the moment before he saw Elena.

A tray of crusty bread had commanded his attention until a flash of orange caught the corner of his eye. She stood three feet away, her back to him. Her hat, dress, and sandals whispered "casual elegance." Her auburn hair and freckled shoulders made him suspect that, like him, she had some Irish blood in her. He navigated the crowd and drew closer to her. She reached into her handbag, treating him to a view of her profile.

She's stunning!

He stopped and stared. Her eyebrow told him that she was a natural redhead. She had a nose with character, the kind women who were born with complained about and others paid money to acquire. Her dress clung to her curves. *There's no way she's single.* He guessed she was forty-three and happily married, with two kids in braces.

She raised her phone, exposing a naked ring finger. His heart thumped. She faced the cakes again and began to type. The closer he got, the more he felt her presence. He parked himself in the best available space, to the left of her shoulder. Bakery aromas masked her scent.

Speak to her before they call her number. What should I say?

He racked his brain until her vintage hat loosened the knot in his tongue. She turned to let him pass. He stood still, silent, a tug-of-war between hope and fear raging inside him. Her smiling eyes had thrilled him, calmed him. He complimented her hat.

Patrick replayed their conversation in his head.

I wonder why she hesitated before telling me she had a boyfriend.

He stopped at a red light on the main street of New Brighton, gave himself a mental pat on the back for having struck up a conversation with Elena, and turned his thoughts to why he was making a side trip to his mother's house.

I'll bet it's been five years since she's worn one of her hats. She can wear it tomorrow for Mother's Day and at the talent show.

He wound his way through a web of side streets and was greeted by a hopscotch patch of concrete weeds in the driveway. His childhood home's gray exterior looked balder than it had a month ago. The boxwoods begged to be trimmed. He unlocked the back door and went inside. The kitchen smelled of Ajax. Prescription drug bottles lined the counter like a platoon of white-hatted soldiers ready for battle. A bouquet of plastic flowers wilted on the table.

Patrick stepped into what until a year ago had been his mother's living room. Between then and four months ago, when she moved into a nursing home, it had been her bedroom. A portable toilet rested beside the twin bed. A wig slept next to a bag of Depends on the end table. He turned into the foyer, squeezed past the stairlift chair, and hurried upstairs.

He entered his mother's bedroom and opened her hat closet. The thirty or so vintage hatboxes stacked on shelves and in piles on the floor reminded him of miniature coffins. He set a batch of three boxes on the bed, lifted their lids, fumbled with tissue paper, and inspected the one he liked in the beam of dusty sunlight.

Some of the hats burst with life, as if they yearned to be reunited with his mother. All of them triggered old memories of her. He gathered the finalists on the cedar chest.

A circular hatbox with *O'Neil's* printed on its pink lid was in the second-to-last batch. Patrick wrestled with the handle and uncovered a hat that resembled the top layer of a wedding cake. Layers of ivory chiffon fabric were wrapped, mummy-like, up the side band. The crown and brimless base were trimmed with green and turquoise flowers.

He sat on the foot of the bed, lifted the hat out of the box, and was transported back to his childhood. He and Maureen walked on either side of their mom to the second row of Saint Joseph's Catholic Church. Heads turned, elbows nudged, and more heads turned. Draped in a cape and crowned with a hat that only she dared to wear, his mother attracted more attention than a bishop. Her jet-black hair, blue eyes, and regal bearing prompted countless comparisons to Elizabeth Taylor.

Music blared from a car passing on the street below. Patrick's mental picture of his mother in her prime morphed to one in her present state. She sat in a wheelchair in the nursing home's dining room, her blue eyes full of wonder and confusion.

Mom's never coming home. His eyes welled up. *I need to let go and sell the house.*

ℒ ℒ ℒ

Elena raced through the flats of Beaver and up Dutch Ridge Road's mile of steep curves into Brighton Township.

Thoughts and images of Patrick swirled in her mind. She applauded herself for making him forget where he was going and imagined women swarming him at an elegant wedding reception.

How can he be single? No woman in her right mind would let him out of her clutches.

She hurried down a long driveway, parked, and searched her handbag for his business card, which she had dropped there, unread, before extending her hand to him and saying goodbye.

Patrick A. Jameson, M.D.
Doctor of Psychiatry
121 Hazel Lane, Suite 302
Sewickley, PA 15143
412-748-9274
pjamesontherapist@gmail.com

A psychiatrist. How intriguing. She turned off the ignition. *I'm holding up Dad's party.*

She zipped Patrick's card inside the lining of her bag, signed her father's card, collected her things, and scurried toward Friendship Ridge Nursing Home. The building's orange brick face seemed to be scowling at her. Air conditioners clung like eye warts to the windows.

Elena passed Michael's Audi in a handicapped parking space and stepped through the home's automatic doors. The aromas of spaghetti sauce and disinfectant joined forces but couldn't defeat the stench of body waste. After signing in, she squeezed onto and off of the elevator, bustled down the hallway, and bumped her father's door open with her hip.

"Hi everyone. Sorry I'm late."

Her hat attracted a chorus of raves. She set her bags on the vinyl chair and held the bakery box up like a trophy. "You would've thought Kretchmar's was giving away cakes."

She laid the box on the bedside table, kissed Michael hello, and hugged her brother-in-law Dan, her niece Catherine, and Catherine's fiancé Jonathon. Sara's twin sons, sophomores at Penn State, would be returning home for the summer early next week. Elena greeted her sister and asked, "Where's Dad?"

Sara, who had inherited their father's chestnut hair and blue eyes, wore a snake-print dress and looked as if she could sprint a mile without breaking a sweat. She pointed a pink-tipped finger at the closed bathroom door. "He's with an aide."

"Good, then I'm not *too* late." Elena glanced at herself in the mirror above the in-room sink and fiddled with her hat. "I'm so glad you talked me into buying it."

"Here, tip your head." Sara pushed the dimple of black straw deeper into the hat's crown. "It's about time you wore it."

"I had no choice."

"Late to bed, late to rise," Sara whispered with a conspiratorial smile. "Michael told me all about your big date last night."

"What did he say?" she asked, trying to sound nonchalant.

"That the food, wine, and atmosphere were magnificent." Sara nodded toward Dan, across the bed. "He'd never spring for the Capital Grille."

Sara's eyes and tone of voice told Elena that Michael hadn't dropped any hints about their engagement. The toilet flushed behind the bathroom door. "How's Dad doing today?" she asked.

"He's excited to see everyone."

"Good, he seemed a little down on Thursday afternoon. Can you believe he's been here almost two weeks already?"

Sara shook her head and sighed. "When did we get old enough to have a parent living here?"

"We aren't old enough," Elena said, hoping that her smile lines were less prominent than her fifty-two-year-old sister's.

The bathroom door lock thwacked open and Elena stepped forward. Her father, looking clean and crisp in his gray slacks and burgundy cardigan, toddled through the doorway behind the rolling walker he called his little red Corvette.

"Lanie!"

"Happy birthday, Dad."

He locked his brakes and raised his arms to her. They embraced and kissed cheeks. She guided his hands to the handlebars and kissed him again. "That one's from Jack and Emma."

They joined the others who stood huddled around the bed as if it were a kitchen table. "You're steady on your feet today," Elena said. "How do you feel?"

"Happy to be alive." He eased his backside onto the edge of the bed and patted his new left hip. "Still a little sore from yesterday. Abby enjoys torturing me."

"In case everyone hasn't heard," Elena said, "Dad's physical therapist, a thirty-something triathlete named Abby, has a crush on him. She calls him Freddie Shaughnessy."

Her father pushed his black-framed glasses up the bridge of his nose and ran a hand through his shock of white hair. "You'd all blush if you heard what she calls me when I disobey her orders."

When the laughter faded, Sara reached for his elbow. "Let's go celebrate your birthday, Dad."

Moments later she led the way through the half-full dining room toward a trio of blue balloons hanging from the back of a chair. Elena chuckled under her breath when she recognized her sister's gray dishes and silver tablecloth from home. Deli lunch boxes, their lids initialed in black marker, served as seating cards. The facility's plastic cups, sweating water, looked like a family of underdressed cousins who had crashed a wedding and exhausted themselves dancing.

Elena buried her gift bag between the two wrapped and ribboned boxes that were perched on the chair at the foot of the table. While unboxing the cake, she remembered forgetting to bring flowers. Her heart sank.

"I forgot flowers for the table," she said loud enough for only Sara and her dad to hear. "I'm sorry."

Her father squeezed her arm and smiled. "You, Sara, and Catherine are my flowers."

"And you're ours." Elena kissed his temple, set the cake in the center of the table, and sat to her father's left, across from Sara.

Catherine and Jonathon, who dressed and ate like J.Crew models, gave Elena and Michael a wedding update during lunch. While they discussed possible dates and the shortlist of locations for their reception, Elena nudged Michael's shoe a few times with her bare foot and gave him a mild version of *the look*. He heeded her warnings.

As lunch was winding down, she overheard Sara say to their father, "You seem happier now than you did."

"I'm adapting." He cleared his throat and glanced around the room before continuing. "The nurses are wonderful, but there's no one to talk to."

"Hang in there, Dad. You'll be home before you know it."

Sara stood and stepped toward the gifts. "Okay everyone, it's time for the birthday boy to open his presents."

When Elena and Sara were in their mid-twenties, their father had established a one-gift limit on his birthday, Christmas, and Father's Day. His excuse, then and now, was that he didn't need anything and they both had better things to do with their money. The Shaughnessy girls, knowing that his primary motive was to curb their sibling rivalry, established a birthday-sweater tradition that had blossomed over the years into one part family joke, one part family Olympics. Their quest for the perfect sweater knew no bounds. Their father played along by gushing about each sweater and wearing it on the birthday of whoever had given it to him.

After extolling the virtues of the checkerboard-patterned sweater he'd received from Catherine and Jonathon and the orange cashmere one Sara and Dan had given him, Elena's father reached for her gift bag. His body language told her that he was oblivious to her hasty card selection and breach of gift-wrap etiquette.

"Black and gold!" He held the striped silk sweater up to his chest and caressed the fabric. "It'll be perfect for Steelers games. Thanks you two." He wiggled to the edge of his seat and kissed Elena's cheek.

Sara lit the "8" and "1" candles and pointed over Michael's shoulder at an elderly upright piano ten feet away. "Elena, will you play for us as we sing?"

"As *we* sing?" Elena teased, rising to her feet. She stepped toward the piano. "Remember," she said over her shoulder, "my ban on public singing excludes birthdays."

She settled herself on the bench and poised her fingers over the keyboard.

A quarter of the way through the song, movement to her left drew her attention. Her voice caught in her throat.

CHAPTER FIVE

Gratitude is the most exquisite form of courtesy.
        –Jacques Maritain

The birthday song filled the air of the cavernous dining room when Patrick rounded the bend. Her hat gave her away.

Elena!

He veered toward her as if he had stumbled upon a parade. *Don't draw attention to yourself.* He braked his mother and her wheelchair to a stop beside a tableful of female residents who were enjoying the festivities fifteen feet away from the piano.

Elena's eyes met his, her mouth fell open. His smile resisted arrest.

She played the final note, rose from the bench, and glanced back at the party table as her father blew out the candles. Patrick, fighting the urge to move closer, was thrilled when she turned and stepped toward them.

His stomach tightened. It dawned on him that Elena might think it strange that she and his mom were both wearing hats. He wished he could make the hatbox disappear from the handle of the wheelchair where it hung. Trying to hide it from her view with his body would only draw attention to it. And telling her that she inspired him to visit his mother's hat closet would either flatter or scare her.

"I never expected to see you here, Elena."

"I thought you were going to a wedding?"

"It's not till later this afternoon." he said, moving to where his mom could see him. She held a Kretchmar's cake box on the lap of her floral housedress.

"Elena, I'd like you to meet my mother, Irene Jameson, the jitterbug generation's Queen of Hats."

"Hello, Irene. I love your hat."

Smiling a childlike smile, his mother removed her hat, set it on the cake box, and petted it like a cat. The fleshy part of her arm jiggled. She studied Elena's face as if she were a niece whose name had slipped her mind.

"Her tongue retired a few years ago," Patrick said, laying a hand on his mom's shoulder. "She still talks, but not like she used to."

Elena gave him a knowing look and bent toward his mother until their eyes were level. "I bet you loved wearing hats back in the day."

His mom lifted the hat in her hands and placed it,

crownlike, on her silver curls. She closed her eyes and smoothed a layer of chiffon fabric along the side band. Her puzzled expression told him that memories swirled in her mind. She opened her mouth to speak but didn't.

"Do you want to say something, Mom?"

Her blue eyes sparkled. She met Elena's gaze. "I got it at a millinery shop in Pittsburgh. Before my boy was born."

"Wow, Mom. You remembered."

She nodded maternally. "You look good with her."

His hand bumped the *O'Neil's* hatbox, sending it swinging. Blood rushed to his face. He settled the box and groped for words.

"I see that Patrick brought you a cake," Elena said, stroking the veiny back of his mother's hand. "Is today your birthday?"

"I can't remember." She turned her head and stared at the piano.

"Mom's giving the cake to the nursing staff as a token of her appreciation."

"That's so thoughtful of you, Irene."

Elena rose to full height and applauded Patrick with her eyes.

He glanced across the room at an aide named Sherry who was feeding a male resident. "She's been here four months now. This place doesn't look or smell pretty, but the care—at least here on the second floor—is excellent."

"That's good to know."

Patrick felt the blood drain from his face. A well-dressed man standing ten feet behind Elena was rocking on the balls of his feet, glaring at him.

Gucci loafers. Not a hair out of place. A jealous Italian.

"I'll let you get back to your father's party."

Elena turned and the man's scowl was replaced by a smile. She waved him over. "Come and meet my new friends, Michael."

She didn't mention Kretchmar's Bakery during her introduction. Patrick shook her boyfriend's hand and guessed he was meeting a politician, a mafia don, or both.

"Sweetheart, Sara wants you to come and have a piece of your father's cake."

Elena nodded at him and caressed Irene's arm. "Thank you for telling me about your hat." She turned to Patrick. "I'm glad to hear how happy you are with your mother's care."

Michael took her elbow and stepped toward the party.

"Goodbye," Patrick mouthed the word.

"Goodbye," she mouthed back.

A moment later Patrick and Irene dodged two meal-delivery carts during their ten-yard dash from the entrance to the dining room to the nurses' station. Two female residents napped like twins on rolling recliners. A cluster of other residents, strangers with familiar faces, sat in their usual spots for passing the time. He greeted a few of them and parked his mother in front of the chest-high counter so that she and her hat wouldn't be visible to Sally Horton, the nursing supervisor, who stood inside the nurses' station with her back to him.

While waiting for Sally to finish speaking to two members of her staff, he replayed his encounter with Elena and her boyfriend and wondered what she saw in him beyond physical attraction and affluence. They seemed mismatched. But so did half or more of his psychiatric patients and their mates.

The huddle of nurses broke up. "Hey ladies," he said, wheeling his mother backwards, "how do you like my mother's hat."

"Look at *you*, Irene," Sally said, stepping out of the nurses' station.

The three women gushed about the hat, touching it as if it would make them younger, prettier, and thinner. Word spread and five members of Sally's team surrounded his mom, who beamed as if she had just won a beauty contest.

When the commotion subsided, Patrick backed her wheelchair four or five feet toward the dining room, stood where his mother could see him, and paused long enough to make eye contact with Sally and each member of her team. He knew that *they* knew a chocolate mousse cake lay inside the box on his mom's lap.

"Searching through my mother's hat closet today took me back to my childhood," he began. "When Mom walked down the main street of New Brighton, men and women turned and stared. What no one knew back then was that she bought all her clothes at thrift stores. As a single mother with no child support, she couldn't afford to shop anywhere else. Her only choice was whether to wear other women's worn-out clothes or the outfits wealthy women were courageous enough to buy, but too afraid to wear." He touched the crown of his mom's hat and smiled. "As you can see, she chose the latter."

Patrick paused. His face grew serious. "I'll close by telling you something you already know. You have one of the toughest jobs in the world. And one of the best. You care for people who once were strong, but now are weak. You feed, bathe, change, and comfort them. You help them to sprout their final blooms." He rested a hand on his mother's shoulder. "Thanks to you, I've seen glimpses of the woman who raised me—her spunk, her flair—the side of her I never thought I'd see again."

He rolled her and her wheelchair forward and helped her to give the cake to Sally.

"Happy Mother's Day, ladies. Thanks for caring for my mom as if she were yours."

The sound of clapping rose behind him. Patrick turned and blushed at the sight of Elena and her family gathered at the entrance to the dining room, applauding. He backed his mother toward the elevator, raised a hand to Sally and her team, and clapped.

Elena carried her father's birthday gifts back to his room, checked her phone, and read a text from Kathleen Riggs:

Today 12:39 PM
They love the house. Keep your fingers crossed. (Your panties and nightshirt are wrapped in the towel under your bed. LOL!)

Elena winced at the thought of leaving her home and garden and dropped her phone in her handbag.

After saying their goodbyes, she and Michael walked in silence to the elevator. He jabbed the down button and whispered sharply, "You couldn't take your eyes off that Patrick guy during his long-winded speech."

She searched for prying ears at the nurses' station and turned back to him. "Don't be ridiculous," she said, matching his tone. "I was admiring his mother's hat."

"Yeah, right," he scoffed. "Then why did you give him some of your father's cake?"

"As a gesture of kindness."

He pressed the elevator button again. "You two acted like you already knew each other."

Her toes choked the thongs of her sandals. "I met him today."

"I didn't see a wedding ring on his finger."

"I wasn't looking at his hands—" *Damn! That didn't come out right.* "Your jealousy gets old, Michael." The elevator dinged. "I've never given you a reason not to trust me."

They squeezed into separate openings and the door closed, triggering the silent rule of elevator silence. Elena shut her eyes and pictured Patrick speaking to the nursing staff.

The nurses couldn't take their eyes off him, either. ... He really loves his mother.

She waited for Michael outside the elevator, walked with him to the security desk, and signed them both out. He took her hand and led the way out of the building and across the driveway toward his car. She resisted the urge to mention his abuse of his mother's handicap placard.

He stopped and turned to her. "I trust you, Elena, but I can't help being jealous any more than you can help being beautiful."

"You *can* help it," she said in as even a tone as she could muster. "But it takes work. Just like marriage."

"I know. I'm sorry. I barely slept last night and embarrassed myself on the golf course this morning." He sighed, running a hand through his hair. "It's making me crazy that we can't tell anyone we're engaged."

"It's only five weeks. They'll fly by."

Michael pulled his keys from his pocket. "I'll drive you to your car."

"That's okay. I'm a few rows back."

"I should finish painting my mom's garage this afternoon. Mama Maria's making lasagna for dinner. She told me to tell you you're invited."

"Please tell her I have a hundred things to do before we move Jack home on Monday. She'll understand, and I'll see her garage tomorrow morning." Elena reached for his hand. "You're a wonderful son for painting it for her."

"Can I come see you tonight, say around nine?"

"Not tonight, Michael," she said in a tired voice. "I didn't sleep well either."

He looked hurt. His eyes pleaded with her.

Should I let him? I could send him home at eleven. No, he'll want to have sex and stay the night. ... Give him something.

She pecked him on the lips and backed a step toward her car. "We can tell your mom about our engagement at brunch tomorrow."

❧ ❧ ❧

After eating the cake Elena had given them, Patrick and Irene played bumper cars getting onto and off of the elevator and strolled a hundred feet down the corridor to the assembly room. Twin oak doors sensed their presence and wheezed open. He wheeled her onto the floor where, two months earlier at the Saint Patrick's Day party, they had danced together for the first time since his wedding.

"Let's wake this place up, Mom."

The light panel's door squeaked open. Staccato clicks echoed off the walls as beams of light poured from the ceiling. With the tables and chairs folded and stacked along the walls, the room looked naked.

He wheeled her the length of the room and up the ramp onto the stage. "It'll be packed during the talent show. We'll have to dance up here instead of down there." Irene nodded her head as if she were a young ballerina receiving instructions before a performance.

He slid the lectern out of the way. "Do you like the new outfit Maureen bought you to wear?"

"I think so."

"You and your hat will steal the show."

Patrick inserted his homemade *Dancing with Mom* CD into the player and pressed the Play and Repeat buttons. The opening notes of Frank Sinatra's "I've Got You Under My Skin" rang from the speakers. He stood behind her and led her in a round of warm-up exercises. After tapping her toes on the wheelchair's steel footrests, she slapped her hands on her thighs as if she were playing patty-cake and grinned when he wiggled the back of her chair.

"Close your eyes, Mom," he said in her ear. "Imagine you're twenty-four again. It's Saturday night. You and your girlfriends just arrived at a nightclub and lit your first cigarette. ... Look. Three men are lined up to buy you a drink.

Did *you* bat your eyelashes at them?" She nodded, smiling. "Listen. The band is playing a Sinatra tune. Let's dance!"

Patrick dashed her across the stage. Her head and shoulders bobbed.

CHAPTER SIX

Parenting is one long exercise in relinquishing control—
or the illusion that we ever had it.

—*Jane Adams*

Late the next morning at Seven Oaks Country Club, Maria
Marino left a trail of perfume and stale tobacco in her wake
as the host led her, Elena, and Michael to their table for
Mother's Day brunch. Her pearls rustled against her pink
silk dress.

Not a single strand of gray colored Maria's blue-black hair.
She looked eighty, but wouldn't be seventy until December.
Fifty-some years of smoking had left her voice as wrinkled as
her face.

Her four sons were her jewels, particularly the eldest who
had painted her garage without being asked. She informed
even the barest acquaintances—waitresses, church ushers, the
clerks at Walgreens—that Michael was the Assistant District

Engineer for Maintenance of District 11 of the Pennsylvania Department of Transportation. It no longer surprised Elena when Maria's sisters and friends mentioned his title down to the last syllable, as if he were the Director of the CIA. She suspected most of them knew more about his accomplishments than their own children's.

Maria sat across from Michael. After stoking his mother's pride by ordering an expensive bottle of champagne, he picked up where he'd left off in the car about a looming retirement at PennDOT. Her face beamed when he announced that he expected to be promoted to District Engineer for Maintenance before Christmas. She drilled him with questions.

Elena pretended to pay attention to their conversation and listened to Louis Armstrong and Ella Fitzgerald sing "Our Love is Here to Stay" from speakers hidden in the ceiling. She wondered how they could make such romantic music together without being a couple.

The champagne arrived. Elena cringed inside and fought the urge to bump Michael's leg under the table as he inspected the bottle, asked questions that didn't need to be asked, and sniffed the cork. The harried waitress finished pouring, buried the bottle in the silver ice bucket, and slipped away.

"I'd like to propose a toast," he said, raising his glass. He smiled at each of them in turn. "Happy Mother's Day to the two best mothers in the world."

They clinked and sipped.

His set his glass down and reached for his mother's and Elena's hand. "There's more big news, Mom."

Her eyes widened. "What?"

"We want you to be the first to know that we're engaged."

"How wonderful!" Maria exclaimed, raising her hand to her chest. Her eyes welled up.

Michael stood and hugged her. "Our thirty-year dream is finally coming true, Mom."

Maria wiped her eyes with the back of her hand. "I'm so happy for the both of you." Rising to her feet, she hurried around the table and hugged Elena.

"Welcome to the Marino family, honey."

"Thank—"

"What am I saying?" Maria interrupted, pulling away from their embrace. "You've been family a long time. I can't wait to tell everyone."

Michael's smile disappeared. A pregnant silence hung in the air as Maria returned to her seat. The restaurant's din seemed to grow louder.

"We can't tell anyone for five weeks, Mom."

Maria looked as if she had won the lottery and been handed a postdated check. "Why not?"

He turned to his fiancée. "She'll explain."

Elena cleared her throat, pleased that Michael hadn't reneged on his promise to let her explain the reason for the delay. She had memorized a script in bed that morning.

"As you know, Maria," she began, "Sara's daughter Catherine got engaged two weeks ago. If we announce our engagement now, we'll draw attention away from her. … Michael was kind enough—classy enough—to agree to wait until the Shaughnessy family vacation next month to break the news. But we couldn't wait to tell you."

"I'm honored to be the first to know." Maria dabbed her eyes with her napkin. Her lips twisted into a resigned smile. "You two've waited thirty years. What's another month?"

Elena suppressed her sigh of relief. "Thank you for understanding."

Maria covered her mouth and coughed. "I won't tell a soul. Not even my sisters."

❧ ❧ ❧

Elena spent what remained of her Mother's Day afternoon juggling errands, laundry, and her kids. The garden center at Lowe's was packed. Jack called to wish her a happy Mother's Day and talked more than usual. Emma apologized for not being home and fretted about her biology final.

After a light dinner alone, Elena escaped to her garden. She thought about her mom and how she would give anything to spend a single afternoon with her. Shifting mental gears, she contemplated the joys and pains of parenthood and mostly laughed, but also shed tears of regret over her failures as a mother.

As the sun set, the two dissenting voices in her head battled to another standstill. She remained torn between her fear of marrying Michael and not marrying him. Her spirits sank at the uncertainty of where she'd be living in three months. She resolved to have a long talk with her father, which she'd been putting off for at least three months, long before he had fallen and broken his hip.

When dusk passed into darkness, Elena parked her cart in its stall of the garage and hurried upstairs to her bedroom. She peeled off her clothes and stepped into the shower. The jets of hot water massaged her neck, shoulders, and mind. She reached for the body wash and sponge and turned her thoughts back to the moment yesterday morning at Kretchmar's Bakery when Patrick had invited her to have coffee or lunch with him.

I wonder how often he visits his mother. He's easy to look at, but my attraction is more than physical. I can't remember a man intriguing me so much. ... Am I losing my mind? How can I want to see him again when I'm not even single? But if I were ...

꼿 꼿 꼿

While driving to Penn State early Monday morning, Michael spent the first hour of their trip on the phone touching base with his section chiefs. Paving schedules and office politics bored Elena. She finished reading a chapter of Jane Austen's *Sense and Sensibility,* closed her eyes, and wondered if his fascination with the seasonal swap between asphalt and road salt would ever wane. She doubted it would and reminded herself that she too worked in the transportation business.

She visualized the SLIPPERY WHEN WET retired road sign—a gift from Michael—that hung in the maternity unit's break room. A second image flashed in her mind, the slick black hair and squinty eyes of the baby boy she had guided down a woman's birth canal Friday afternoon.

Michael finished his call. "Sorry I've been neglecting you."

She opened her eyes. "No problem."

He turned on the radio. "Today and tomorrow are your Mother's Day," he said over the sound of U2's "Mysterious Ways."

"I won't be able to relax until tomorrow evening, when Jack and Emma are both home and settling in."

"With the two of them working in Pittsburgh this summer, you'll be like three ships passing in the night."

"I've already told them we're having dinner together at least three nights every week. And Sundays."

Elena leaned forward and opened the Explorer's vanity mirror. While taming her hair, she pondered her children's relationship with their father. It saddened her that James made so little effort to see them.

"You spend more time with them than James does," she

said. "If I weren't around, he'd probably pay a mover to take them back and forth to school."

"At least he helped them get their summer internships."

She closed the visor and reached for Michael's hand. "Speaking of help, thanks again for taking today and tomorrow off from work. It means a lot to me."

"I can't wait to become their step-father."

Elena glanced at the dashboard clock. "Emma's biology final started ten minutes ago. I hope it's going well."

She reclined her seat, closed her eyes, and pictured the Christmas photo card she'd received last December from Meryl Dixon, her ex-husband's wife. Fifty-two-year-old James Simmons stood on the deck of a Norwegian Cruise Line ship holding hands with his jeweled, tanned, and plasticized sixty-year-old wife. Elena relished the memory of tossing the card in the fireplace.

She'd been ashamed but relieved when her marriage ended three years ago. Meryl had run James' orthopedic surgery group for fifteen years. She now ran his life. Despite incriminating evidence, he never admitted to the affair. They were married fourteen months after Elena had sent him packing.

She opened her eyes. Her gaze slid across the wall of rock that had been sculpted by dynamite to clear a path for the highway. *Being replaced by an older woman is worse than being replaced by a younger one*, she thought. *But it's better than being replaced by a man. ... Or is it?*

Her mind drifted back to a week after James' wedding when, after declining Michael's previous four invitations, she had agreed to have dinner with him. She'd felt old and ugly, cast off, lonely. Michael had been divorced for nearly twenty years and was generally regarded as Beaver's most eligible bachelor. Before she knew it, weeks and months had passed and they were a couple again. She hadn't been strong enough to break things off.

His phone rang, jarring her from her reverie.

"It's the boss again." He tapped the screen. "Hi Mom."

While listening to him answer and re-answer Maria's questions about their engagement and wedding plans, Elena tried to gauge where his relationship with his mother stood on the spectrum between love and control. She wondered the same thing about her own relationship with Maria. Clear answers eluded her.

Maria's open arms and ears had been a godsend to Elena during her first few motherless years. She had dined often at Maria's table and spent evenings alone with her when Michael went out with his friends. She regretted breaking her heart thirty years ago when she had broken his and wished she could quantify and repay the emotional debt she owed to her.

Elena's thoughts turned to her emptying nest. The combination of her mom's early death and her own divorce had heightened her need to be a good mother. Jack and Emma remained her highest priority and the primary source of her identity. She wanted them to thrive on their own, but not until she ironed out more of their wrinkles.

My time is running out.

She slipped off to sleep.

❧ ❧ ❧

The next night, shortly before midnight, Elena wept as she paced laps around three sides of her bed. She leaned toward the dresser mirror, stuck her tongue out, and inspected its red tip. Returning to her horseshoe path, she replayed the evening's events in her mind.

Wine and laughter had flowed as she, Michael, Emma, and Jack cooked dinner together. A Caesar salad was followed by an entrée of penne pasta in a garlic butter sauce topped with grilled chicken and a medley of spices. The scent of magnolias wafted across the deck. The conversation was better than the food. She forgot her worries.

As dusk descended, it surprised her that neither of her kids showed any signs of wanting to leave the table. Their phone-free hands and eyes thrilled her. It wasn't until they offered to do the dishes and began to clear the table that she suspected something was awry. When she asked what was going on, Jack told her in a kind but matter-of-fact tone that he had decided to live that summer at his father's home in

Wexford. He explained that he'd get thirty more minutes of sleep each night and spend half as much time and gas commuting to his internship at PNC Bank. He finished by promising to mow her lawn every week.

Emma's brave mask had melted before Jack turned to her. Tears rolled down her cheeks as she announced that one of her Alpha Phi sorority sisters at Case Western had invited her to live in the guest bedroom of her parents' home in Mount Lebanon. She'd be six miles instead of thirty from her internship at the UPMC Center for Integrative Medicine. She apologized again, hugged her mom, and promised to visit often.

Elena stared at the moon, wanting to wail. She longed to tell Jack that she loved him twice as much as his father ever had or would and that Meryl and his dad would drive him crazy within a week. She wanted to accuse Emma of abandoning her and having an ulterior motive—to spend nights at her boyfriend Christopher's apartment. Instead, she bit down hard on the tip of her tongue and tasted blood.

This was supposed to be our last summer together. I need them more than they need me. ... Where is the line between love and control?

A tear soaked through her blouse and felt cool on her chest. Elena wiped her cheeks with the back of her hand, lowered her gaze to the half-eaten cherry pie in the middle of the table, and took a deep breath.

"It kills me to say this," she said, her eyes alternating between Jack and Emma, "but my most important job as your mother is to teach you to be independent. Teach you to not need me. ... Teach you to fly."

She smiled through her tears. "Please come home for dinner on Sundays."

CHAPTER SEVEN

You'll repent if you marry, and repent if you don't.
–*Publilius Syrus*

The next morning Elena hit the snooze button and dropped her head back on the pillow. She tried in vain to keep the fragments of two dreams from blurring together and drifting up the chimney of her mind. The conscious remains of the night smoldered inside her brain. She recalled waking up at a little after three, having another good cry, and resigning herself to the reality that Jack and Emma wouldn't be living at home this summer.

Emotional stretch marks hurt like hell, but an empty nest never killed anybody. Pick yourself up.

The dawn light guided her into the bathroom. After peeing, showering, and going through her usual morning routine, she covered the dark circles under her eyes with concealer. She slipped into a pair of scrubs, wolfed down a bowl of Honey Bunches of Oats, blew a kiss at her mother's photo, and hurried to the garage.

The four days she'd been off work had felt like ten. Her walk from the parking lot to the Mother-Baby Unit equaled her five-minute commute to the hospital. The collage of sights, smells, and sounds comforted her. She greeted her co-workers, squeezed her lunch into the refrigerator, and resumed directing an old crew of nurses and a new cast of mothers and babies in humanity's oldest drama.

❧ ❧ ❧

Late that Saturday morning Michael stopped at a traffic light in downtown Pittsburgh and turned to Elena. "You know the saying, 'Diamonds are a girl's best friend?'"

"Yes?"

"Well, I want you to love your diamond almost as much as you love me."

She smiled with clenched teeth. Now wasn't the time to explain why she couldn't love a diamond the way she loved a person. He drove forward. A wave of nausea rose from the pit of her stomach. Her mind raced. She took a long, slow breath and rubbed her belly the way she had when Jack and Emma kicked inside her womb. Michael seemed to be oblivious to her distress.

He turned into a parking garage and stopped to grab a ticket from the automated attendant. They spiraled up the ramp, adding to Elena's dizziness. She closed her eyes and pictured a diamond ring on her finger. A surge of adrenaline coursed through her body, quelling her inner storm. She let out a sigh and unclenched her fists.

"The ramp made me dizzy," she said, in case he'd noticed her discomfort.

"Maybe it's menopause."

She pointed to her left. "There's a space."

He parked and they walked toward the elevator. This was the closest he had ever come to witnessing one of her panic attacks. Since Wednesday evening, when he informed her that he'd made an appointment to look at diamonds today, she had suffered four of them, including this mini-attack.

Anxiety added to her anxieties, but she dreaded the thought of taking medication. Anti-depressants depressed her. Twenty- five years had passed since her second treatment for panic disorder. While riding a wave of anxiety in bed last night, she imagined a diamond ring on her finger and the feeling of panic diminished as if a whistling teakettle had been lifted off the stove inside her brain.

At first Elena had thought it was a fluke, a lucky break. Then, in her garden this morning, she admitted to herself that she felt naked without a wedding ring on her finger and missed all that a diamond represented: security, beauty, purity, strength, everlasting love. Michael had flaws, but so did diamonds—and so did she. The tide of the war in her head had shifted. She now feared not marrying him more than she feared marrying him.

"Don't forget what I told you last night," she said, stepping off the garage elevator. "It takes a woman more than an hour or two to pick out a diamond."

He took her hand and led her out of the garage, across Liberty Avenue, and into the Clark Building. An ancient elevator deposited them on the fourth floor of Pittsburgh's diamond district. They walked down a deserted corridor lined with shops that looked nothing like mall jewelers. He stopped in front of a smoked glass door painted with gold lettering.

Nardelli Diamond Merchants
–By Appointment Only–

The whine of a high-speed drill leaked through the oak door across the hall. *It sounds more like a dentist's office than a jewelry store*, Elena thought. The drill stopped and started. "Remember," he whispered in her ear, "Anthony Nardelli doesn't cut or set diamonds or sell to the public. Let me do most of the talking."

Michael studied the biometric identification pad and placed the tip of his index finger on the amber circle of light. Twin bolt locks snapped open.

They stepped inside a diamond store that hadn't changed since the 1950s. Fluorescent light bounced off the U-shaped array of empty display cases. She half expected an elderly Jewish man to pop up from behind the vintage cash register, lower a gold-chained monocle from his eye, and welcome them in Dutch-accented English. Footsteps fell behind the shop's rear wall.

A man she assumed to be Anthony Nardelli sauntered through the swinging door, grinning a grin that could melt a diamond off a woman's finger. "Welcome, Michael and Elena. Congratulations on your engagement," he said, swaggering around the horseshoe display case. His white T-shirt and black Armani jeans accentuated his non-facial assets. Meticulously unshaven, his neck and fingers draped in more jewelry than she wore in a week, he was virile in the way only Mediterranean men can be. She guessed he was forty-five, a bachelor.

He and Michael hugged and kissed cheeks. Bypassing a formal introduction, he turned to Elena, greeted her as he had Michael, and remained standing close enough to blow in her ear. She thought about drifting a step or two away but opted to let him trespass inside her personal space. He smelled delicious, and she didn't want to offend him. She ignored the men's commentary on the weekend's PGA golf tournament and listened to their body language.

Five minutes ago Elena had known only three things

about Anthony Nardelli: he was Italian, the cousin of one of Michael's longtime golf buddies, and a jeweler. She now understood much more. For one thing, Michael would never trust him alone with her. For another, she no longer worried whether the diamond dealer could be trusted with the secret of their engagement. Her instincts told her that he knew and had many secrets.

She wasn't surprised when Michael, the senior male, shifted the conversation to business. "Anthony," he said in a rolling Italian-American voice, his hands waving in the air. "I trust that you'll treat Elena and I like *family*. We already know the diamond cartel's 4-C bullshit, so let's skip formalities. Show us what you got."

"From what you told me on the phone, Michael," Anthony Nardelli said, rubbing his palms together, "I picked out ten diamonds you two'd be proud to own." He started toward the swinging door. "Come back to my office."

While walking between the men, Elena wondered what they had discussed on the phone and why Michael hadn't consulted her beforehand. They entered the office, passed an uncomfortable-looking white sofa, and stopped at a round glass table. Their host pulled out two acrylic chairs. "Please make yourselves comfortable," he said, motioning for them to sit.

They declined a drink and settled into their seats. The diamond merchant stepped to a corner of the office and squatted in front of an antique safe. Not wanting to smudge the glass tabletop, Elena tucked her purse under the chair and rested her hands on her lap. Dean Martin crooned "You're Nobody 'Til Somebody Loves You" from the Bose sound system that lay by itself on the stainless credenza. She fiddled with her bracelets and reminded herself not to ask about price. Her intuition told her that each of the diamonds would be in Michael's price range and that the men would negotiate in private. The safe clicked open and closed.

Humming along with Dean, Anthony Nardelli sat beside Michael and shook diamonds from a red Cartier pouch onto a black velvet display pad. Elena tingled with excitement as he coaxed the last stone with a finger, silently counted to ten, and arranged them in a row from smallest to largest.

After sliding the pad toward his customers, he offered a loupe to Michael, who declined it in a tone of voice that said, *I'd never question your integrity.* The jeweler laid the loupe above the diamonds and handed a pair of tweezers to Elena, inviting her to have a look.

She pinched the sides of the largest stone between the tongs and raised it toward her eyes. "This one's enormous."

And gaudy.

She set the diamond and the tweezers on the pad, picked up the loupe, and smiled at Anthony Nardelli.

"Do you mind?"

"Not at all."

She slid the stainless cover away from the lens and raised the loupe to her closed right eye. Using her left eye and hand, she lifted the same diamond with the tweezers, positioned it a few inches below the glass, and switched eyes.

"Wow. What a difference. It's so much clearer. Facets within facets."

Smooth on the surface but turbulent underneath. Just like me.

The men were silent. Elena felt their eyes on her. She dropped the gem in the palm of Michael's hand and repeated the drill with each of the other diamonds. After handing him the smallest one, she asked, "Which one do you like best?"

He set the diamond down and raised the largest one between his thumb and forefinger. "Other than size, they all look the same to me." He returned the stone to the pad. "Which is *your* favorite?"

She used the tweezers to gather all but the smallest diamond into a cluster. "These ones are all too big." She pointed at the lone diamond. "I bet this one's the best of the lot. It's practically flawless and not at all small." She turned to Anthony Nardelli. "How many carats is it?"

"One-and-a-half."

"And the largest one?"

"A hair over three-point-two."

Elena thanked him, lifted her purse off the floor, and said to Michael, "Let's sleep on it for a few days before we decide."

❧ ❧ ❧

"I'll make a deal with you," Michael said to her forty minutes later, after they had ordered lunch at the Sewickley Hotel.

"What?"

"I'll let you choose the diamond if you'll let me tell my brothers about our engagement."

"No, Michael, you agreed to wait. And when you proposed, you said I—"

"I say we buy the biggest diamond." He looked away and raised his hand to flag a waiter.

The biggest one is huge, Elena thought. *Way too flashy for me. Do they all cost the same? Where does Anthony Nardelli get them? ... Drugs? Mafia?*

Michael asked for more water.

"When you proposed," she said in an even voice, "you said you wanted me to pick out my diamond."

"We haven't had sex since I proposed." He ran his hands through his hair and sighed heavily. "It's been eight days. Why are we already acting like we're married?"

CHAPTER EIGHT

Dancing is a wonderful training for girls,
it's the first way you learn to guess what a man
is going to do before he does it.
–*Christopher Morley*

Two evenings later, on a stormy Monday, Elena greeted her
father in his room at Friendship Ridge, set her umbrella and
purse on the radiator along the wall, and slid the vinyl chair
toward his recliner. "You look like a Steelers coach in your
black and gold sweater, Dad."

He winked at her and smiled. "Don't tell Sara I wore it
before your birthday."

Elena turned an imaginary key against her lips. "It'll be
our little secret."

They watched the NBC Evening News in silence until
it broke for a commercial. "It's bingo night, Dad," she said,
lowering the volume with the remote. "I dodged a caravan

of walkers and wheelchairs downstairs in the lobby. What do you say we show your neighbors some of our Shaughnessy magic?"

Her father took off his glasses, held them up to the light, and breathed steam on the lenses. "How far is it?"

She thought a moment. "About as far as it is from your house to the Beaver Library. We can rest on a bench along the way."

He finished wiping his glasses with his handkerchief. "Okay, I'll give it a go. Too bad it's bingo and not cards."

Thunder rumbled outside. Elena's imagination leapt back to her childhood. "Remember how we used to play gin rummy while Mom cooked dinner?"

He waggled his eyebrows at her the way he had when she was a girl. "I remember playing, but I don't remember winning."

"*You* taught me to play," she said with a proud chuckle. "Every weekday at five-thirty I'd race home on my red Schwinn."

He scratched his chin. "A boy's bike with a banana seat. I bought it at Snitger's."

"You told me it was from Santa."

"It was—"

She matched his grin. The news came back on, a story about falling oil prices. Watching without listening, Elena tingled with nostalgia at the memory of the unbridled joy she'd felt the day her father had removed the training wheels from her bike. The look of pride on his face as she wobbled down the driveway would forever be etched in her mind.

He closed the recliner and moved like a tired seal on land toward the edge of the seat. "I'll never forget the day you gave the Anderson boy a bloody nose."

"He wouldn't stop calling me 'Danny Partridge.'"

"Danny who?"

"The redheaded kid on *The Partridge Family*."

"Oh. I made you help the Anderson boy to his feet and shake his hand. ... He was a grade or two ahead of you. What was his name?"

She shook her head in wonder. "How do you remember these things, Dad? ... Brian Anderson was twelve. I was eleven. A year later he was six inches taller and I wouldn't have stood a chance."

"A year later he asked you to dance."

Elena looked at him curiously. "Brian Anderson was the first boy to ask me to dance. How did you know?"

"Your mother swore me to secrecy, but I think the statute of limitations has expired."

"You're a character, Dad." She squeezed his arm. "You always know how to lift my spirits. I wish Michael and I could ..."

"Could what?"

"Have such playful banter."

He kicked off his slippers. "Please hand me my shoes, Lanie."

She reached for a pair of black canvas slip-ons and

squatted in front of him. "Lift your foot." She slipped his left shoe on and patted its tongue.

"How is Michael?" he asked, raising his other foot.

"He's golfing in the rain with his Monday evening league."

"I sensed tension between you two at my birthday party. Is everything alright?"

"Just a little tiff." She weighed whether to say more, but decided against it. It had been a long day and she was tired. Setting his foot on the floor, she stood and backed his rolling walker toward him. "Let's go win some prizes."

Moments later they approached a crowd of residents gathered outside the assembly room. Clouds of perfume melded into a floral fog.

"You made it, Dad," she said in his ear.

"My hip is begging me to sit."

"Out here or inside?"

He stepped through the doorway. While strolling toward a square of tables at the center of the church-sized room, Elena was reminded of the night she had chaperoned Jack's first middle-school dance. She wondered where all the men were. "I see you got your second wind," she said, taking her father's elbow. "Or are you prancing for the ladies?"

"They're all *old*."

She led the way to two women seated in wheelchairs and milled around behind them. Dressed in their Sunday best, they seemed to have their wits about them. She suspected their only malady was that the shelf date on their legs had expired. "Look, Pauline," one of them said to her tablemate, "Betty is wearing her fake pearls."

Dad would have a heart attack if we sat here.

Frank Sinatra's "I've Got You Under My Skin," began to play. Elena's eyes were drawn to movement near the piano at the corner of the room. She recognized Irene's hat.

Patrick! They're dancing. … How sweet of him.

"Let's watch the dancers, Dad," she said, tugging on his arm. She pulled out two chairs at the next table, helped him into one of them, and sat down. Irene, clutching an armrest of her wheelchair with one hand and snapping her fingers with the other, beamed as Patrick zigged and zagged her around an area twice the size of Elena's dining room.

They're in their own little world. Having so much fun. …

"That's Duke Ellington's 'Take the A Train,'" her father said during the opening notes of the next song. "That young man has excellent taste in music."

Elena nodded at her dad and scanned the room. Toes were tapping, heads were bobbing. She turned back to the dancers as Patrick raced his mother toward the baby grand piano's open mouth. Braking to a stop at the last second, he pulled her wheelchair backwards in a sweeping *S* curve.

"Your mother and I used to get lost in each other on the dance floor, Lanie." He leaned closer. "I wouldn't be surprised if you and Sara were conceived after a night of dancing."

They exchanged knowing looks and resumed watching the dancers.

I hope they cancel bingo. I could watch them—him—all night. … I keep telling Jack and Emma that the way a man treats his mother is the way he'll treat his wife. I wonder if he'd give Dad and me a dance lesson. …

Another song began with a piano introduction Elena remembered from her childhood. "Isn't that one of those Bossa Nova songs you and Mom used to play?"

"Yes." Her father tapped his foot to the beat. "Sergio Mendes. 'The Look of Love.'"

Patrick pushed Irene forward three small steps, pulled her backwards two large ones to a home position, and spun her wheelchair a quarter turn, counterclockwise, from twelve to nine o'clock. He repeated the sequence of three pushes, two pulls, and a quarter turn until they completed a full circle. Then he glided her forward with the same three small steps, but on their trip back home, he swished and swerved her as if he were a matador and she a red cape.

Patrick completed another circuit and took a sideways step to his left. Gripping the wheelchair's nearer handle in his right hand, he spun his mother in tight circles during the song's climax, a flurry of tender pleas in which the male and female singers took turns beseeching the other to never go. At the twelve o'clock of each twirl, Irene lifted her foot a few inches, as if to salute the bull.

The song ended. Elena and her father joined a smattering of residents in clapping. Patrick waved at the bingo crowd to acknowledge the applause. His eyes met hers. She knew from years of delivering babies what sheer joy looked like.

❧ ❧ ❧

Elena called her dad late that Wednesday morning and arranged for them to take a walk outside during her lunch break. She worked only a few minutes away and wanted him to get some exercise and enjoy the May sunshine.

A half-hour later, while waiting for the elevator to take them downstairs, she overheard Sally Horton say to an aide, "Housekeeping is cleaning Irene Jameson's room. A new admission is coming at two-thirty."

Elena stepped away from her father and approached Sally. "I couldn't help hearing you mention Irene Jameson's name. Has she moved back home or to another facility?"

"No," Sally said, sadness in her eyes and voice. "Irene passed away last night at the emergency room."

"Aw." Elena's breath caught in her throat. She fought to keep her eyes from welling up. "She and Patrick were dancing together just Monday evening."

"I know. They were so excited to dance in the talent show this afternoon."

CHAPTER NINE

Thank God for your mother.
–David O. Selznick

That Friday morning Patrick stepped inside a funeral home for the first time since his late wife Kate's death six years ago. He arrived at J&J Spratt Funeral Home forty-five minutes after his mother's private family viewing had begun. He departed fifteen minutes later feeling orphaned, adrift.

While driving across town to Holy Family Catholic Church, he consoled himself by considering how much worse the past few days would have been if his mom hadn't insisted years earlier that she not be laid out at a funeral home for what she called "public consumption." He knew that vanity had factored into his mother's desire for privacy. Still, he admired her willingness to buck convention. It was with traces of this Irene—this mom—that Patrick had reconnected on the dance floor these past two months.

He parked where the funeral director had suggested and wandered to the aisle seat of the left front pew, where his sister Maureen, her husband Frank, and twenty-four-year-old daughter Jennifer completed his immediate family. He joined them in kneeling, prayed for the strength to get through the day, and reflected on a painful reality.

Many of the people who were gathering behind him had treated his mother differently since her first stroke five years ago. Some of her family members and friends had gone so far as to ignore her altogether, as if dementia had killed her. He recalled how much the Jekyll-and-Hyde transformation of his mom's personality had disturbed him at first and reminded himself that she hadn't been singled out. As a psychiatrist, he'd long known that the stigma of mental illness was real and that it stemmed mostly from fear. But it still hurt.

He sat back on the pew and glanced at his watch. *Eight more minutes.*

Patrick scratched his chin and pondered the cultural customs and religious rites that hovered, mistlike, over death. He understood and respected that most people found consolation in these public expressions of tribute and grief. But it all felt like a spectacle to him, a cross between Memorial Day and Halloween. Casketed corpses spooked him. With their coiffed hair and ballooned, masked, and costumed bodies, they struck him as spiritless ghosts of real people. He planned to be cremated and have his remains scattered over his favorite waterfall.

He gazed at the crucifix hanging on the wall behind the altar and turned his thoughts back to Tuesday morning when Sally Horton had called to inform him that his mother was showing symptoms of a urinary tract infection. Two calls later, when dusk was drifting into night, he learned from another nurse that his mom had taken a turn for the worse and would be transported to the emergency room. He left a message on Maureen's phone, rushed to the hospital, and greeted his semi-conscious mother when the EMTs lowered her gurney from the ambulance to the ground.

It didn't take the ER physician long to diagnose pneumonia and explain to him that his mom's lungs were filling with fluid and any attempts to stem the tide would only prolong her suffering. Patrick, fulfilling his mother's wish that extraordinary measures not be taken, signed a consent form authorizing an injection of morphine. The doctor told him what to expect and when to expect it. A nurse administered the drug.

When Patrick and his mom were alone in the ER cubicle, he closed the curtain, turned off the light, lowered the bedrail, and sat sideways, facing her. "I'll help you, Mom," he said, stroking her cheek.

Her breathing began to ease and quiet as the morphine kicked in. Her eyes remained open.

He brushed a few stray locks of hair off her forehead and half-spoke, half-sang, "There's no other—*like* my mother."

Her hint of a smile compelled him to repeat the lullaby, this time in a singsong voice. Changing the tempo and pitch with each verse, he weighed whether to ask her an important question. During many of his visits going back about eighteen months, including Monday evening before they danced together, he had asked her playfully, *Do you know who I am?* Without fail, she'd study him a while, a puzzled look on her face, and answer, *You're my boy. Patrick.*

Finishing another verse, he leaned his head closer to hers. "There's no other, like my mother," he said, this time speaking the words. His chest rose and fell.

"Am I your boy, Patrick?"

Her vacant eyes clung to the ceiling, her breathing shallowed to a rasp. He squeezed her hand, as if to save her from drowning.

Maternal love flickered in her eyes.

The heart monitor fell silent.

"Goodbye, Mom." He kissed her cheek and cried.

Patrick jumped in his seat as the organist played the opening notes to "Be Not Afraid." He wiped his eyes, nodded at the crucifix, stood, and faced the back of the church. Four funeral attendants rolled his mother's casket to the altar. When the choir finished, the priest began the Mass.

Patrick shed sporadic tears throughout the ceremony.

After Communion, he knelt, closed his eyes to pray, and wept instead. He leaned his backside against the pew, laid his arm on the railing, and rested his forehead on it. Maureen draped an arm across his heaving shoulders. Mucus poured from his nose.

When the worst had passed, he slid back onto the pew bench, wiped his eyes and cheeks with his handkerchief, and blew his nose. The closing song began. The attendants surrounded the coffin. The funeral director guided him to join the procession out of the sanctuary.

Patrick walked alone, staring at the back door of the church. When the casket stopped, he took a deep breath and turned toward the crowd of fifty or so relatives, neighbors, friends, and colleagues who approached Maureen. He recognized people he hadn't seen in decades.

Renee Ballard, his practice manager and best female friend, was first in line. After hugging him, she slipped one of her husband's white hankies into his hand and whispered, "Wipe your nose or everyone will see your boogers."

He burst into laughter, dabbed his eyes, and wiped his nose, just in case.

"What would I do without you, Renee?"

"Muddle along, I guess. The office is filling fast with food and cards." She embraced him again. "Don't forget to forget your fears and practice what you preach."

"Yes, Doctor Ballard," he teased.

Patrick's encounter with Renee helped him to relax and open himself to receiving the hugs, handshakes, and words of consolation that followed.

Betty Hathaway, his late wife's mother, stood last in line. Despite her petite frame, she gave him the best hug he'd had since their last visit three or four months ago. "I'm so sorry about your mother, Patrick. You're living proof that Irene was a great woman."

"Thanks, Betty."

"They're ready to move things along," she said, glancing birdlike to either side of him. "I'll have you over for dinner soon. Let me know if there's anything I can do."

"I will."

She stepped away. He felt a tap on his shoulder and turned.

"Elena!"

They skipped hellos and hugged.

"Thank you so much for coming."

Her lips twitched. "I'm so sorry about your Mom."

"Sorry to interrupt you, Patrick," the funeral director said, tugging his elbow. "We'll be departing for the cemetery in five minutes."

"I'll be right out."

He turned back to Elena. Her hunter green scrubs brought out the color in her eyes.

"I'll let you go," she said, handing him a card.

"Thanks." He took her elbow and started toward the door.

❧ ❧ ❧

After his mother's burial and a small family luncheon, Patrick stopped at his mom's house to retrieve her lockbox, which was hidden in his old bedroom. The closet door creaked open. His mom's slacks, halved over hangers, hung like a flat rainbow across the cast iron pipe. Retired linens and blankets bulged from the top and side shelves.

He knelt on one knee, cleared a path through the two-high, two-deep stacks of shoeboxes, and found the lockbox. Pulling it out of the closet, he bumped and toppled a bedspread that was stuffed inside a clear, zippered bag on the bottom shelf to his left. A vintage suitcase stood upright behind where the bedspread had lain.

He slid the black valise out of the closet and brushed his fingers across the ragged corners and frayed leather handle. *It looks like something out of a 1950s movie. It's heavy. I wonder what's inside.* He laid it flat on the floor and thumbed the latches. The clasps snapped open. He lifted the lid.

"What the fuh—"

CHAPTER TEN

The deepest search in life, it seemed to me,
the thing that in one way or another was central to all
living, was man's search to find a father.
– *Thomas Wolfe*

Patrick raced home as if the vintage suitcase lying on his passenger seat contained a bomb.

The next hours passed in a blur. The collective aroma of the hundreds of books lining the floor-to-ceiling shelves in his library failed to mask the odor of history leaking from the piles of papers and photographs strewn across his desk. He sifted through clues to the mystery that had haunted him since he was a child: the story of his father, Mitchell Jameson, and how he had abandoned Maureen, him, and their mother forty-seven years ago.

The grandfather clock struck in the hall, breaking Patrick's concentration as he reread his mom's diary entries from the weeks prior to his birth. He rubbed his eyes with his hands and counted eleven more chimes. His stomach rumbled.

He tucked the stationery box full of his mother' old diaries into a corner of the satin-lined valise, which lay open on the hardwood floor to his left. His eyes slid from the red-lettered "CONSTABLE'S SALE" notice to the tattered edges of a roll of blueprints for a fictitious home. He picked up the bundle of love letters from Mitchell to Irene, straightened them against the desk, and set them beside the stack of eight-by-ten black-and-white wedding photos.

Patrick stretched his legs under the desk, gazed at the wall of books to his right, and reviewed what he had learned. A month after her twenty-ninth birthday and five years before becoming his mother, Irene O'Malley had eloped to Tennessee. Including the priest, five people were present at the wedding ceremony. The morning after, Irene discovered the first of her husband's many lies when they remained in Chattanooga instead of departing for a European cruise. Over the next two weeks, Mitchell's three-month-old Pontiac was repossessed and his coal business was sold for a dollar to get out from under debt. Within a month Irene was pregnant with Maureen.

Of the fifty or more pages in his mom's handwriting, three stood out. Across the top of each she'd written _Physical Abuse_. One sentence stuck with him: _I crouched down and covered my stomach to protect Patrick._

He clenched his eyes shut and succeeded in not imagining his mother battered and bruised. His thoughts skipped to another shocking discovery: Mitchell Jameson had claimed he wasn't his biological father. The photographs proved otherwise.

How hard it must have been for Mom to look at me and be reminded of him. ... She sacrificed so much more than I ever dreamed.

Patrick now understood why his mother, who had used the information in the suitcase as evidence in her case for an annulment in the Catholic Church, had told Maureen and him so little about their father. *Mom must have kept all of this because she wanted us to know the truth. After she was gone.*

He opened his eyes and reached for a black-and-white snapshot of his mother walking out of a church holding Maureen's hand. The photograph had caught his eye a few hours earlier when he noticed that his mom was wearing the same hat he'd recently brought her to wear at Friendship Ridge. Looking again at the month and year date-stamped on the bottom border of the photo, he shook his head in amazement. He'd been born nine months later.

Awash in feelings of love and respect for his mother, Patrick rose to his feet, turned out the lamps, and walked to the kitchen. He dug two magnets out of a drawer and hung the picture of his mom on the refrigerator. It stood alone.

Moments later, while brushing his teeth, he remembered Elena's card. He hurried to the closet, pulled it from the inside pocket of his suit jacket, and tore open the envelope.

With Deepest Sympathy was printed on ivory paper in slate gray ink. The card's classic elegance didn't surprise him. He opened it.

> *Dear Patrick,*
>> *Your dear mother was blessed to have you as her son and final dance partner.*
>> *When things settle down for you, my dad and I would like to take you up on your offer of a dance lesson. If bribery is necessary, would a Kretchmar's cake do the trick?*
>> *No rush. (412) 528-8793*
>
>> *Warmly,*
>> *Elena*

Patrick reread Elena's note twice. Her words felt like a hug.

🐾 🐾 🐾

Late the next morning Elena and Michael were a few miles into their planned, five-mile walk through the streets of Beaver when her phone swished, announcing an incoming text message. "It's probably Emma," she said, pulling the phone from the pocket of her shorts. She held the screen at reading distance and didn't recognize the phone number.

Today 11:54 AM
Thanks for the card and for coming to my
mother's funeral mass. It was very thoughtful
of you. I'd be happy to give you and your
father a dance lesson.

A rush of warmth washed over Elena. She slipped the
phone back into her pocket and reminded herself that she and
Patrick were only friends.

"Who was that?" Michael asked.

"Something to do with dad. Who else will be at the
Falcona's party tonight?"

❧ ❧ ❧

When they finished their walk in her driveway, Michael told
Elena he'd be back at two-thirty, suggested they shower
together then, and headed home to mow his grass. The
thought of what he wanted them to do after showering left
her cold. Walking toward the house, she wondered if her
recent lack of libido stemmed solely from her conflicted
feelings about marrying him. Or was menopause finally
creeping in?

Ten minutes later, after tugging a shopping cart free at the
Beaver Supermarket, she stepped out of the way and typed a
response to Patrick's text.

Today 1:04 PM
My Dad went to the talent show on
Wednesday. He said you and your Mom
would have won first prize, hands-down.

Elena dropped the phone into her purse, passed a few
shoppers, rounded the bend, and squeezed a loaf of bread
before setting it in her cart. She worked her way to the meat
case and was comparing packages of chicken breasts when
her phone announced another text.

1:09 PM
She's the only girl I've ever danced with whose
feet were safe from mine.

Elena chuckled under her breath and tried to think of a
witty response. She warned herself not to reply too quickly. It
might give him the wrong impression.

After paying for her groceries, she wheeled her cart to the
sidewalk, parked it in front of her Explorer, and typed:

1:31 PM
I bet you've broken a lot more hearts than
toes. How are you holding up?

She pressed Send, returned home, and was putting eggs
in the refrigerator when Patrick's next text arrived.

1:37 PM
I'm sad to lose her, but glad she passed suddenly and won't suffer any more. She was eighty-one. It was her time.

Elena speculated that, based on his mother's age, Patrick may be older than he looked and older than she. She finished putting the groceries away and typed:

1:41 PM
It's so hard to lose our parents. My dad asked me yesterday why I've been hugging him so much lately.

After pressing Send, she sat on a stool at her kitchen island, sliced an apple, and surfed the *Fine Gardening* website. Her phone swished again.

1:45 PM
While you're dancing with him, you'll be hugging him without his knowing it. When would you like your lesson?

1:47 PM
Whenever you're feeling up to it. Weeknights are less hectic than weekends. What type of Kretchmar's cake would you like?

Bribery isn't necessary. But if you insist, the
nurses LOVE chocolate mousse cake.

1:49 PM
Oh, so you're a re-gifter?

Elena hurried upstairs, undressed, and stepped into the
shower. A minute later she planted a wet footprint on the bath
rug and reached for her phone on the sink.

I must be hearing things.

She climbed back into the shower and chided herself for
acting like a schoolgirl. *You're forty-nine. Engaged to be
married.*

After dressing, she went downstairs to the living room
and leafed through the latest edition of *Food Network
Magazine.* She hoped her re-gifter comment hadn't offended
Patrick.

Her phone swished, her heart leapt.

2:23 PM
Sorry for the delay. My sister called. I only
re-gift cakes.

Michael will be here any minute, she thought and typed:

2:25 PM
I need to run. Take care of yourself and let me
know when you're available for the lesson.

She remembered that Michael wanted them to shower together and have sex. *How can I say no without starting a fight? ... His impatience is growing faster than a marigold.*

Patrick's number flashed on her phone's screen.

2:27 PM
Keeping busy is one of the best remedies for grief. How about this Wednesday evening at 7:00?

2:28 PM
That works for me. Should we meet in the bingo hall?

A car door closed outside. Elena switched her phone to vibrate and dropped it into her purse. "We're only friends," she said under her breath.

CHAPTER ELEVEN

Least said, soonest mended.
–Irish Proverb

The following Thursday evening an orchestra of crickets chirped a lusty symphony and wild honeysuckle flavored the breeze across Sara's deck. The candle's flame cast a restless glow against the bottle of Merlot.

Elena finished pouring and raised her glass. "Cheers to the Shaughnessy sisters."

"Cheers."

They clinked and sipped.

Sara reached for a Godiva dark chocolate truffle. "How are Jack and Emma?"

"Good. They've been home more than I feared."

"I told you they would. How do they like their jobs?"

While Elena gave an update on Jack's internship, Sara's

eyes bounced back and forth between her and the *Brides* magazine lying on the table.

"Emma likes her job, too. What's the latest on Catherine's wedding dress?"

"The selection is huge," Sara said, her eyes lighting up. "Much bigger than when we were brides-to-be." She flipped to a marked page and slid the magazine toward Elena. "Isn't that off-the-shoulder neckline fabulous?" Before Elena could respond, Sara tapped her finger on the dress's hemline. "*Look* at the scalloped lace trim."

It didn't take long for Sara's monologue to bore Elena. She listened with one ear and reminded herself that she planned to wear an elegant but simple dress at her second wedding, and, when the time came, to let Emma choose a dress without her interference. If asked for her opinion on wedding matters, she'd give it, but she didn't want to go overboard the way some mothers did.

Sara segued to the subject of bridesmaids' dresses. Elena poured more wine and stole glances at the sky, trying to capture the instant when dusk passed into night. Experience told her that the rising full moon would make for a busy day at work tomorrow. Her thoughts swung back and forth between the public announcement in a few weeks of her and Michael's engagement and the private revelation to her sister tonight that Patrick Jameson had taught her to dance with their father.

"Weddings are so much more complicated now," Sara said, closing the magazine and pushing it and the candle toward the center of the table.

"I danced with Dad last night."

"*What?*" Sara asked, her voice and eyebrows rising. "He can barely walk."

"We borrowed a wheelchair. You should have seen him snapping his fingers to 'Fly Me to the Moon.'"

Sara's lips curled into a sly smile. "Does this have anything to do with the man you saw dancing with his mother? The guy who gave the cake to the nurses."

Elena nodded. The fingers of her right hand strummed, harplike, across the grooves of the wrought iron table. "His name is Patrick Jameson. His mother died last week, but he insisted on following through on his offer to give Dad and me a dance lesson."

"Is he single?"

"Yes, but I don't know why. He and Dad hit it off immediately. They went on and on about jazz, books, and the Steelers. Imagine the look on Dad's face when he asked Patrick where he went to college and learned that he's a Notre Dame graduate."

Stop blabbing. She took a gulp of wine.

"Do you think he's interested in you?"

Elena shook her head and lowered her gaze to the candle. "He met Michael at Dad's birthday party."

Feeling her sister's eyes on her, she slid the truffles closer and studied them as if a gold coin was hidden in one of them. She'd blame the wine if Sara mentioned her reddening cheeks.

"Behave yourself," Sara said, a blend of amusement and authority in her voice.

"I forgot how to misbehave a long time ago."

Sara nudged Elena's knee with hers under the table. "No you didn't."

Elena recrossed her ankles, bit into a truffle, and let the chocolate melt in her mouth. "Remember how Dad used to dance with us at family weddings?"

"They're some of my fondest memories of him."

"Mine too. I wish more men from our generation knew how to lead a woman around a dance floor."

"Dan and I haven't danced in years," Sara poured herself more wine. "We should take lessons before Catherine's wedding."

Elena hummed the melody of "The Girl from Ipanema."

"That was one of the songs we danced to last night. Wouldn't it be fun to learn how to tango or salsa?"

"Why don't you and Michael take lessons?"

"He says he will as soon as I go skydiving with him." Her eyes widened. "*That's* never happening."

☙ ☙ ☙

Later that night Elena slipped into a nightshirt, brushed her teeth, and stacked the decorative pillows from her bed onto the chair. The Merlot had cast a silken spell in her mind. She fetched her journal from the bottom drawer of the nightstand and crawled under the sheet, propping her back against two pillows.

She tugged on the ribbon page marker, flipped back a few pages, and read what she had longed to share with Sara but couldn't.

After our dance lesson, Patrick handed Dad a CD. Printed in indelible black ink beneath "Dancing with Mom" were the words, "and Dad." He told us his mother would be happy he was passing the dance baton on to the two of us.

He escorted us to the second floor and (as promised) re-gifted the Kretchmar's chocolate mousse cake to the nurses. He said it was from Dad and me and that we had paid him a handsome presenter's fee. He caught himself and explained that it was the fee that was handsome, NOT the presenter.

Patrick is smooth but not at all slippery. How refreshing. After he said goodbye to Dad, he pulled me aside and asked if I'd meet him outside at the gazebo in ten minutes—he had a favor to ask of me. I agreed.

I didn't keep him waiting more than five minutes. It felt like thirty.

We sat alone and talked about nothing for a while. Then he asked me if I'd visit an art gallery in Pittsburgh with him and share my impressions of two paintings he was having a difficult time choosing between. "I'm no art expert," I told him. He said he wanted a woman's perspective and that he knew me well enough to know I had good taste. I accepted. It's exhilarating to have a man solicit my opinion. (Yes, even a younger one. He's 47.) It's much more gratifying than compliments about my appearance.

Who knew sitting under a gazebo in front of a nursing home could be romantic?

Elena flipped the journal closed, turned off the lamp, and smiled herself to sleep.

Chapter Twelve

From a little spark may burst a flame.
    –Dante Alighieri

Elena took the Friday before Memorial Day off and spent the next four days gardening, bickering with Michael, finalizing plans for his fiftieth birthday party, staying away from the house during real estate showings, and cooking. She hosted a barbecue on Monday afternoon for her and Sara's family. Michael left early to golf. The girls helped her clean the kitchen.

After everyone left, she typed a text:

Today 8:32 PM
Hello Patrick. Would you mind if we made a few stops in the Strip District after we visit the art gallery on Saturday? I need to buy some bulk ingredients.

She pressed Send, filled the dryer with a load of towels, and got the rest of the house back in order. Her phone announced an incoming text.

Today 9:14 PM
Hi Elena. I don't mind. Thanks again for agreeing to help me select the painting.

She reread Patrick's text aloud: "Hi Elena. I don't mind. Thanks again for agreeing to help me select the painting."

The words struck her as impersonal, like something a psychiatrist would say to a patient who had agreed to help him choose plants for his office, not something he'd say to a new female friend who'd agreed to help him select a painting for his home.

She dumped the load of dry towels onto the sofa and began to fold them. With each towel she added another possible hidden meaning behind Patrick's text.

Calm down. He was probably just being polite.

She went upstairs, hoping a good night's rest would untangle the knots in her mind. After tucking herself into bed, she reflected on the ways men are like dogs and women are like cats. She wanted to purr, but her mind was a blur.

❧ ❧ ❧

Elena returned home from work the next day and plugged her phone into the charger on the kitchen counter. An unwritten statute of limitations had passed on what she now referred to as Patrick's "Thank You" text. She could no longer reply anything along the lines of, "You're welcome." It would send the wrong message. He could infer that she was disorganized, disinterested, or daft. And that was just the "D's."

The word disturbed popped into her head as she stripped out of her nursing scrubs, prompting her to slam the brakes on the Ferris wheel spinning inside her head. She needed to quit obsessing and either be content with waiting to hear from him again or steer the conversation in a new direction.

Elena hurried to the garden, pulled weeds, and compiled a list of safe topics she could raise with him: art, dancing, jazz, bakeries, food, books, psychology, football, flowers, and cars. She didn't want him to misunderstand her intentions. She wondered what her intentions were and what her curiosity about Patrick said about her relationship with Michael.

Fear compelled her to do nothing. Nothing but wait.

The shades of gray covering the walls of her mind darkened between then and Friday. Patrick's businesslike text on Monday and lack of communication since then had signaled to her that his intentions were platonic. Maybe he sensed that she'd developed a crush on him and wanted to let her down gently.

The darkest shade of gray—black—coated the floor of Elena's mind. Maybe Patrick was the type of man who liked to hint at a chase but run from a catch, like a fisherman more adept at setting hooks than handling fish. She'd read articles and been warned by her single girlfriends about men whose favorite sport was luring women into their nets only to keep them dangling beside the boat, or worse, to throw them overboard once they'd been filleted.

Her intuition told her that Patrick wasn't that type of man. But her intuition wasn't always right.

❧ ❧ ❧

That Friday evening Elena and Michael were engaged in a heated discussion about diamonds when her phone vibrated against the teak table on her deck. She picked it up and read a text from Patrick:

> *Today 8:49 PM*
> I look forward to seeing you tomorrow morning.

It's a good thing Michael's not sitting beside me, she thought and typed:

> *Today 8:49*
> And I you.

She pressed Send and met Michael's gaze across the table. "It's a big decision," she said, repeating what she had said a moment earlier.

According to the mental tally she'd kept since they met with Anthony Nardelli nearly three weeks ago, this was the sixteenth time he had pressured her to decide on a diamond. Two weeks ago she lost track of how often he had urged her to renounce her moratorium on sex.

When it came to sex, time was her ally. But when it came to diamonds, time was on his side. They'd be departing for Hilton Head in eight days. It took time for a jeweler to set a diamond. A week ago Michael had boasted of someone at Orr's Jewelers agreeing to expedite the setting of her diamond. Ten minutes ago he'd grumbled about a rush fee that would go into effect on Monday.

"Come on, Elena. Imagine all the oohs and aahs you'll get with a three-carat diamond on your finger."

"It's way too flashy for me."

Michael won a partial victory when she selected the smallest of the diamonds and gave him her mother's gold engagement ring on which to have it set. He didn't complain when she declined his request for sex and sent him home shortly after ten.

Elena hurried to bed, exhausted. Moments after laying her head on the pillow the resonant voice in her heart expressed its disappointment in her and grew silent in defeat. Then, for what seemed like an hour, the voice in her head cackled, applauding her for selecting a diamond and coming to her senses about marrying Michael. She breathed a sigh of relief when it finally quieted.

Her thoughts turned to Patrick. How could she be smitten with a man she'd spent a total of two hours with and, at most, thirty minutes alone—a man she had hugged only once, in a church after a funeral? It struck her that they had met the morning after Michael had proposed to her. She wondered if her attraction to Patrick had been driven by fear, like a drowning woman lunging toward a mirage she'd mistaken for a raft.

Am I that close to the edge? I need to quit acting like a teenager. I'll be fifty in October. … If he asks to see me again, I'll say no and tell him I'm engaged.

శ్రీ శ్రీ శ్రీ

The village of Sewickley, nestled midway between Beaver and Pittsburgh, buzzed with a school's-out energy the next morning, the first Saturday of June. The pale blue sky was dotted with sheeplike clouds. A trio of bicycles was parked on the Beaver Street sidewalk in front of Starbucks when Elena and Patrick stepped outside carrying cups.

"Where are you parked?" he asked.

She pointed across the street. "In the lot behind the shops. My meter won't expire until two."

"Good, we'll have time for lunch. I'm parked over here." He guided her around the corner and up Locust Place. The Sewickley Hospital was visible through the trees a few blocks ahead.

A cold shiver ran down Elena's spine. It dawned on her that Michael planned to have her diamond set at the Orr's Jewelers store in Sewickley. *What if Anthony Nardelli meets him today on short notice?*

"What's one of your favorite stories from inside the delivery room?" Patrick asked.

"I have so many." She scratched her forehead. "Let me think."

What if Michael sees my car? What if he sees us together this afternoon? ... Don't panic. She remembered taking her medication after breakfast. *Answer his question.*

"Here's one," she said. "One woman was nine-and-a-half months pregnant with her first child. Nearly every woman arrives early for a scheduled inducement. But not *this* woman. She and her husband showed up an hour late for her 6:30 AM appointment. When I asked her why, she complained that her hair and makeup weren't cooperating." Elena paused for effect. "You should have seen her hair and makeup that afternoon."

He laughed. "She sounds like one of my patients."

Patrick stopped beside the passenger door of a black sedan, pulled a key fob from his pocket, opened the door, and held his hand out for Elena's coffee.

She gave it to him, gathered the skirt of her white sundress, and got into his car.

"Thanks," she said, reaching for her cup. "I've helped at least a dozen first-time fathers off the floor. Who says men are the stronger sex?"

"Not I, said the psychiatrist to the maternity nurse."

He closed her door and walked around the front of the car. After settling into his seat, he flipped the switch for the sunroof, removed his sunglasses, and turned to her.

"Elena, I have a confession to make."

She couldn't read his eyes. "A confession?"

He nodded. "It's true that I'm struggling to decide between the two paintings. And I would like your opinion." He hesitated, his cheeks reddening. "But the main reason I asked you to come with me today is that I wanted to see you again."

Elena bit her lip to contain her smile. "I'm flattered, Patrick, but—"

"I promised myself I'd tell you the truth before we left Sewickley."

He looked at the steering wheel and appeared to be collecting his thoughts. She fiddled with the green beads of her necklace and tried to guess what he'd say next.

He turned to her again. "We met four weeks ago today. Within minutes of meeting you my attraction to you was more than physical. ... Your outer and inner beauty reminded me—remind me—of Audrey Hepburn. You inspired me to make a sidetrip to my mother's house to pick out the hat she was wearing when you met her."

Goose bumps raced up Elena's arms. "Really?"

He nodded again and scratched behind his ear. "We haven't spent much time together, but I feel like I know you and that you know me." His eyes searched hers. "Does that make sense?"

"No. I mean, yes." Her heart pounded in her chest.

"I haven't felt this connected with a woman since my wife died six years ago."

She pressed her knees together to stop their shaking. *Six years a widower.*

His face sobered. He gazed out her side of the windshield and said softly, "Her name was Kate. She had a brain aneurysm in her sleep one night."

A sigh escaped Elena's lips. She gripped her coffee cup with both hands.

His chin fell to his chest. "She never woke up."

"How tragic."

Their eyes met, his filled with sorrow, hers with sympathy.

"Kate was barely forty. Five months pregnant with our first child." He looked away. "A baby girl."

Elena, torn between her desire to comfort him and her fear of crossing an invisible threshold of intimacy, squeezed his arm just below the elbow.

"I'm so sorry, Patrick."

He thanked her and stared blankly at the silver Mercedes parked in front of them. She cringed, imagining what he must have felt when he woke up and discovered that his wife and baby were dead.

A long minute passed in silence.

Three teenage boys skateboarded past them on the street. The sound of laughter and rolling wheels faded. Elena patted Patrick's arm and folded her hands on her lap.

He turned to her. "Sorry for unleashing all of that on you. I—"

"There's no need to apologize."

Her lips curled up. The tension in his face relaxed.

"I went off script from the little speech I had prepared for you."

She raised her eyebrows, inviting him to elaborate.

"I planned to tell you that I realize you have a boyfriend, that you've done nothing to lead me on, and that I'd like for us to continue to become friends."

"I'd like that too, Patrick."

❧ ❧ ❧

He turned into the parking lot behind Beaver Street at ten to two, the trunk of his car loaded with fresh pasta, shrimp, and cheese for Michael's birthday party. A painting, double-wrapped in brown paper, took up most of the backseat. Elena's right knee bobbed up and down as she guided Patrick to an open space across from her Explorer.

A piece of yellow paper flapped in the breeze under her windshield wiper. *A note from Michael! What if he's waiting for me?*

She lowered the sun visor, opened the vanity mirror, and leaned forward, her eyes sweeping the parking lot.

Flyers!

She breathed a sigh of relief. Identical pieces of paper lay on the windshields of two cars to the left of hers and one a few spaces to the right. She tugged on her earrings and closed the mirror and visor.

Patrick shut off the engine and turned to her. "Before you go, Elena, I have something for you." He reached behind her seat, lifted a Pottery Barn bag onto the leather console between them, and tilted it toward her.

"Towels?" she asked, her eyes wide.

He shook his head and smiled. "They're there to hide what's underneath."

"You clever man."

She removed two white hand towels from the top of the bag and revealed a circular box lying on its side. "What a pretty box," she said, sliding it onto her lap. She raised the lid an inch or so, pulled it out from under the box's string handle, and folded back the tissue paper. Her breath caught in her throat.

"Your mother's hat!" She held it up as if it were a crown. "It's beautiful."

"She'd be happy for you to own it. ... Try it on."

Elena placed the hat on her head and tucked her hair behind her ear. Her eyes asked him how she looked.

"It looks spectacular on you."

"I feel so honored." She leaned across the console and kissed him on the cheek. "Thank you, Patrick."

"You're welcome. Excuse my reach." He opened the glove compartment, pulled out a black-and-white photograph, and handed it to her. "That's my mom wearing your new hat."

"Irene was gorgeous."

He pointed at the date stamp on the bottom of the photo. "Guess who was born nine months later?"

"You?" He nodded. "Wow, Patrick. You're the only person I know from our generation who has a picture of their mother date-stamped nine months before their birth."

"There's more," he said, tapping the photo. "The first time I remember ever seeing this hat was a half-hour after we met. And the first time I ever laid eyes on this picture was the day my mom was buried."

"No way?"

"Yes way."

CHAPTER THIRTEEN

A woman in her forties makes a succulent dish.
–Sicilian Proverb

The next afternoon, before Michael's birthday party, Elena hurried across her driveway to Jack's Subaru. She reached into the open driver's side window, handed him a napkin full of cookies, and tousled his damp brown curls. "Thanks for hiding the For Sale sign in the garage and going to pick up your grandfather."

He set the cookies on his lap. "How many did they bake?"

"Take a guess."

"Seventy people are coming?" She nodded. He tapped the steering wheel, squinting his blue eyes up at her. "Seven hundred?"

"Excellent guess, Banker Boy. Sixty dozen."

He flashed the smile Dr. Contes had perfected years ago. "Why so many?"

"To make a splash. And to give women the thrill of stashing a napkin full of them in their purses."

Elena explained how to sign her father out of Friendship Ridge and finished by saying, "Give him a once-over and try to make him look like his old self."

"Okay, Mom," he said, shifting into reverse. She patted the hood and checked her watch. The first guests would be arriving in about an hour.

She walked around the garage, climbed the stairs to the deck, and couldn't remember her lawn ever looking so festive, her garden so lush. *The quiet before the storm*, she thought, leaning against the railing. *This is the largest event I've ever hosted. ... And probably the last one here.* A pang of nostalgia jabbed at her heart. She felt like an actor touring the stage of an empty theater before her final performance.

That morning, Michael's mother had greeted two men from the party rental company with a plateful of cookies and persuaded them to arrange everything to her specifications. Nine round tables, each dressed and surrounded by eight white wooden chairs, were laid out in the shape of a diamond. The table at the base of the diamond rested about thirty feet outside the entrance to the white, high-peak food tent.

Elena gazed proudly at her creative contribution to the party, the centerpieces that lay atop the red-and-white checked linen tablecloths. Red peonies from her garden sprayed out of yellow-and-red cans of Mancini sweet roasted peppers.

She stepped into the kitchen and heard Maria's leathery voice in the living room. *She's instructing her girls. I wasn't invited.* Elena slipped a mini lady lock into her mouth and brushed the evidence from the corners of her lips. Her sandals clopped down the hall.

"Come in, honey," Michael's mother said, turning to her.

"I didn't want to interrupt your flower arranging." Elena joined Maria's two sisters and three daughters-in-law huddled in the middle of the room.

"Remember girls," Maria continued, "Italians don't eat to live, we live to eat. Why are we better than the best caterer?" She didn't wait for a response. "Because we're *family*. It's you and your daughters' jobs to make sure everyone's still talking about Michael's party a year from now. Make it look easy. Don't tell anyone we worked our butts off for a month."

Maria glanced at her watch. "Okay, it's time for Elena and I to get our dresses on. Remember girls, keep your makeup fresh. The bathrooms will be busy. I put a hand mirror on the windowsill above the kitchen sink. Josie's in charge now." She blew them a kiss.

Michael's Aunt Josephine started toward the kitchen with her crew in tow.

Elena followed Maria upstairs. "I'm so glad it's not a surprise party," she said, closing the door to her bedroom.

"Me too." Maria removed her red dress from its hanger

and laid it on the bed. "Remember, honey, our job is to make sure everyone eats too much and has fun. Neither of us are allowed to lift a finger after the first guest arrives."

"You haven't let me do anything all weekend."

They undressed down to their undergarments. Maria stepped into her dress, pulled it up her body, and turned her back to Elena.

"Can you zip me?"

"It feels strange to not have cooked or baked anything," she said, pulling the zipper. She fastened the clasp.

"You know how I am about food." Maria held Elena's arm and stepped into her other shoe. "You bought all that food yesterday in the Strip District."

"That's only money, like writing a check to a caterer."

"We're having the party at your house. And you worked so hard in your garden."

"I do that every year."

"Here." She handed Elena her most prized possession, the strand of pearls her late husband Albert had given her on their twenty-fifth wedding anniversary. Elena, moving behind Maria, wrapped the pearls around her neck and hooked the clasp.

"I wouldn't let Michael or his brothers do anything either," Maria added.

Elena slid her gray cocktail dress up her body and slipped her arms through the sleeves. She looked in the dresser mirror and loved how the silk chiffon fabric hugged her curves.

"Maria, why don't Italian women let the men do anything?"

"To please them. It's how our mothers and grandmothers taught us."

Maria zipped Elena's dress and pointed at her in the mirror. "You look beautiful."

They smiled at each other's reflection.

"Honey," Maria said, caressing Elena's shoulder, "today isn't just Michael's fiftieth birthday party, it's a preview of your wedding."

※ ※ ※

When the final guests arrived at five-forty, the hankie Elena had used to wipe smeared lipstick from Michael's cheeks matched the checked tablecloths. The fragrances wafting from the garden and the guests were no equal to the aroma of garlic permeating the air. Some boasted of not having eaten since breakfast. The two cookie tables rivaled the bar in popularity.

At six o'clock, Aunt Josie spread the word that the antipasto tables were ready. Guests swarmed into the food tent, where Michael's sisters-in-law reenacted the miracle of the loaves and fishes. Lana Marino, the petite wife of

Michael's brother Marco, kept the bread table looking like the window display of an Italian bakery. Rose and Isabella Marino and their daughters replenished platters of Italian cold cuts, sliced sausages, hard, soft, and semi-soft cheeses, olives, tomatoes, bruschetta, roasted eggplant with peppers and cucumbers, artichoke hearts, and roasted peppers and anchovies.

When everyone's appetites had been whetted, Michael's two aunts served the entrée course from oval chafing dishes—shrimp scampi over angel hair pasta, baked manicotti, and Maria's famous meatballs.

After dinner, Luciano Pavarotti sang Verdi's *Rigoletto* from the speakers and guests flocked again to the cookie tables. Elena chuckled under her breath when she caught Sal Gallo loosening his belt.

She and Michael meandered from guest to guest and table to table like a pair of butterflies working their way around flowerbeds. Everyone raved about the food and grumbled of having eaten too much. Elena overheard Maria mention to him that five cases of Sicilian red and two of Sicilian white remained.

When they finished mingling, he led her behind a hydrangea bush. "Great party, huh?"

"Fabulous."

"Congressman Jenkins and his wife are the only ones who ate and ran." He kissed her on the lips. "Today is one of the happiest days of my life."

"Good for you, Michael. Your mother is in her glory, too."

"I couldn't talk her out of showing off my baby pictures. Can you believe how hairy I was?"

"*Yes.*"

He matched her grin and took her hand. "Care to join me in the bathroom for a quickie?"

"Maybe later," she teased, nudging him toward the deck.

Elena worked her way to Sara's table and sat next to her father, who was chatting with Emma.

"Having fun, Dad?"

He nodded and swallowed a bite of cannoli. "The food is delicious, but the company is even better," he said, patting his granddaughter's hand. "Emma was just telling me all about her medical research."

Elena turned her gaze to her daughter and saw her own eyes and narrow nose with a pointed tip, along with the shade of red hair she had had during her days at Georgetown.

Emma slid the errant strap of her coral sundress onto her shoulder and rolled her eyes. "I've never seen so much bling in my life," she said, loud enough for only her mother and grandfather to hear.

"I know." Elena leaned toward her. "How does my face look?"

Before Emma could answer, Maria rested a hand on Elena's shoulder and said in her ear, "We'll sing to Michael after this song. Let's go stand in front of the cake."

"Okay."

Elena rose to her feet and they started toward the food tent.

"Do you mind if I lead the singing?" Maria asked.

"Not at all."

A two-tiered red velvet cake sat on a round table beside the entrance to the tent. Michael's Aunt Josephine lit the oversized "5" and "0" candles and scurried away. Elena turned to face the crowd.

Everyone is having so much fun. My garden is the perfect backdrop.

When Frank Sinatra sang the final notes of "The Best Is Yet to Come," Maria nodded at her son Max on the deck, who nodded back and pointed a remote at the stereo. The music stopped, but the guests continued to speak as if it hadn't.

Maria gave a thumbs-up to her sister Stella, who lifted her spoon and led her family in a chorus of clinking glasses. The tinkling spread, reached a crescendo, and descended slowly. All eyes rested on Maria and Elena.

"Thank you for celebrating Michael's fiftieth birthday with us," Maria said into a cordless microphone. Smiling as only a proud mother can, she scanned the crowd for him. "There you are, all the way in the back. Come up here so we can sing to you."

Michael wound a path through the tables, looking handsome in his perfectly pressed white shirt, gray summer-wool slacks, and black Ferragamo loafers—Elena's birthday gift to him. He embraced them in a three-way hug and turned and waved at the crowd.

"After we sing to him, Michael would like to say a few words."

Maria raised her right arm and led the singing.

When the song ended, Michael blew out the candles, accepted the microphone from his mother, and stretched his arms toward his guests.

"Thank you very much."

He paused. Three or four wives shushed their husbands.

"I don't feel a day over fifty," he said in a deadpan voice.

Friendly laughter rose and fell. He turned to his mother and kissed her cheeks.

"Mom, I spent the past week narrowing the hundred things I should thank you for down to three." His eyes bounced from Maria to the crowd and back. "First of all, thank you for bringing me into the world and loving me. ... Second, thank you for teaching me most of what I know. ... And last but not least—" He rubbed his stomach and grinned. "Thank you for being the best cook in the world."

He wrapped his arm around her shoulders. "How about a hand for Mama Maria?"

Maria blew kisses and bowed like a diva.

As the clapping faded, Michael's face grew serious. "I wish my father could be here with us this evening." He pointed at the sky. "Dad, I know you're watching down on us. ... Between games of bocce."

The crowd's collective *"Aw"* jumped to a "Hah!"

Michael's command of the audience surprised Elena. She'd never seen him speak in front of a group of more than eight or ten people.

The guests quieted. His uncle Vinnie sneezed. Michael waved at his brothers, who stood along the deck railing from oldest to youngest waving back at him.

"For those of you who don't know, Mom gave each of her boys *real* Italian names. I'm Michelangelo. Max is Maximo. Matt is Matteo. And Marco is Marco. *He's* the baby!"

Another burst of laughter rang out.

Michael took Elena's hand and kissed her on the lips. "Last but not least, let's give a hand to our hostess this evening, Elena Shaughnessy, a woman whose beauty surpasses all the flowers in her garden."

When the clapping stopped, he punctuated the silence with two deep breaths. The audience leaned forward.

"Ladies and gentlemen, friends and family, I'd like to make an announcement."

Elena, sensing what was coming, fought the urge to cover his mouth with her hand. "No," she whispered without moving her lips. His eyes stopped short of hers and drifted back to the crowd.

"Elena and I are engaged to be married."

The guests rose as one and cheered. Elena didn't return Michael's kiss. She slipped her free hand behind her back, dug her nails into her palm, and pretended to smile.

The bastard couldn't wait another week? Couldn't warn me it was coming?

When the din subsided and everyone returned to their seats, he continued, "I proposed to Elena a month ago at the Capital Grille in Pittsburgh. We decided then to keep our engagement a secret until tonight."

Like hell we did!

Michael handed the microphone to his mother and pulled a black velvet box from his front pocket. He snapped the lid open, lifted the three-point-two-carat diamond, and slid it onto Elena's finger.

CHAPTER FOURTEEN

Keep your eyes wide open before marriage,
half shut afterwards.
–*Benjamin Franklin*

Champagne corks popped. The opening notes of Frank Sinatra's "Love and Marriage" blared from the speakers. Well-wishers hurried toward the tent. Arriving first, Marco and Matt served as a human buffer and began to marshal the guests into a semblance of a receiving line.

"The cake! The cake!" shouted henna-haired Aunt Josie, looking like an ambulance fighting her way to the scene of an accident.

"A circus," Elena muttered.

"What?" Michael asked, leaning his ear to her mouth.

Turning her back to the crowd, she gave him *the look*. He flinched. She nudged him toward the parade of guests and appeared to be elated when his cousin, Gina Fortunata, enveloped her in a hug.

After congratulating them and gushing about her diamond, each guest received a double-cheek kiss from Maria and a piece of cake from Aunt Josie.

Emma and Jack were thrilled, Elena suspected, mostly because they thought she was. Sara raved about the diamond and teased her for keeping the engagement a secret from her. Michael gloated when Catherine thanked them for taking some of the attention and pressure off her and Jonathon.

When the line had dwindled to four people. Elena caught a glimpse of her father rolling his walker toward them.

Moments later they embraced. "If you're happy, Lanie," he said in her ear, "then I'll be happy."

She looked into his eyes and shook her head to confirm what she sensed he already knew. He nodded, his face reflecting her pain.

"We'll talk soon, Dad. Let's get you off your feet."

After escorting him back to his seat, she scurried around the tent and the garage to her front door, careful not to make eye contact with anyone. She climbed the stairs two at a time, locked the door to her master bathroom, and sat and sobbed.

Four or five minutes passed.

She was repairing her face when Michael shook the doorknob. "Elena, people are starting to wonder where you are."

Tell them I clogged the toilet trying to flush your diamond! she wanted to scream.

"I'm fixing my makeup. I'll be down in a minute."

After she rebuffed his third attempt to hold her hand, he stopped trying. She spoke to him only when forced to for the sake of propriety and on two occasions, when she was certain no one could see or hear, she hissed, "You don't respect me."

When the last guests departed and Maria and her girls shifted into clean-up mode, Elena told him he had five minutes to say his goodbyes. He griped about a fictitious seven AM meeting. Neither of them spoke as she walked him to his car.

He leaned to kiss her goodbye.

"You couldn't wait another week?" she said, turning away.

"I waited a month. Catherine and Jona—"

"You couldn't buy the diamond *I* picked out?"

"Everyone but you loves it."

"It's gaudy. You bought it for you, not me."

He sighed, his eyes fell to the street.

She glared at him until he met her gaze. "Don't call or text me tomorrow."

৯২ ৯২ ৯২

The next morning Elena awoke exhausted but relieved that she had scheduled the day off. She slipped into a pair of shorts, went downstairs to make coffee, and found a note on the kitchen table.

Elena,
We cleaned til after 2. Everythings done. My first
wedding present to you! The only thing you need to
do is sign the party companies paperwork. Their
coming between 10 and 12.
Maria

Elena sought refuge in her garden after breakfast. A few hours later she thanked the party rental drivers for returning the For Sale sign to its hole in the front lawn and gave them a fifty-dollar tip to split. Other than water and bathroom breaks and a ten-minute lunch, she gardened until dusk.

While eating yogurt and pretzels for dinner, she checked her phone for the first time in hours and was surprised to learn that Michael had obeyed her request not to contact her.

She showered and tucked herself into bed. A twist of nausea swirled in her stomach. She rushed back to the bathroom, shook a Xanax from the pill bottle, pinched it in half, and swallowed it with a sip of water. A week ago she had filled the prescription, the first anti-anxiety medication she'd taken since her early twenties. The only thing worse than taking it was not taking it.

Elena climbed into bed again and turned her thoughts to whether Michael was intelligent enough to understand the extent to which he had trapped her. How could she break off their engagement and justify herself by complaining that he'd bought her too big a diamond and waited four weeks instead of five to announce the news?

During the twelve hours between eight and eight that Tuesday, Michael barraged her with forty-seven texts, five phone messages, and two rambling emails. After the first incoming wave of texts, Elena turned off her phone. That evening she broke her silence via email.

> Michael,
> Your groveling is unmanly and unwelcome.
> I need more time to think things over.
> Elena

She tossed and turned in bed that night. The battle lines of her mental debate about whether to marry Michael were redrawn. The arguments were heated. She vacillated between the two entrenched positions and wondered which of her inner voices was her conscience.

She feared they both were.

Marrying Michael would mean she could forget her worries about housing, financial security, and spinsterhood. Breaking off the engagement would crush him and Maria, and her friends and family, with the exception of her father, would think she was crazy.

She chided herself for becoming involved with him again in her moment of weakness after James' wedding. Michael had disrespected her thirty years ago. He disrespected her now. Their values were incompatible. She didn't love him enough to marry him.

Before the alarm sounded on Wednesday morning, Elena decided to listen to her heart. Sacrificing happiness for security was too big a price to pay. She didn't want to be a part of the mass of mankind that Henry David Thoreau had claimed 'lead lives of quiet desperation.' She'd call off the engagement, buy a townhouse, and work to stretch her identity beyond the roles of wife, mother, and nurse. She gave herself forty-eight hours to map out a plan for breaking the news to Michael and everyone else.

❦ ❦ ❦

Early that evening Elena pulled garden gloves onto her ringless hands and hurried to a patch of blue-bearded irises. She stabbed a bamboo stake into the soil, lifted one of her top-heavy girls, and propped it against the wood. Pulling another stake from the cart, she lunged it toward the ground. The tip grazed her clog.

"Ouch!"

She kicked off her shoe, knelt on one knee, and studied her baby toe.

No blood.

Shifting into a sitting position, she wrapped her arms around her knees and closed her eyes. The events of the past hour replayed in her mind.

The sound of the doorbell had startled her. She glanced out her bedroom window, saw Michael's Audi parked in the driveway, and sat on the bed, waiting for him to leave. The doorbell rang a second and third time. He pounded on the wooden screen door.

She debated whether to continue to wait for him to leave or to get it over with and break off their engagement now. He rang the doorbell a fourth time.

She ran downstairs and scowled at him through the sidelight. The circles under his eyes were as dark as his hair, his tie was askew below his unbuttoned collar, and his hands and feet were restless. She opened the door enough to confirm that the screen door was locked.

"Let me in, Elena. We need to talk."

"Talk to me here."

"Do you want the old lady across the street to hear us?"

"Martha's in Chicago."

"You know I'd never hurt you."

"You hurt me Sunday night."

She saw movement to her left and turned. David and Tina Johnson were walking their Jack Russell Terrier up Seventh Street toward her house. Elena opened the door and flicked the screen door's hook out of its eyelet.

She backed into the foyer. "Have a seat on the couch."

The screen door whined open. Michael stepped inside and walked across the living room. She sat on the side chair nearest the foyer, her hand clenching her phone.

Let him speak first.

She weighed her words, trying not to look at him. A half-minute passed in silence.

"I'm sorry, Elena. I couldn't wait another week to announce our engagement. I bought you the biggest diamond to show everyone how much I love you. Please forgive me."

"It's not that easy, Michael. You disrespected me."

He closed his eyes and took a deep breath. "I'm sorry, Elena. I couldn't wait another week to announce our engagement. I bought you the biggest diamond to show everyone how much I love you. Please forgive me."

She counted as he repeated himself seven more times. His sorrowful, sing-song tone brought back memories of the minutes before her mother's funeral Mass, when a group of women had prayed the rosary aloud.

He paused and began again. After she counted to sixteen, Michael stood and stepped slowly toward her. She rubbed the indentations her nails had left in her palm. He knelt at her feet, laid his head on her lap, and bawled like a baby.

Her defenses weakened.

A half-hour later they showered together, washing the sweat of passion off each other's bodies.

CHAPTER FIFTEEN

Respect yourself and others will respect you.
–Confucius

Elena met her kids at the Cheesecake Factory for dinner the following evening. The conversation centered on their impending vacation to Hilton Head Island in South Carolina. After failing to convince her to push back their departure time on Saturday, Jack and Emma let out a collective groan and agreed to sleep at home tomorrow night. Elena reminded them again to baby Michael's Audi during the trip.

Jack begged off dessert and left for a date with his new girlfriend. Having split a Chinese chicken salad, the girls each ordered a slice of cheesecake.

"We'll walk off the calories on the beach," Elena said.

"I look forward to our walks and talks, Mom."

Emma's phone vibrated on the table. She glanced at the screen and scrunched her nose.

"How are things with you and Christopher?" Elena asked.

"My love life sucks," she said, rolling her eyes.

Elena reached for her daughter's hand.

Emma poured out a tale of woe. Christopher Morton, her twenty-two-year-old boyfriend, had decided at the last minute not to attend Michael's birthday party and, a day later, not to join them on vacation. She suspected his excuse about a last-minute project at work wasn't entirely true and complained that when he wanted something, he was attentive and charming, but more often, he was aloof. Until a week ago, she had painted him as the perfect boyfriend.

"He doesn't reply to half my texts, but he expects me to respond immediately to his. What's worse is he calls me 'College Girl' in front of his friends. It's humiliating."

"How does he react when you confront him?"

Emma blew the hair out of her eyes. "I haven't. Not yet."

"You haven't?" Elena asked, trying not to sound judgmental.

"I'm afraid of losing him." She smiled at the server to hide her anguish. Her frown returned when he departed. "What should I do, Mom?"

Elena took her first bite of caramel pecan turtle cheesecake and considered her response. The ecstasy in her mouth threatened to spread to her face. She pulled the napkin from her lap and a prong of her engagement ring snagged her skirt. She worked it free with her other hand and said, "You always called the shots when you had boyfriends in high school. Remember how one part of you liked that and another part of you didn't?" Emma nodded. "It sounds to me like Christopher is calling all the shots."

"I know and I hate it." Emma stabbed her fork into her chocolate raspberry truffle cheesecake. "Adult relationships are so complicated."

Elena raked loose pecans with her fork. "Honey, if you put up with Christopher's disrespectful behavior, you'll only get more of it. It may even get worse. Why don't you hold him accountable?"

"I want to, but I'm worried I'll come across as a bitch."

"Would you rather be a pushover?"

Emma shook her head and sighed. "What should I do?"

Elena slid her plate to the middle of the table. "Take two bites of this and marry a pastry chef."

"Very funny, Mom," Emma said, trying to laugh. She took a bite and pushed both plates toward her mother.

Elena sampled the cheesecake, complimented it with her eyes and lips, and swallowed.

"If I were you, here's what I'd do. … I'd sit down with him and tell him two or three things he needs to change. Inexcusable things, like ridiculing you in front of his friends. The things that, each time you let him get away with it, you lose an ounce of self-respect."

Emma lifted the tall, masculine-looking pepper shaker

and clacked it twice against its salty sibling. "I know I should confront him, but ..."

"But?"

"Christopher's handsome, successful, and way more sophisticated than the guys at Case Western." She reunited the shakers. Her eyes wandered toward the bar. "I'm lucky to have him as my boyfr—"

"No, he's the lucky one." Elena took Emma's hand and pulled it gently toward her. "Never feel inferior to a man."

"I know, Mom."

Elena softened her expression and searched her daughter's eyes. "If Christopher is a good man, he'll respect you for standing up to him and start treating you better. If he's not, he'll become a bigger jerk and you'll be glad to be rid of him. Either way, you'll win."

The corners of Emma's lips turned up.

※ ※ ※

At work the next day, Elena worried about the example she was setting for Emma. Eight words from dinner last night echoed in her mind's ear: *If I were you, here's what I'd do.*

She alternated between scolding herself for not practicing what she preached and telling herself the advice she'd given her daughter didn't apply to her because of the difference in their ages. Emma was young with her whole life ahead of her. She was middle-aged, transitioning to life's down slope.

After dinner that evening, the table on Elena's deck was littered with dishes and glasses, a bottle of Chardonnay, a serving tray, and an open Nordstrom gift box. Michael's peace offering, a green dress, was a size six, one size too small. Ten minutes ago they had begun to repeat themselves about how they'd spend their week on Hilton Head Island. Without thinking, she spun her engagement ring on her finger.

"Why is it that everyone but you loves your diamond?" Michael asked, looking at her hand. He reached for the wine bottle. "Most women would be thrilled to own it."

Her eyes met his. "I'm not most women."

He finished pouring and exaggerated a sigh. "What, it's not good enough for you?"

She sipped her wine. "It's plenty good."

"Then why don't you like it?"

"Do you ever listen to me?"

"More than you know."

She fought the urge to tell him what she thought of his listening skills. The knot in her stomach tightened.

"It may not be too flashy for your taste, Michael, but it is for mine. Why didn't you buy the one I wanted?"

"They cost the same."

She crossed and uncrossed her arms. "If the smaller one cost half as much, I'd still prefer it."

He looked away in a huff. "You don't know a good thing when you have it."

"Maybe not, but I know a bad one."

She stood and stacked dishes on the tray.

It's now or never. Swallow your fear. … Do it now.

She slipped the ring off her finger and set it on the table in front of him.

Michael opened his mouth but didn't speak. The blood drained from his face.

"I'll exchange it for the one you wanted."

She shook her head.

"Why not?"

"Because we're not getting married."

Chapter Sixteen

To a father growing old
nothing is dearer than a daughter.
–Euripides

Twenty minutes later Elena rushed to her father's side, tears rolling down her face. "Oh, Dad," she said, pressing her forehead against his temple.

"What's wrong, Lanie?"

"I broke off the engagement."

"I'm sorry, honey."

He aimed the remote at the television, lowered the recliner's leg rest, and pulled a handkerchief from his pocket. "Here." He handed it to her and patted the thigh below his good hip.

She split her weight between the arm of the chair and his lap and buried her face in the crook of his neck. He smelled like himself, only older. His heart thumped against her chest.

"Why didn't I listen to you two years ago when you warned me to be careful?"

"Now, now. Now, now." He brushed the hair out of her eyes.

"And now I've hurt him. And Maria. ... *Again.*"

"Far better to hurt a man before you marry him."

He kissed the crown of her head and rocked the recliner for a silent moment. She clung to him, taking deep breaths.

"Michael has good qualities," he said in a gentle tone. "But I've always thought he ..."

She wiped her eyes. "What, Dad?"

"I've always thought he was full of himself." The chair swayed back and forth. "Insecure. ... More sizzle than steak."

She drew her head back until their eyes met. "You left out mama's boy."

"That too."

They exchanged grins. Elena shifted more of her weight onto the arm of the chair and rested her head on his shoulder. "Why didn't you say anything?"

"I didn't want to interfere," he said, his whiskers tickling her forehead.

"Michael and I had some unfinished business from thirty years ago, but I never should have let our relationship go this far." Elena balled the hankie in her fist. "He did me a favor, Dad."

"A favor?"

She paused, gathering her thoughts. "I knew in my heart that I didn't love him enough to marry him, but I couldn't bring myself to act on it until he shocked me to my senses at his party. I had no idea he was going to announce our engagement then. And he bought the diamond he wanted instead of the much smaller one I had picked out."

"A man who doesn't respect you doesn't deserve you, Elena." He patted her shoulder. "I'm proud of you for finding the courage to break off the engagement."

She sighed. "I made the right decision, but I'm an emotional wreck."

"Give it time, Lanie. Give it time."

They rocked in silence for a moment. She pictured herself relaxing on the beach, the sun on her skin, the waves at her feet.

Her father cleared his throat. "I hope Michael doesn't do anything stupid."

She sat up and turned, looking him in the eye. "Like what?"

"Put yourself in his shoes. This is the second time you got away. His heart is broken, his pride shaken. He may lash out at you like a wounded animal. … Be vigilant, Elena."

"I will."

She stood and stepped into the sandal that had slipped off her foot a few minutes ago.

He inched forward in his seat. "I suggest you ignore him. That way, you won't risk saying or doing anything to provoke him. And you won't risk raising his hopes."

She nodded, acknowledging the wisdom of his advice. "Any suggestions on what I should tell Jack and Emma?"

"Tell them the truth—that you're human enough to make a big mistake and smart enough to learn from it." His eyes brightened. "They'll respect your decision. You'll be setting a good example for them."

She folded his handkerchief and handed it to him. "Thanks for listening, Dad."

He grinned from ear to ear. "Thank *you*, Lanie."

"For what?"

"For sitting on my lap for the first time since you were twelve."

❧ ❧ ❧

The next morning, thirty miles south of Pittsburgh, Elena caught her first glimpse of the rising sun. She reset the cruise control and glanced at Jack beside her and Emma in the backseat.

I could watch them sleep for hours. … They took the news so much better than I expected. When did they grow up and become adults?

She scanned her mirrors for black Audis and turned her thoughts to the relief she'd felt an hour earlier when Michael hadn't shown up in her driveway with his bags packed.

He better not show up at Hilton Head.

CHAPTER SEVENTEEN

A woman has got to love a bad man once or twice
in her life, to be thankful for a good one.
–Marjorie Kinnan Rawlings

Michael never showed up in South Carolina that week. Elena returned home tanned and rested on Saturday evening.

She took her dad out to lunch the following afternoon for Father's Day. Afterwards they toured Franciscan Manor, an assisted living residence that reminded her of a posh hotel catering to widows. The facility's residents looked healthier and more alert than his current neighbors and seemed to enjoy living there. He put down a deposit.

They stopped at Bruster's for hot fudge sundaes on their way back to Friendship Ridge, where she gathered his laundry, typed a note on her phone to buy razor blades and toothpaste, and slung her handbag over her shoulder.

"Why don't you take a nap before Sara picks you up for dinner?"

"I probably will," he said, leaning forward in the recliner. "Thanks for everything today, including the music player thingamajig you gave me." He pointed at the white box on the table beside him. "What's it called again?"

"An i-pod."

"Eye pod," he said with a puzzled look. "Did an optometrist invent it?"

"You're a hoot, Dad."

"It's wonderful to hear you laugh again, Lanie." He squeezed her hand. "I'm glad you had fun on your vacation. And I'm proud of you for ignoring Michael."

"That was easier to do when three states separated us." She sat on the edge of the bed. "My bigger concern right now is how to tell everyone that I've broken off the engagement. Do you have any suggestions?"

He muted the television. "It's nobody's business."

"I know, but I have to say something. Without bashing him."

"Hmm." He wrinkled his nose in thought. "Why not just say you got cold feet?"

"Isn't that too vague? Wouldn't tongues wag to fill the void?"

"Tongues will wag no matter what you say. You don't have to justify yourself to anyone but yourself." He ran a thumb across his lips. "The less you say the sooner the storm will pass."

"I got cold feet," she said, trying the words on for size.

She rose from the bed. "Once again, Dad, Happy Father's Day." She kissed his cheek. "I love you."

"I love you, too."

She started toward the door.

"Before you go, Elena." She turned back to him. "I meant to tell you earlier. Patrick Jameson visited me yesterday."

§2 §2 §2

Patrick paced his living room floor later that afternoon. This was where he did his best thinking. He had developed his pacing habit within weeks of Kate's death. Years ago, on two occasions, he'd smelled her scent and felt her presence here. Now, rarely a week passed without his pacing laps around his most treasured possession, the antique Tabriz Persian rug they had splurged on a week before moving in.

When Patrick yearned to feel close to Kate, he'd stroll around the hardwood perimeter of the room and relive a scene from the evening of their move-in day, when, during their six or seven attempts to get the rug to lay flat and straight, their emotions had shifted from anticipation to frustration, determination, exhaustion, and jubilation. Afterwards, they spread two towels on the rug and had a champagne and pizza picnic. They made love for dessert.

Thoughts of Kate had entered Patrick's mind that Father's Day afternoon, but they didn't compel him to pace.

For the past three weeks Renee Ballard had pestered him to call and introduce himself to her sister's friend, Jennifer Pearson, a forty-four-year-old divorced dermatologist. Renee argued that getting to know Jennifer would take his mind off his mother's passing and the burden of settling her affairs. After failing to convince him, she redeemed the handwritten red coupon he had included with her Christmas bonus.

* Good for Anything *
(Provided it's reasonable.)

Patrick and Jennifer had lunch together yesterday at Mambo Italia in Sewickley. He found her attractive, liked her sense of humor, and was considering asking her out on a real date. But she wasn't the reason he paced that Father's Day afternoon.

Each time he passed the painting Elena had helped him select, he paused to admire it and resumed walking and reflecting on his visit with her father yesterday afternoon. Patrick had surprised himself when he acted on impulse and invited Fred Shaughnessy to see Branford Marsalis in concert at the Pittsburgh Jazz Festival. At first he attributed it to being caught up in the moment with a fellow jazz lover. But last night he began to suspect an unconscious motive. Fred would keep his connection to Elena alive.

Early this afternoon Patrick had spent a few hours sorting through the contents of his mother's valise and compiling notes about the father he'd never met. He now wondered whether a second unconscious motive—paternal deprivation—lay behind his decision to invite Fred to the concert. He had always longed for but had never had an important father figure in his life. Elena's father seemed to possess the qualities he would seek in such a man.

While pacing, Patrick tried to gauge Elena's likely reaction to learning that her father would be attending the jazz festival with him. Would she consider it strange, scheming, unsafe, kind, or dashing of him? He racked his brain but couldn't decide. He debated whether to call Fred and cancel their plans.

No. I'll tell her the truth.

He hurried into the kitchen, sat on a stool at the island, and typed on his laptop:

Hello Elena,

I hope you're having a wonderful Father's Day with your Dad. I donated my mom's hat collection to Friendship Ridge yesterday afternoon. Susan, the activities assistant I gave them to, said future Hat Days will be much livelier. She predicted that some of the women will fight over their favorite hats. Imagine the headline in the *Beaver County Times*:

Feathers Fly at Friendship Ridge
Hatted Ladies Duke It Out

I visited your father afterwards. He remembered me and treated me like an old Irish drinking buddy. I enjoyed listening to his stories, especially his tale of being at Three Rivers Stadium when Franco Harris made his *Immaculate Reception.*

Your Dad is the only person I know who's more passionate about jazz than I am. I couldn't resist inviting him to see the Branford Marsalis Quartet perform at the Pittsburgh Jazz Festival next Sunday evening.

Would you like to join us? I'll bring my mother's wheelchair. For him, not you.

Patrick

He pressed Send and felt the same thrill he'd felt in seventh grade each time he slipped a love letter into Karen Fleming's locker.

❧ ❧ ❧

Elena returned home from visiting her father that afternoon and spent a few hours on the phone catching up with friends. None of them hinted at being aware that she had broken off the engagement. She'd been tempted to say something the first few times Michael's name came up in conversation but decided against it. She was still on vacation. Her news could wait until tomorrow.

After eating yogurt, an apple, and dark chocolate for dinner, she finished reading the Sunday paper and checked her email. A week ago in Hilton Head, after Michael had flooded her with texts and voice messages, she'd blocked his phone numbers. He adapted by sending her a daily email. A cocktail of fear, guilt, and curiosity conspired to motivate her to read them. She clicked on today's email:

Dear Elena,

Father's Day is the day of the year I think most about the family we never had together. Speaking of family, my mom misses you almost as much as I do. She's still the only one I've told. Thanks for not telling anyone outside your family. It gives me hope.

I exchanged the diamonds yesterday afternoon and dropped off the new one at Orr's. I can't wait to give it to you. I kick myself every day for letting my ego get in the way of my common sense. Once again, you're right that I shouldn't have announced our engagement, especially without running it by you first.

To show you how much I love you, I've decided to extend my deadline by a week. You now have until next Sunday night to change your mind. At a minimum, you'll need to meet me in person by then to talk things over. Otherwise, you'll leave me no choice but to reveal your secrets.

When and where can we meet?

Yours Always,

Michael

Mostly the same old drivel. Exposing my secrets would burn his bridges to me. He'd never do that.

She distracted herself by looking at the vacation photos on Emma's Facebook page. Her laptop pinged a few minutes later.

Her heart raced as she read Patrick's email. After reading it again, she called Sara and asked to speak to their father. She teased him for not telling her about his plans to attend the jazz festival and laughed when he made the excuse of being afraid she wouldn't let him go because of his hip. She informed him that Patrick had extended the invitation to her and asked whether he'd prefer to have a boy's night out. He encouraged her to join them.

Elena finished the call and resisted the impulse to respond immediately to Patrick. She set the timer on her phone for an hour and worked in her garden, thinking of what to say. When the alarm sounded, she hurried to the kitchen and typed:

Hello Patrick,
 Thanks for visiting my dad yesterday and inviting me to join you two at the jazz festival next Sunday. I haven't seen my father this excited in months. He assured me I wouldn't be in the way.
 What time would you like us to meet you at our parking lot in Sewickley? What can I bring?
 Elena

Elena reread what she had written and laughed out loud. "*Our* parking lot? You big flirt."

She pressed Send, closed her eyes, and recalled the moment two Saturdays ago when, after hugging Patrick goodbye in the parking lot, she had agreed to let him know if she was ever single. An earlier memory from the same day ran through her mind. While driving to meet him that morning, she had decided not to mention her engagement because it was a secret.

What should I tell him next Sunday?

CHAPTER EIGHTEEN

Jazz washes away the dust of everyday life.
—Art Blakey

The cloud of barbecue billowing from a barrel across the street tickled Elena's nostrils. She settled into a folding chair to Patrick's left and checked her watch. Just under an hour from now the Branford Marsalis Quartet would be performing on the stage that ran the width of Penn Avenue in the heart of Pittsburgh's Cultural District. Jazz fans of every age and stripe were gathering, transforming the street and sidewalks into a human collage.

Patrick finished assembling the wooden table he'd slid from a bag moments earlier. After pulling wineglasses from the picnic basket and a bottle of Sauvignon Blanc from the cooler, he uncorked the wine, poured and served it, and raised his glass to his guests.

"Cheers to my new jazz-loving friends."

"Cheers."

Elena clinked glasses with him and her father, who sat to Patrick's right. She sipped her wine and played with the chocolate lab belonging to the pregnant couple beside her. The dog gave her the cover she needed to watch Patrick arrange a plate of cheese and crackers and bowls of fresh strawberries and whipped cream. His masculine presence and humble confidence captivated her.

He handed each of them a dessert-sized Chinet plate and a napkin.

She reached for a strawberry. "It's wonderful to not have to do anything but show up."

"You're a gracious host, Patrick," her father added. "Thank you for inviting us."

"The honor is mine," he said. "Last year I brought a biography of Thomas Jefferson to the festival."

Her dad tilted his head back, gazed at the face of a low-rise building, and pointed a few stories up. "Look at how the green paint contrasts with the orange brick and brings out the detail of the cornices." He shook his head. "They don't make them like that any more."

"They don't," Patrick agreed. "Speaking of which, I envy you for having seen Miles Davis perform with John Coltrane and Bill Evans. When you mentioned it earlier, my attention was split between listening to you and finding a place for us to sit. Would you mind beginning again at the beginning?"

"Not at all," he replied. "I saw them in 1959 at the Village Vanguard in New York City."

Elena was dazzled by Patrick's eloquence and the manner with which he asked her father questions and commented on his responses. The conversation segued seamlessly into a discussion of the jazz scene during the late 1950s and early 1960s. She sprinkled in a few snippets of jazz lore to show that she had more than a passing interest in and knowledge of the subject. She studied Patrick's hands, facial expressions, and elocution. *He strings sentences together the way Miles strang trumpet chords,* she thought. *I could listen to him talk all night. Smart is sexy.*

Twenty or so minutes into the conversation, her father set his wineglass on the table and exhaled a deep breath. "I'm all talked out for now." He lifted the sports page from his lap. "I'll let you two visit."

Patrick turned to her. "He could write a book."

She returned his smile. "Did you know he plays the trumpet?"

"He mentioned it in passing last Saturday."

"Dad was a highly accomplished musician. Back in the early sixties, he played in a mixed-race quintet that did weekend gigs at Pittsburgh jazz clubs, including the Crawford Grill."

"All the jazz greats played there."

She leaned closer and lowered her voice. "The first few years after my mom died, he played a tribute to her every evening after dinner."

"I'm not surprised. I recommend music therapy to all of my grieving patients. One widow played Beethoven piano sonatas from eight until ten every morning. On the second anniversary of her husband's death, she told me the piano had saved her life."

He crossed an ankle over his knee. His eyes narrowed. "Did your dad play the same song every evening?"

A how-did-you-know look spread across Elena's face. "Art Farmer's 'When Your Lover Has Gone.'" She looked at the stage and hummed the melody under her breath. "I can picture him setting the needle on the album and raising his trumpet to his mouth."

She met Patrick's gaze. "Are you familiar with the song?"

He nodded. "I have a few versions of it in my iTunes library. I collect jazz ballads."

"Hmm." She sipped her wine. "I've never heard of anyone collecting jazz ballads."

"They're my favorite subgenre of jazz. Some of them—" his eyes fell to the ground before returning to hers— "Some of them speak to me."

"Oh?" She inched her chair closer, as if he were about to tell her a secret. "What do they say?"

"Different things, depending on the song and my mood."

He scratched his chin in thought. "Beneath each ballad's wistful sadness—its melancholy—I hear a hint of hope."

Her eyes smiled up at him. "Beautifully said, Patrick."

A faint blush colored his cheeks. He stood, refilled her and her father's wineglasses, and pulled a second bottle from the cooler. While he opened it and poured into his own glass, she examined his profile and backside as if she were a photographer studying the angles, curves, and inner state of a model. She discovered his manly legs and a scar under his chin.

Even his crow's feet are kissable.

"So, what's it like to run a hospital maternity unit?" he asked, sitting down.

"Well—" Elena thought a moment— "Imagine the joy and the responsibility of being the first person to see and touch a newborn baby. You feel as if you know the little guy or girl by the time they wail and you lay them on their mother's breast."

"The look in your eyes tells me you love your job."

"I do. I love babies." Her smile faded a notch. "But it can be grueling. Physically and emotionally."

"I bet you've seen it all."

She glanced at the pregnant woman to her left, turned back to Patrick, and said just above a whisper, "Imagine performing an emergency C-section with insufficient anesthesia."

"Ouch."

"The worst is when a family expects to cry tears of joy and cries tears of sorrow instead."

His brow furrowed. "I couldn't do your job, Elena."

"And I couldn't do yours." She rubbed her temple as if she had a headache. "Mental illness spooks me."

He reached for a cracker and a piece of cheese. Questions raced through Elena's mind. There was so much she wanted to learn about him. His work. His past. His present.

He swallowed. "What made you decide to become a nurse?"

"My mother was one."

"Maternity?"

"No, surgical."

He wiped his mouth with a napkin. "How long ago did she pass away?"

"When I was fifteen. Breast cancer."

His lips turned down. "How awful."

"It was hardest on him," she said, pointing at her father, whose face was hidden behind the newspaper. "He had to finish raising my sister and me."

"Did he ever remarry?"

"No. I'm not sure he even dated."

Patrick's eyebrows rose and fell. "Losing your mom as a teenager had to be much worse than my never meeting my father."

"Why do you say that?"

"I didn't know what I was missing. But you did. And still do."

Elena sat forward in her seat and gazed at the half of her father's body that was visible to her, from the gray slacks at his hip to his bare ankles. She pictured herself slipping his black canvas shoes onto his feet late that afternoon. A lump rose in her throat.

"I can't imagine never having met him," she said, her voice trailing off.

Patrick sipped his wine contemplatively. "If I had a father like him, Father's Day would be one of my favorite days of the year instead of the second worst."

She opened her mouth to speak, closed it, and thanked her brain for bridling her tongue. The anniversary of his wife's death was his least favorite day of the year. She wondered when it was.

"Mother's Day is difficult for me," she said.

He nodded acknowledgment. "I'm sorry for sounding like a therapist, Elena, but I'm curious to learn how losing your mother as a teenager shaped the woman you've become.

She sat back in her chair and gathered her thoughts.

"If you're comfortable talking about it," he added.

"I could talk to you for hours about anything, Patrick." Blood rushed to her cheeks. "Well, *almost* anything."

He reached for a strawberry and their knees bumped. The base of her spine tingled.

Get ahold of yourself.

She took a gulp of wine, hoping it would cool her down. It didn't.

Answer his question.

"My mother's death made me more independent and introspective than I otherwise would have been. ... And a better Mom and gardener."

"Independence and introspection run through my veins, too."

He slid the cooler, picnic basket, and table toward them to make room for two fortyish men who were searching for a place to sit.

When he finished, she turned to him and said, "It's hard to believe your mom has been gone now for over a month."

"It is. I just put her house on the market."

She heard a mix of resignation and peace in his voice. "It was sweet of you to donate her hats to Friendship Ridge. Your mock newspaper headline about feathers flying cracked me up."

"Can you imagine little old ladies duking it out over their favorite hat?"

Her cocked head and brow didn't dent his straight face.

"You don't believe it could happen?" he asked, his head and brow mirroring hers.

"Anything's possible, I guess."

"Elena, a catfight is nothing compared to a hatfight."

She laughed, nearly spilling her wine. "You have a great sense of humor."

"You think I'm kidding?"

"I *know* you are." She scrunched her nose at him.

They shared a laugh and drank a silent toast.

The drummer finished his sound check and walked behind the stage. Elena checked her watch. *Eight more minutes.* She searched the bowl for the best strawberry and reviewed what she planned to tell Patrick about Michael.

I want him to know that I'm single. If I were him, I'd want to know about the engagement.

She sat back, strawberry and napkin in hand, and turned to him. "I broke off my relationship with Michael a few weeks ago."

Patrick's Adam's apple disappeared and reappeared. Covering his mouth and clearing his throat failed to mask his pleasure.

Goose bumps ran up her arms. "We were engaged," she said, compelled by her conscience.

The gleam in his eyes extinguished like blown candles. "Oh?"

"Briefly."

His face grew pale.

"I broke it off."

He raised his wineglass to his lips and stared at the stage.

She curled her toes in her sandals and prayed for the concert to begin.

An awkward minute passed.

Her father closed and folded the newspaper and rested his hand on Patrick's arm. "I understand you're a widower."

"Yes."

"I was forty-six when my wife died. I never found anyone who could fill her shoes. Do you have a girlfriend?"

Patrick brushed a fly off his nose and hesitated a moment. "My practice manager fixed me up with her sister's friend recently, but it's too soon to say she's my girlfriend."

"Good for you," Elena blurted out.

***

Later that night, after walking her father to his room and arranging for an aide to help him get ready for bed, Elena started toward the exit. Images swirled in her mind of Patrick's polite but guarded behavior after the music had begun. She signed out at the front desk, stepped out of the building, and recalled feeling invisible in his backseat while he and her father talked jazz during their drive back to Sewickley.

Why did I have to tell him that Michael and I were engaged? Why did he mention that other woman? I wonder how pretty she is? How young? How accomplished? Just my luck. Now that I'm single, he isn't. Thank God they just met.

"What am I thinking?" she whispered aloud. "It's too early for me to even consider getting involved with another man."

She reached into her handbag, fished for her phone, and turned the ringer on.

Eight unread texts and one voice message. I hope the kids are okay.

She read Emma's text first.

> *Today 10:09 PM*
> I'm having Christopher issues. Please call me.

She read the last of Sara's texts.

> *Today 10:12 PM*
> It's an EMERGENCY!

She dialed Sara's number and jogged toward her car.

"Elena!"

"What's wro—"

"Michael called me. You need to get over here now. Meet me on the deck."

Five minutes later, her red sandals slick with dew, Elena stepped onto her sister's deck.

Sara greeted her with a hug. "You'd better sit down."

"No, I've been sitting all night." She leaned the seat of her white shorts against the railing. "What did he want?"

"We talked for over an hour," Sara sat in the chair nearest Elena. "Mostly about how lost he is without you. At one point, he cried and begged me to help him win you back."

"He's pathetic."

Sara's eyes fell to the candle. "He told me one of your secrets and claimed he has more."

"*What* secret?"

Sara met her gaze. "That you were investigated by the Pennsylvania Department of Health. Something about a baby girl who almost died."

"Shit!" Elena plopped into a chair.

"He went on and on, but I couldn't understand all of it. Why didn't you tell me?"

"Because—" She wiped her eyes with the back of her hand. "I was embarrassed. Scared to death."

"I would have supported you."

"I know." Elena's eyes apologized. "Did he tell you I wasn't found guilty of anything?"

"He said you got your hand slapped and were lucky to keep your job."

"My name was cleared."

"What happened?"

Elena exhaled a deep breath. "Almost a year ago—July tenth—we were staffed at the state minimum due to vacations. Judy Hastings called off at the last minute. I had to shift a new RN from neonatal to delivery." She wiped her eyes again. "I did everything possible to help her and an arrogant young obstetrician avoid a disaster."

"Is the baby okay?"

"She's fine. But her father is somehow related to Arlen Hunt, the personal injury lawyer from Pittsburgh who's always on television. They sued the doctor and the hospital." Elena sighed. "Lawsuits lead to investigations. The hospital settled out-of-court and was able to keep everything hush-hush."

"How awful."

Elena gripped the arms of her chair. "I still have nightmares."

CHAPTER NINETEEN

Revenge is sweet and not fattening.
–Alfred Hitchcock

Elena retraced her path around Sara's house, climbed into her Explorer, and jammed the key into the ignition. "Why did I believe his Sicilians-never-tell bullshit?" She backed out of the driveway. "Who else will he tell? What else will he tell?" She braked hard and stepped on the gas. "How can I retaliate?"

Eight blocks later she turned onto her street and narrowed the list to her two favorites: she could spray-paint "ASSHOLE" in orange across the hood of his Audi or tell his friends and their wives about his bouts of erectile dysfunction.

Elena parked in the garage and reminded herself that she could only fantasize about striking back at him so forcefully. The one thing she wanted more than revenge was to avoid an all-out war.

She stepped into the kitchen and glanced at the clock. Eleven ten was too late for her, but not for her daughter. She pulled her phone out of her purse.

While Emma ranted about Christopher, Elena said little but did much. She scoured the kitchen sink, cleaned the inside of the microwave, organized the Tupperware cabinet, and had started on the junk drawer when Emma ran out of breath and asked, "What should I do, Mom?"

"Do what you told him you'd do. Break up with him immediately and don't look back. A man who doesn't respect you doesn't deserve you."

Moments later, after saying goodbye, Elena plugged her phone into the charger and opened her laptop. *I wonder what the bastard has to say for himself.*

She clicked on Michael's daily email:

Elena,
    If you had met with me to talk, I wouldn't have acted on my threat.
    My patience is wearing thin. I'd hate to reveal more of your secrets to more than just Sara.
    Don't keep me waiting.
        Yours Always,
        Michael

A chill ran down her spine. She checked the back and front door locks and hurried to her bedroom.

She brushed her teeth, took her medicine, slipped a nightshirt over her head, and thought she smelled placenta. Her stomach turned. She started toward the bed and whispered, "Baby Alexa lives."

She crawled under the covers and squeezed her eyes shut. "Baby Alexa lives."

Repeating the affirmation failed to prevent last summer's delivery room fiasco from replaying in her mind.

Drenched in sweat, the mother had wailed like a banshee. The fetal heart monitor signaled distress. It was too late to perform a Caesarean. Fear and failure poured from the doctor's eyes. He nodded at Elena and stepped back. She took his place and girded herself, wishing she could save precious seconds by just reaching in and pulling the breached baby out. But she knew better. Her instincts kicked in. She confirmed that the umbilical cord wasn't around the neck, maneuvered the body into position, birthed one leg at a time, tugged to release the butt, worked her hands to the slippery shoulders, and pulled.

Pulled as if the baby were hers.

The newborn's face blushed blue. Elena clamped and cut the cord, cleared the throat, and blew life into the infant's mouth and nose. She massaged her tiny chest and blew again. And again. And again. …

Baby Alexa lives.

She cried herself to sleep.

At dawn the next morning Elena sat Indian style on an Adirondack chair on her deck. Steam rose from her coffee mug like smoke from the mouth of a cannon, warming and dampening her chin and cheeks. By accident, the gray yoga pants she'd thrown on moments earlier matched the Georgetown T-shirt she'd slept in.

"Feeling sorry for yourself never got you out of a jam," she said under her breath. She blew on her coffee and swallowed a sip. "You're wounded, not defeated. You knew before you earned your nursing pin that birthing babies is a bloody business."

She pictured her file of thank you cards from patients and letters of commendation from superiors. "Everyone but you knows how good a nurse you are. ... So what if Michael tells everyone? You were cleared of any blame. You'll look bad, but he'll look worse. Everyone will see him for the asshole he is."

Elena tightened her grip on the sides of the mug and closed her eyes. *He wants me back. He'll give me a few days to surrender. ... What other secrets could he tell?*

She racked her brain and thought of four things she wouldn't want him to divulge. If revealed, none of them would put her in jail. But each of them was personal, intimate, and nobody's business but her own. She reminded herself that

Sara knew all but one of the secrets, ranked them from bad to worst, and identified where his revelations would shift from trying to win her back to punishing her for not coming back. She envisioned her worst-case scenario and winced.

He'd need to grow a new set of balls to go there.

She set the mug on the arm of the chair and rubbed her temples, trying to get inside his head and think what he was thinking.

Telling Sara allowed him to rattle me and, at the same time, contain the damage. He knows she'd never tell a soul. Bullies are cowards. Is he too much of a coward to tell anyone else? … Maybe, but the time for ignoring him has passed.

She untangled her legs and set her feet on the deck.

I need to go on the offensive.

While finishing her coffee, Elena considered her options and ruled out all but two of them. She could rebuke him in a strongly worded email and threaten to fight fire with fire. This might keep him at bay for a week or two, but it wouldn't solve her problem.

Her other alternative was to meet with his mother.

Maria loves me like a daughter. I'll apologize for breaking her heart again. Michael will do whatever she tells him to do. … If nothing else, she'll listen to me, woman-to-woman.

Elena squeezed the mug between her thighs. "What if she's already telling him what to do?"

CHAPTER TWENTY

A woman's heart is a deep ocean of secrets.
–*Gloria Stuart*

"The back room is empty," Elena said, pointing over Maria's shoulder.

"Good. We'll be alone."

Elena finished stirring cream into her coffee, held her breath, and passed Maria's invisible cloud of perfume and stale tobacco. She walked through the twin French doors into Café Kolache's meeting room and stepped aside. "Sit wherever you'd like."

Maria set her purse on the second table to her left. Elena closed the doors and rehearsed her opening line. She settled into a chair across from Michael's mother, lifted a Kretchmar's Bakery bag from her handbag, and slid it across the table. "Here's a little peace offering."

"Ah, my favorite," Maria said, eyeing and sniffing the pair of pecan rolls. "I have something for you, too." She pulled a small gift bag out of her purse and laid it on the table. "I'll give it to you later, after we talk."

Elena studied the pink bag and hoped her mother's wedding ring lay inside.

"I want to take you home and feed you, Elena. You're nothing but skin and bones."

"I've lost five pounds and I never want them back."

Maria coughed her phlegmy cough. "I'm worried about you, honey."

"I'll be fine." Elena blew on her coffee. "How have you been?"

"I've been a wreck. This is the fourth time I left the house in over two weeks." She pulled a tissue from her purse, sniffled into it, and rested her free hand on Elena's. "Two Mondays ago I didn't bother getting out of my nightgown."

"I'm sorry for—"

"I wanted to call you a hundred times, but I kept telling myself to mind my own business." She shook her head and smiled. "I'm *so* happy you called."

"I'm sorry for hurting you, Maria. That's one of the reasons I wanted to see you today. To apologize. I know how much you've always wanted Michael and me to be together."

"I still do."

Maria lifted her coffee cup to her mouth. Her eyes

searched Elena's. "This morning you said you needed my help. What can I do?"

Elena took a deep breath to steel herself. "Did you know that Michael revealed a secret of mine to Sara last night?"

Maria's brow wrinkled. "Michael told a secret?"

"Yes."

"I taught my boys to keep secrets."

"I know." Elena wondered if the telltale signs of maternal disappointment on Maria's face were real or a mask. She knew where a mother's first loyalty lay.

"Sicilians don't tell secrets," Maria muttered.

"Michael does. Your Sicilian code of honor is why I trusted him." Elena paused to let her words sink in. "My secret had to do with a difficult delivery, a near-disaster at the hospital. I thought maybe you knew."

"No, honey."

Elena shared an abbreviated version of the Baby Alexa story. The distress in Maria's eyes and hands convinced her that Michael's mother was hearing it for the first time. When she finished, Maria said, "I'm sorry you had to go through that. And that Michael blabbed it to Sara."

"My children aren't perfect either." Elena reached for her coffee. "Michael has threatened to expose other private, confidential matters of mine. And not just to my sister."

"What's he trying to do, push you away for good?"

Elena shrugged her shoulders and stared through the French doors at nothing.

She'll help me. Give her a minute to absorb everything.

She turned to Maria. "The coffee went right through me. Excuse me while I use the ladies' room." She pushed her chair back and grabbed her handbag. "Can I get you anything?"

"No thanks."

Elena returned a few minutes later, smiling. "Michael won't be single for long."

"He never is. But you're the one he loves." Maria's eyes brightened. "Think of all the good times you two had. Why throw it all down the drain?"

Elena filled her mouth with coffee but didn't swallow. Drowning her tongue, she figured, would prevent her from saying the wrong thing.

Maria flashed the smile Elena had seen her use hundreds of times to soften people up before persuading them to do something she wanted, such as eating a second helping of her cooking. "Michael is lost without you." She patted Elena's hand. "He needs you."

Elena swallowed her mouthful of coffee in two gulps. "Another woman will snatch him up."

"But he loves you, Elena. Won't you give him one more chance?"

"I'm sorry, Maria," she said softly, but with resolve. "I can't."

Maria's eyes fell to the table. The lines in her face deepened as she fought back tears.

A silent moment passed.

"Here," she said, sliding the gift bag toward Elena. "I want you to have this no matter what happens with you and Michael."

Elena pulled tissue paper and a black velvet jewel box from the bag. She opened it and gasped. "Your pearls!"

Maria nodded, smiling.

"But Maria, you love your pearls. Albert gave them to you on your twenty-fifth anniversary."

"That was a long time ago." She coughed her cough. "I don't go anywhere to wear them."

Elena lifted the strand of pearls from the box and admired them with her eyes and fingers.

I can't accept these. It wouldn't be right. ... How can I not hurt her feelings?

She stood, cupped the pearls in her hand, and stepped to Maria's side, hugging her. "I'm so honored. ... Thank you."

"You're welcome, honey."

Elena, returning to her seat, swirled the pearls into the box and closed the clamshell lid. The corners of her lips turned down. "I'm sorry, Maria," she said, inching the box across the table, "but I can't accept your pearls."

Maria looked crestfallen. "Why not?"

"It wouldn't be right for me to pass them on to Emma someday. She doesn't have any Marino blood." Elena let go of the box and slid her hand back across the table. "Please save them for one of your granddaughters to wear on her wedding day."

Maria's eyes glistened like wet chocolate, their pity pouring inward. She slipped the box into her purse and lifted a fresh tissue. "I'll never stop hoping and praying that you two get back together."

"Then keep hoping and praying. But forgive me if I disappoint you."

"A mother always forgives her children, even when she doesn't understand them." Maria squeezed Elena's hand. "Don't worry about your secrets, honey. I'll take care of Michael."

CHAPTER TWENTY-ONE

A ship in harbor is safe,
but that is not what ships are built for.
–John A. Shedd

Patrick's office was tucked between the offices of a podiatrist and an endocrinologist on the third floor of a medical building in Sewickley. Two factors had compelled him to choose the location fifteen years ago: its privacy and its bird's-eye view of the Ohio River. He understood the stigma of mental health and believed in the healing power of nature, especially water.

Rarely a day at the office passed without him asking a patient to gaze at the river, imagine him- or herself as a storm cloud hovering above the surface, and pour their emotional rain into the water. All of his patients knew the correct answer to the question he asked, somewhat tongue-in-cheek, at the end of each session: *And what do the trees along the riverbank keep telling themselves?*

This too shall pass.

Patients often compared his two-room office suite to the den and kitchen of a lake house. Its blend of masculine lines and feminine curves was timeless. Renee Ballard enjoyed telling new patients that he had designed and decorated the office himself. When pressed for details, Patrick would only admit to selecting the nautical artwork, filling the shelves with books, and giving Renee free rein to rearrange things.

Late on a Monday afternoon at the beginning of July, a week and a day after the Pittsburgh Jazz Festival, he approached Renee's kitchen-island desk and handed her a few letters that he had signed.

"Are you ever going to tell me about your date?" she asked.

"After Theresa's session."

He hurried back into his office. The door from the outer hallway clicked open. He turned and stood beside the still-swinging white galley door.

"Hello Theresa," Renee said.

"Hey Renee."

He heard the women hug and thought, *Theresa sounds better than I expected.*

He walked to the wall of windows, watched a barge chug upriver toward Pittsburgh, and debated again what to tell Renee about his date on Saturday night.

She's going to strangle me. ...

At four fifty-nine Renee tapped on his office door and smiled at him through its porthole window. He waved her in, greeted Theresa at the door, and led her to the blue leather sofa that was perched at an angle for a downriver view. He sat in his gray leather listening chair, which was positioned at a ninety-degree angle to the sofa with an upriver view.

Theresa spent most of the session venting about Frank, her husband of nineteen years, who wasn't present enough to her emotionally, except on the second and fourth Saturday of the month when they had sex.

At five fifty-three Patrick escorted her back to Renee, returned to the wall of windows, and read his session notes into his dictation recorder. "Theresa Hamilton: Marital collapse averted during her family vacation to the Outer Banks. Action steps to stop the cycle. One: recognize progress in admitting and addressing her root fear—repeating her parents' marriage. Two: measure progress via an assessment—*correction*— self-assessment of her targeted behavior between sessions. Namely, the cessation of conscious and unconscious nagging and other behaviors that push Frank away. Three: guide analysis of alternatives and decision on optimal mode and timing of her constructive confrontation."

Hearing heels, Patrick stopped the recorder, slipped it into his pocket, and turned toward the office door. It swung open and closed.

"Not bad for a Monday," Renee said, stepping across the tan area rug toward him. "I ran our patient demographics for the second quarter."

"Good. What stands out?"

"Nothing major. Sixty-eight percent female. The median age fell a year to forty-seven. Once again, anxiety edged out depression and grief."

She handed him a two-page report and sat at the end of the sofa nearer the river. "Speaking of which, you had five grief referrals."

"Good grief," he said, raising his hand to his forehead, Charlie Brown-like. She groaned teasingly at his tired joke and brushed a loose thread from her mustard-colored pencil skirt.

"Okay, Patrick, it's your turn to report. How many of the half of our patients who are women between forty and sixty are currently in love with you?"

"The same three miserably married ones," he said, walking to his chair. "The same as the number of male patients who'd marry you tomorrow if you were single."

Renee smiled and tucked a swath of her shoulder-length brunette hair behind her ear. "There's now a fourth one."

"Who?"

"Andy Cole. He knows that I'm at least ten years older than him and happily married. He reminds me of a young Sean Connery. Too bad he's too old for Cassandra or Jessica."

"It's a good thing Andrew's too old for your girls. He has issues with women."

"Enough shop talk," she said, crossing a leg over her knee. "What did Jennifer wear on Saturday night?"

He paused to remember. "A royal blue sundress that had a pair of wide white stripes running around the skirt part."

"Nice. And her shoes?"

"Black sandals with heels."

"How high?"

"I'd guess two inches."

Renee uncrossed her leg and leaned toward him, her face serious. "Does she have potential?"

"She does, but—" He gazed upriver.

"But what, Patrick? …"

He didn't speak.

"Please don't tell me 'but she's not Kate.' Not again." Renee shook her head and sighed. "Be glad you're not a woman trying to find the perfect man."

He unbuttoned and rebuttoned the left sleeve of his white linen shirt. "Can I help it that I know what I'm looking for?"

"You're way too picky."

"I'm glad I was picky twelve years ago when I hired you," he said, repeating his customary response to her accusation.

"You're reneging on your promise to Kate that if anything happened to her you'd search until you found another woman to love."

The words hung in the air.

How much should I tell her?

Renee let out another sigh. "You barely try anymore. Before you met Jennifer, your last date was what, fourteen months ago?"

"Thirteen," he said, trying not to sound defensive.

Renee's expression shifted from exasperation to concern. She walked past him, pulled a book from a shelf, and handed it to him.

Midlife Grief
The Quiet Depths

Patrick Jameson, MD

She stepped to the sofa and half-leaned, half-sat on its arm. "You mourned and wrote for two long years. Since then, I've tried to fix you up with at least a dozen women. You've received hundreds of cards and emails from grieving men and women thanking you for helping them to live again." Her eyes pleaded with him. "Why won't you live again?"

He turned his head toward her, but his body, like a buoy anchored to the surface of the river, continued to face upstream. "I'm alive."

She narrowed her eyes. "How many times have you told a patient that fear is the enemy of love?" He shrugged a shoulder. "Why won't you take your own advice?"

"It seems to work better for my patients."

Renee sat on the edge of the sofa. "You're stuck, Patrick. One part of you yearns for companionship and the love of a woman. Another part of you is afraid of betraying Kate." She smoothed her skirt and waited until he met her gaze. "You're afraid of intimacy."

He squirmed. "But—"

"But nothing."

Her disapproving, big-sister look faded slowly.

"You're too good a man to be alone. Give a girl a chance."

He turned in his chair and faced her, his feet planted on the floor. "There's something I need to tell you, Renee. Something I should have told you three weeks ago but was afraid to."

"What?"

"It wouldn't be right for me to start anything with Jennifer." He leaned his arms on his thighs. "Not when I have feelings for another woman."

"Who?"

"Remember the woman I met at the bakery in Beaver a few months ago?"

"The nurse who went to your mother's funeral Mass?"

He nodded. "Her name is Elena."

"I thought she had a boyfriend?"

"She had a fiancé."

"A *what?*"

"You heard me."

She looked at him, bewildered. "You broke up an engagement?"

"No."

"Patrick, this woman can't be ready to date. You need someone who's emotionally available."

"I know. That's why I kept my feelings for her a secret from you until now."

He sat up, crossed his ankles, and let out a breath he didn't remember holding. "When I'm with Elena, I feel things I've only ever felt with Kate."

Renee's eyes widened. "That's something I never thought I'd hear you say."

"Me neither. I was on the verge of giving up hope."

She sat back, rested her elbow on the arm of the sofa, and shook her head. "Your timing is terrible. Do you want to be this woman's rebound relationship?"

"Our timing may be perfect."

She couldn't suppress a laugh. "That's a rationalization if I've ever heard one."

"Don't forget, Renee, Kate had a boyfriend when I met her. We never kissed until five months later." He folded his hands between his legs. "While Elena's emotional wounds heal, we can cultivate our friendship."

Renee gave him a who-are-you-kidding smile. "You know how you like to tell patients that human feelings aren't airless balloons lying asleep in a bag and that they're more like water balloons—slippery and prone to leaking and breaking?"

"Yes?"

"Well, given your monklike existence these past six years, I'd think your water balloon was ready to burst."

He pressed his thighs together. "My balloon is lying in wait for the right woman."

She matched his grin. "I don't know what to say, Patrick. I'm thrilled that you're so taken with a woman. What does Elena say?"

"She doesn't know."

Renee's mouth fell open. "I don't know whether to laugh or cry."

"She knows I'm interested in her, but not how much." He stood and stepped to the wall of glass. "I think she's interested in me."

"You two need to have a long talk."

"I plan to on Saturday." He turned to her. "I'm going to invite her to see Cirque du Soleil with me. What could be a tamer first date than a matinee circus?"

"A candlelit dinner."

"Why do you say that?" he asked, puzzled.

"Because a lot of girls rate the magic of a circus just below the magic of a kiss."

❧ ❧ ❧

That evening Elena and her father sat at a table for two in the dining room of his new home, the Franciscan Manor assisted living residence. She counted five male residents and felt as if she were in a Ritz Carlton ballroom attending a banquet honoring past-chairwomen of the Daughters of the American Revolution.

Her dad swallowed his first bite of raspberry almond cake. "They never served anything like this at Friendship Ridge," he said, grinning.

"I know. I counted five bouquets of fresh flowers on the way here from your room. Their florist bill must be astronomical."

He leaned toward her, a conspiratorial look on his face. "Do you know why this place is swimming in flowers?"

She thought a moment. "To mask unpleasant odors?"

"That too, but it's not the main reason." He set his fork on his plate. "The flowers, food, and fancy furniture are like props on a theater stage. They're there to make the residents' children feel less guilty."

She shook her head in wonder. "Only you would see through the veneer."

His eyes swept back and forth across the room. "I'm happier here than I was at the other place. But it still isn't home."

She patted his hand. "Hang in there, Dad. You'll be back home before you know it."

"I'd already be there if I hadn't been stabbed in the butt in Korea."

She reached for her coffee. "When's your next chess match with your new friend Joe?"

The twinkle returned to his eyes. "Tomorrow after breakfast. A dollar a game."

He nodded at each of three women who scooted past him, single-file, behind their walkers. Elena wondered if they had taken the long way out of the dining room to prance past him. He leaned closer and said just above a whisper, "This place is full of girls who think they're beauty queens. Joe told me the beauty shop offers fifty shades of gray."

They shared a laugh. Elena knew from the look on his face that he meant no reference to the book, *Fifty Shades of Grey*.

"Hey Dad, I saw on the activities' calendar that they hold a dance every Wednesday evening. Would you like to be my dance partner again?"

"Sure." He lifted a bite of cake to his mouth.

Her mind drifted back to the evening Patrick had given her a dance lesson. ... *Will I ever hear from him again?* ...

"How are the kids?"

Her fork clattered against the plate. "They're fine. They still like their summer jobs. Emma broke up with her boyfriend last week. And Jack broke a record—he's been dating the same girl now for over a month."

"Good for him. What's her name again?"

"Maggie."

"How about your house, any nibbles?"

Elena shook her head and scraped icing onto her fork. "Everyone loves it, but they're scared off by how old it is. That and they think they'll need to hire a gardener."

"It's a gardener's paradise." He nodded encouragement. "Don't worry, it'll sell."

She set her napkin beside her plate. "I went house hunting yesterday."

"See anything you like?"

"A bungalow on 2nd Street with potential. And a condo near the courthouse." She stifled a sigh. "It's hard to let go."

"Don't worry, honey, it'll all work out. A change will do you good." He sipped his coffee. "Is Michael behaving himself?"

"Yes."

"Has the gossip died down?"

"Pretty much, as far as I can tell. Other than with Sara, the kids, and a few girlfriends, I've stuck to my story about getting cold feet."

He cupped his hand over hers. "I'm proud of you, Lanie."

They finished their coffee. She escorted him back to his room, put his laundry away, and kissed him goodbye.

A half-minute later, while Elena waited for the elevator, a female resident stepped toward her behind a purple rolling walker. *She looks familiar.* The older woman's inimitable smile gave her away.

Elena smiled back. "Mrs. Krebs?"

"Yes?"

"My name is Elena Shaughnessy. You taught me a long time ago. Probably too long ago to remember—"

Mrs. Krebs' face lit up. "Elena Shaughnessy! No kindergarten teacher forgets red-headed girls who punched every boy in her class."

They laughed and hugged.

"You look fabulous, Mrs. Krebs."

"Thank you, Elena. You've blossomed into a beautiful woman. Please call me Dorothy."

"I'd be honored to, Dorothy. My father just moved in on Saturday. Fred Shaughnessy. Have you ever met him?"

"Yes, but not since you were in my class. Didn't he used to run the Westinghouse plant?"

"He did." The elevator dinged. "I'll look for you on my next visit. We can catch up and I'll reintroduce you to my dad."

"Please come by my room. Two-thirty-five." Dorothy raised her left hand and waved two, three, and five fingers.

Elena held the elevator door open. "I'll make a note in my phone."

"I'll make tea for us in my microwave."

"Would this Wednesday evening after dinner be too soon?"

"Not at all."

They hugged again and said goodbye.

Elena stopped at the bank on her way home and battled bugs in her garden until dark. After showering and shaving her legs, she slipped into a T-shirt and a pair of panties, climbed into bed, and propped her back against the pillows. She opened her laptop. Two emails caught her attention.

Pain before pleasure.

Dear Elena,
   I look for you every evening at Starbucks. Six-thirty. The clock is ticking.
   Love,
   Michael

"Will he ever go away?" She deleted the email and clicked on Patrick's.

Hello Elena,
   Life is a circus.
   If I promise not to be as big a clown as I was at the concert, will you go with me to see Cirque du Soleil this Saturday afternoon?
   I'll call you tomorrow evening to discuss.
   Patrick

Where did that come from? I wonder why he's not taking that other woman.

CHAPTER TWENTY-TWO

Love is friendship set on fire.
–French proverb

"Classic with an edge," Elena whispered to herself. She turned in front of her dresser mirror for a profile view and liked how the sleeveless periwinkle sundress gathered at the waist, accentuating her breasts. Hands on hips, she struck an end-of-runway pose and grinned.

"Not bad for forty-nine."

She moved closer to the mirror and adjusted her headband. The pale yellow silk had a smattering of periwinkle polka dots and a tied-scarf look that straddled the line between dressing the outfit up and down. That had been her plan Tuesday night after Patrick's call, when she splurged on it at Nordstrom.com. She checked her makeup, tugged on her earrings, and remembered him telling her at the art gallery how much he liked dangly earrings.

Wait till he finds out I'm the queen of dangly earrings. She met her own gaze and blinked. *Calm down, girl. Tomorrow is the one-month anniversary of your broken engagement. ONE month. You don't even know why he invited you instead of that other woman.*

A car door closed. Elena hurried to the side of the window and pulled the white sheer back an inch or so. Patrick opened the passenger door and bent over.

The blasted door is blocking my view. … Flowers!

He stepped onto the front walkway. She closed the sheer, scrambled to the mirror, and gave herself a final look. The heels of her yellow sandals clicked against the hardwood floor. She kicked them off at the top of the stairway and scooped them into her hand. He tucked the flowers behind his back and rang the doorbell.

She turned the bend in the stairs. They smiled at each other through the screen door.

"Hello Elena."

"Hi Patrick."

He can't take his eyes off me. Hold onto the railing or you'll trip. Stop grinning like a schoolgirl.

She dropped her sandals onto the floor and slipped her feet into them without looking.

"Welcome," she said, pushing the screen door open.

He stepped inside and gave her a one-armed hug. She luxuriated in the feel of his body against hers and the scent of his cologne.

"These are for you," he said, unveiling a wide-hipped glass pitcher that reminded her of something Jackie Kennedy would have served lemonade from at a poolside table.

"Cornflowers and daisies are great together." She dipped her face into the flowers and stole a peek at his baby-blue cotton shirt and gray dress shorts. They fit him perfectly. Taking a half step back, she looked him in the eye and smiled. "Thank you."

"You'll be the best dressed woman under the tent today." His eyes rose from hers. "I like your headband. It's feminine. Hat-like."

She touched the silk at her temple. "It keeps my waves in check."

His gaze swept from the living room at his left to the dining room at his right. "You were being modest when you described your home to me on the phone. It's beautiful, inside and out."

"Thanks. If you'd like, I'll give you a tour of the downstairs when we get back."

"Will you throw in a tour of your garden, too?"

ॐ ॐ ॐ

The lights inside the blue and yellow tent dimmed, quieting the crowd. Patrick tapped the screen of his phone. Elena rehearsed in her mind the question she had been wanting to ask him for days, the question she'd promised herself she would ask before the performance began.

I need to know. Their eyes met. *Ask him now.*

"Patrick, are you still dating the woman you mentioned at the jazz festival?"

He shook his head. "Nothing ever got started."

Her toes danced in her sandals. She fought to contain her smile. Her eyes and her silence asked him to say more.

"We met for lunch and went to dinner once." His eyes fell back to his phone. "She wasn't my type."

"I see." The smile in Elena's heart spread to her lips.

"Here's what the Cirque du Soleil website says." He leaned closer to her and read aloud from his phone:

> *"Deep within a forest, at the summit of a volcano, exists an extraordinary world—a world where something else is possible. A world called Varekai. From the sky falls a solitary young man, and the story of Varekai begins. Parachuted into the shadows of a magical forest, a kaleidoscopic world populated by fantastical creatures, this young man sets off on an adventure both absurd and extraordinary. On this day at the edge of time, in this place of all possibilities, begins an inspired incantation to life rediscovered. The word Varekai means "wherever" in the Romany language of the gypsies, the universal wanderers. This production pays tribute to the nomadic soul, to the spirit and art of the circus tradition, and to the infinite*

passion of those whose quest takes them along the path that leads—" Pitch darkness blinded them for an instant. *"—that leads to Varekai."*

Patrick's phone went dark. He slid it into his pocket. His elbow touched hers and lingered, sending a warm shiver through her.

"You have a great reading voice."

His nose and lips grazed the curtain of hair covering her ear. "You made me blush."

She brushed her shoulder, catlike, across his upper arm. "Only women blush in the dark," she whispered back.

Exotic bird calls accompanied the forest of shadows bursting to life on the stage.

His hand found hers.

❧ ❧ ❧

Elena and Patrick stepped out of the tent, squinting to shield their eyes from the sun. He tugged on her hand and led her away from the main stream of pedestrian traffic.

"Did you like it?" he asked, his voice laced with boyish verve.

"It was magical. The acrobatics, contortions, music, costumes, and props were woven into a theatrical web."

"Great image. Have you ever seen humans fly like that?"

She shook her head. "I added flying to my bucket list."

"I haven't stopped flying since I saw you on your stairs."

She sensed from his reaction that her smile had told him everything she wanted him to know.

He glanced at his watch. "It's a little before three. Would you like to see one of my favorite places in Pittsburgh?"

"Sure. What is it?"

"I'll surprise you."

Twenty minutes later Patrick turned left off Forbes Avenue onto Craig Street, where the campuses of the University of Pittsburgh and Carnegie Mellon overlap amid an array of funky shops and restaurants. "There's a space," he said, as much to himself as to her. He braked to a stop, reached for the back of her headrest, and backed into the narrow space.

"When did you learn to park like a valet attendant?"

"Here in Oakland, during medical school."

Elena closed the vanity mirror and visor. "Where are we going?"

He pointed across the street at a single-story building sandwiched between an Indian restaurant and an endodontist's office.

CALIBAN BOOK SHOP
USED & RARE BOOKS BOUGHT & SOLD

"I love used bookstores," she exclaimed.

"Caliban gets my vote as the best bookstore between

New York and Chicago." He checked his sideview mirror. "I'll get your door for you."

A moment later he pulled his credit card from the parking meter and asked, "What's your favorite book of all time?"

They stepped off the curb and waited for traffic to clear.

"*Anna Karenina.* Oprah's Book Club recommended it several years ago. I finally took the plunge last winter."

"Great choice." He took her elbow and started across the street. "Tolstoy paints such poignant pictures with words."

"He made me feel as if I were Kitty, living in nineteenth-century Russia, falling in love with Levin."

Patrick opened the door for her. "Books can take you anywhere."

She nodded agreement, paused in the shop's entryway, and followed him to the nearest wall of books, which was marked with a sign that read, "NEW ARRIVALS."

She brushed her fingers across the spines of a vintage set of Charles Dickens' novels. "What's *your* favorite book?"

"*Les Misérables.* Have you read it?"

"No, but I've wanted to ever since I saw the play." She pulled a copy of Paula Byrne's *The Real Jane Austen: A Life in Small Things* from the shelf. "It's my all-time favorite play."

"Anyone who loves Leo Tolstoy's writing will love Victor Hugo's. I've read it three times over the past six years."

"It's that good?"

Their eyes met. "It's that powerful."

He flipped a book open and they browsed a while in silence.

"Come with me." He took her arm and led her through a floor-to-ceiling tunnel of books. "Welcome to the wall of fiction."

He searched the alphabetized stacks and pulled a hardcover from the shelf. "This is the original Modern Library edition. Here, have a look."

VICTOR HUGO
LES MISERABLES

COMPLETE AND UNABRIDGED
A MODERN LIBRARY GIANT

The book's acetate cover glistened and crinkled in her hands. "It looks almost new." Elena raised it to her face and breathed in. "But it has that wonderful old-book smell."

"I call it book perfume." He tapped a forefinger on the front cover at a sketch of a man standing in front of a cottage. "Don't the dust jacket and the plastic cover add to the effect?"

"They really do."

She returned the book to him. He slid it back in the shelf and said, "Let's ask where the gardening section is."

  

Twenty-five minutes later Elena stood at the front counter purchasing two books: a mint-condition copy of Harry Randall's 1969 classic, *Irises,* and Jennifer Helvey's *Irises: Vincent van Gogh in the Garden.* Patrick lifted her bag from the counter.

"What did you get?" she asked, dropping her wallet into her purse.

The shop door jingled. "I'll show you in the car."

When they arrived at his passenger door, he pulled *Les Misérables* from the bag and held it out to her. "I'd like you to have it as a keepsake from today."

"That's sweet of you." She accepted the book and kissed his cheek. "Thank you."

"If you loved the play, Elena, you'll love the book." The smell of curry filled the air. "Would you like to have a late lunch?"

"Sure."

I don't have to be anywhere until Monday morning, she thought.

He glanced up and down the street "How does the café inside the Carnegie Museum sound?"

"Terrific."

What an incredible first date this is turning out to be.

"Let's drop these off first." He took the book from her, opened the door, and laid her bag on the seat.

Tucking *Les Misérables* under his arm, he reached for her hand and started toward the museum a block away. A young man in a robe and flip-flops jaywalked across the street, prompting them to reminisce about their college days. Elena liked how Patrick walked on the street side of the sidewalk at a pace that accommodated her heels.

He's chivalrous, but not over the top.

They entered the Carnegie Museum of Art and turned into the crowded café. After they ordered their meals at the counter, he led her to a corner table for two that had just been cleared along the wall of windows. It overlooked a pool-sized fountain, two metal sculptures, and Fifth Avenue.

He set their wineglasses down, pulled the table away from the wall, and slid it toward her when she was seated.

"That's good. Thanks." She laid the copy of *Les Misérables* on the table.

He sat beside her and raised his glass. "To a memorable afternoon."

"Yes, most memorable."

They clinked and sipped and talked about books and writers until a server delivered Elena's Cajun shrimp salad and Patrick's turkey croquettes. While eating, they discussed movies. He ranked *Casablanca, Schindler's List,* and *The Graduate* as his three favorites and admitted to liking romantic comedies. Neither of them were fans of horror or science fiction.

He cleared the table, stepped away, and returned, first with two fresh wineglasses, and then with a slice of cheesecake that he set in front of her. A single fork lay on the plate.

Sitting down, he picked up the copy of *Les Misérables* and asked, "Would you mind if I read one of my favorite scenes from literature to you?"

"I'd like that."

He opened the book about a quarter-inch from the beginning and flipped back through the pages. "As you know from the play, Jean Valjean spent two decades in a French prison for stealing a loaf of bread and trying to escape from jail. At this point in the novel, he's in his mid-forties—about our age—on the day he was released from prison. After walking all day and being declined lodging everywhere, he showed up at the door of a bishop who offered him food and a bed at no cost."

"I remember the bishop scene in the play."

"Here it is." He marked the spot with his finger and turned to her. "Ready?"

She nodded and he read aloud:

> *The bishop turned to the man:*
> *"Monsieur, sit down and warm yourself: we are going to take supper presently, and your bed will be made ready while you sup."*
> *At last the man quite understood; his face, the expression of which till then had been gloomy and hard, now expressed stupefaction, doubt, and joy, and became absolutely wonderful. He began to stutter like a madman.*

*"True? What! You will keep me? You won't
drive me away? A convict! You call me Monsieur
and don't say 'Get out, dog!' as everybody else
does."*

Patrick read as if he were auditioning for both parts in
the play.

*... As the cathedral clock struck two, Jean
Valjean awoke.*
*What awakened him was, too good a bed. For
nearly twenty years he had not slept in a bed, and,
although he had not undressed, the sensation was
too novel not to disturb his sleep.*

Patrick's reading and the story of how Jean Valjean
couldn't resist the temptation to steal the bishop's silver
enthralled Elena.

The next morning, the police arrived at the priest's door
with a knapsack full of silver and a guilty looking Jean Valjean
in custody. The bishop proclaimed the former convict's
innocence and admonished him for forgetting to also take
the silver candlesticks he claimed to have given him. Jean
Valjean shrank back in shock when the gendarmes released
him and the bishop not only forgave him, but also gave him
the sack of silver and asked him to use it to make himself an
honest man.

Elena hung on the bishop's parting words:

> *"Jean Valjean, my brother: you belong no longer to evil, but to good. It is your soul that I am buying for you. I withdraw it from dark thoughts and from the spirit of perdition, and I give it to God!"*

Patrick closed the book and set it on the table.

"Bravo!" she said, clasping her hands together. "You brought Victor Hugo's words to life."

"Can you see why I love the book?"

"Yes. I can't wait to read it." She slid the plate of cheesecake toward him. "Other than my father when I was a little girl, you're the only man who has ever read to me."

"I thought maybe you'd think it was strange of me." He nodded sideways toward the young couple seated at the table beside them. "Especially in public."

Strangely romantic, she wanted to say but didn't. "Not at all."

She watched his smile grow, mirroring hers, then veering toward mischief.

"Speaking of strange," he said, patting his chest, "my heart has been acting funny lately."

She raised her eyebrows in mock seriousness. "Any probable cause, Dr. Jameson?"

"A girl."

"A *girl*?"

She interpreted his nod as a further invitation to play. His expression sobered. "Would you mind giving me a little relationship advice?"

"I'd be glad to." She reached for her wine. "Tell me about her."

"Her name is Elena," he said, his face lighting up. "She has a terrific personality and sense of humor. She's highly intelligent. And a great conversationalist."

"Is she pretty?"

He shook his head slowly, left then right.

"She's stunning."

Elena bit her lower lip. *And so are you.* She used both hands to guide her wineglass back to the table. "Do you two have much in common?"

"A bunch."

"Like what?"

His eyes drifted from the fountain back to hers. "A shared love of music, books, theater, and nature. Intellectual curiosity. … We're both Irish. And we each lost a parent at a young age." He leaned closer, a bittersweet look on his face. "But …"

"But?"

"… She recently ended a serious relationship. Her heart needs time to heal."

"I see." Elena lifted the fork and dipped it into a back corner of the cheesecake. "Have you told her how you feel about her?"

"I've dropped hints." Patrick raised his wineglass to his lips and searched her eyes over the rim. "I wish I knew whether she has feelings for me."

Elena fought the urge to reach for his hand. "What does your gut tell you?"

"That she does."

Elena slid her wineglass and kissed it softly against his. "Always trust your gut."

He took her hand in his. "Just when I was about to give up hope, you appeared out of nowhere in your Audrey Hepburn hat." He laced their fingers together. "You make me laugh. And think. And wonder."

"I wonder too, Patrick. ..."

"Most of what I wonder thrills me. For example, if our conversations are great now, will they be outstanding in the future?" His smile faded. "But I also wonder whether it's smart for us to begin a relationship so soon after you broke off your engagement."

He released his hand from hers, reached for the fork, and stabbed it into the cheesecake.

Elena stared at the fountain and considered what and how much to tell him about her relationship with Michael. *Be upfront with him,* she told herself. *But don't scare him away like you did at the concert. ... Don't let his psychiatrist questions get you to open up about why you broke things off thirty years ago.*

She met Patrick's gaze. "Michael was my first love. I got back together with him in a moment of weakness two years ago, shortly after my divorce. Before I knew it, we were a couple again." She sipped her wine. "I won't bore you with the details now. I'll just say that if I had married him a little part of me would have died each day on the inside."

Patrick slid the cheesecake toward her. "Thanks for sharing that with me."

He rested his chin on his steepled fingertips and studied the streetscape, looking more like a therapist than he ever had to her. Unable to read his face, she tried to imagine what he was thinking.

He turned to her. "I have an idea, Elena."

"Am I going to like your idea?" she asked, the playful lilt in her voice masking her nerves.

"I think so." He unsteepled his fingers and rested his hands on the table. "Let's spend the next three months as friends only."

"Only friends?"

"Yes. You weren't married to Michael, but you're still going through a divorce of sorts. Your emotional wounds need time to heal." He scratched his temple. "I have patients and friends who've rushed into relationships to avoid dealing with the pain of a breakup. And others who never did their inner work who still aren't emotionally available ten or more years after their relationship ended."

She nodded knowingly. "My boss hates men."

"It would be foolish for us to hurry into a relationship and risk losing our friendship. Starting out as friends will give us time to get to know each other better without all the pressures and expectations of romance and sex." He folded his hands on his lap. "What do you think?"

She smiled at him. *Most men invest their energy in getting a woman into bed. He wants to invest his in our friendship.*

"I agree completely."

"It took me six years to find you, Elena. I can wait three more months."

CHAPTER TWENTY-THREE

Immature love says, 'I love you because I need you.'
Mature love says, 'I need you because I love you.'
–Erich Fromm

Two evenings later Elena and Sara studied their menus outside Mario's Woodfired Pizzeria in downtown Beaver. The umbrella above their table flapped like a sail in the breeze. Baskets of red geraniums dangled from the awning. A trio of teenage boys strutted past, leaving a trail of cologne and bravado in their wake.

Elena set her menu on the table and pulled a perspiring bottle of DaVinci Pinot Grigio out of her handbag. "I realize it's Monday, but will you have a glass of wine with me? I feel like celebrating."

"Sure." Sara peered over her reading glasses. "What are we celebrating?"

"Two things, but before I forget, wasn't Mrs. Krebs your

kindergarten teacher?"

"Yes," Sara exclaimed, closing her menu. "I meant to tell you that I found Dad and her sipping iced tea this afternoon on Franciscan Manor's front porch."

Elena's smile widened. "I sensed an immediate connection when I introduced them. Aren't they cute together?"

"Yes, but it felt strange to see Dad courting a woman."

"I know, but who better than Mrs. Krebs to capture his fancy?"

"How long has she been a widow?"

"Going on twenty years."

Sara opened her menu again. "Can you imagine the two of them having sex?"

"Why not, once Dad's hip and Dorothy's knee are back in commission?"

"I just hope neither of them gets hurt."

Elena raised a brow. "During a night of wild sex?"

"Ha-ha-ha!" Sara laughed. "I was referring to their hearts, not their limbs."

A waitress delivered wineglasses, uncorked the bottle, and looked relieved when Elena asked her to come back in five minutes to take their order.

"What are we celebrating?" Sara asked again.

Elena finished pouring the wine and said in a hushed tone, "Yesterday was the one-month anniversary of the day I broke off the engagement."

"It's already been a month?"

"It felt like three." She raised her glass and clinked it against her sister's. "To new beginnings."

Elena's chair screeched against the brick pavers, sliding a few inches closer to Sara. "There's something else I want to celebrate."

"What?"

"A new friend."

Sara's eyes grew wide. "Who?"

"Patrick Jameson."

"The guy who took you and Dad to the jazz concert a few weeks ago?"

"Yes."

Sara's knee bumped Elena's under the table. "I *knew* he was interested in you."

"He took me to see Cirque du Soleil on Saturday afternoon."

"Why didn't you tell me?"

"I wasn't sure how you'd react."

Sara assumed a wise older-sister look. "It *is* early for you to be dating."

"Patrick insisted we keep our relationship platonic for three months. Or longer, if I need it."

Sara grinned. "You'll need it before then. Is he gay?"

"He's a psychiatrist."

"A gay psychiatrist?"

"No. He's a widower. During our drive home, he told me I'd look hot dressed up as Batgirl in a black mask, cape, and over-the-knee boots."

"How platonic of him."

The sisters laughed as only sisters can.

Sara's eyes narrowed. "I saw him in a suit at Dad's birthday party. He's definitely your type—tall, light, and handsome."

Elena fanned her face with her menu. "I know."

"Behave yourself, little sister."

"As a psychiatrist and a widower, Patrick understands the importance of giving emotional wounds time to heal. He doesn't want us to rush into a relationship and risk losing our friendship."

"Won't the anticipation drive you wild?"

Elena closed her menu and set it on the table. "I'm giving him a cooking lesson tomorrow evening. Afterwards, we're going to set boundaries in a platonic pact."

"Platonic pact? I've never heard of such a thing."

"Neither had I. He's helped patients create them as a safeguard against jumping into a rebound relationship. Speaking of which, he's convinced Michael was my rebound after James."

Sara scratched her neck. "I never thought of it that way."

"Neither had I. Maybe because of our history together." Elena sipped her wine. "Patrick has a brilliant mind, he's almost as intuitive as a woman, and he listens better than anyone I know, including Dad."

"Psychiatrists are professional listeners. I couldn't imagine being married to one. Having him delve into my psyche and sort through my emotional baggage, some of which I don't even know I have." Sara crossed her arms and pretended to shiver. "I'd feel naked."

"I'm not worried. I need all the help I can get."

The waitress arrived, took their order, and scurried away.

Sara pushed her chair back. "Care to join me in the ladies room?"

"No." Elena pulled her phone from her bag. "Emma's struggling with her breakup."

Poor girl." Sara grabbed her purse and stepped toward the restaurant's entrance.

Elena read three texts from Emma and typed:

Today 7:14 PM
You'll be fine. Just ignore him. He's trying to
m—

"Hi Elena."

The phone bounced off the table and landed on her lap.

"Michael." She gripped the phone in both hands.

"My mother's over by the door," he said, pointing to his right. Maria and Elena exchanged smiles and waves. "She's putting our name in for an outdoor table."

"Sara's in the ladies' room. She'll be back any second."

Michael squatted on his haunches, his eyes level with her chin. "Mom was right, Elena, you're looking thin. But you'll always be beautiful to me. And I'll always want you and need you."

She drew her hand back before he could touch it.

"Will you please give me one more chance?"

§ § §

After dinner, Elena assured Sara that she'd be fine, hugged her goodbye, and walked a half block to the Beaver Supermarket. She wandered through the store, plopping two blocks of cheese, a family pack of steaks, a Pepperidge Farm coconut cake, chocolate ice cream, and a jar of caramel topping into her cart.

He gained the weight I lost. He's the one who's suffering. She placed the groceries on the checkout belt and felt a knot of fear and guilt in her stomach. *Who am I kidding? All it took was two minutes in his presence for my wounds to gape open.* She squeezed the bridge of her nose, silencing her inner voice.

She swiped her debit card, carried the bags to her car, and drove home in a daze. After putting the groceries away, she sat at the island and covered her face in her hands.

He rattled me. I'm not as far along as I thought. Relationships are risky.

She opened her laptop and typed:

Patrick,

I'm sorry, but I need to cancel our plans for tomorrow evening. I'll be in touch.

Elena

After pressing Send, she ran upstairs and poured her hopes and fears into her journal. Expressing her feelings in writing eased her mind, but she remained as conflicted as ever.

Curiosity compelled her to go downstairs to see whether Patrick had responded. He had.

Hello Elena,

My cooking lesson can wait. I'll survive as a mediocre chef until my instructor is available. My body temperature has been at least five degrees above normal since Saturday. I won't be in any condition to negotiate our platonic pact until my fever breaks.

Take as long as you need.

Patrick

Elena searched the music library on her laptop for James Taylor's "Fire and Rain" and set it to play on repeat. While listening, she reread Patrick's email twice and replayed her encounter with Michael at the restaurant.

The opening guitar solo played again. She sang along and contemplated the fire and rain Michael had brought into her life. Midway through the song, she stood and roamed around the kitchen, belting out the notes. The song ended and began.

She grabbed the dish towel from the stove handle and wiped the tears from her face.

"So I ran into Michael. So what? We both live in Beaver. Our paths had to cross eventually. … I told him no without even blinking. Why am I fretting? I should be celebrating."

Elena tossed the towel onto the counter, cut a large slice of the semi-thawed Pepperidge Farm cake, and topped it with two scoops of ice cream.

So what if I put five of the ten pounds I lost back on. I need to get my curves back. My mojo. I need to trust myself and be Elena.

She dropped the knife and scooper into the sink and stepped to the island. The dust jacket of *Les Misérables* caught her eye. She pictured Patrick reading it to her at the Carnegie Café.

He's so thoughtful and full of life. I can't squander my opportunity to build something with him.

She lifted a bite to her mouth and typed:

Hello Patrick,
    I'm sorry to hear about your fever. Do you think it'll break by Thursday evening?
    If not by then, when?
    I'll bring dessert. Remember to have a pound each of fresh pasta, butter, and lump crabmeat. … *And* to be platonic.
    Elena

She pressed Send, finished her cake and ice cream in bed, and read *Les Misérables* until she drifted off to sleep. The open book slept above her heart.

CHAPTER TWENTY-FOUR

One cannot think well, love well, sleep well,
if one has not dined well.
  –Virginia Woolf

Elena received a dozen red roses at work that Thursday afternoon. Michael's card was signed, "I love you and need you." The same note had accompanied Tuesday and Wednesday's dozen. She held the vase by its neck during her drive home from the hospital.

While turning into her driveway, she stopped and said hello to her neighbor, Martha Morrison, who was walking her poodle. Martha informed her that Michael had driven down their street at least ten times on each of the previous two evenings. Elena told her the roses were from him, promised to bring her a bouquet of flowers from her garden that weekend, and pulled up her driveway.

"He's like a shark that smells blood," she muttered to herself. "But I'm not bleeding."

She dropped the roses in the trash can, saved the vase, and hurried upstairs to shower and dress for Patrick's cooking lesson.

82 82 82

"It looks fabulous in here," Elena said to Patrick early that evening as they stood in his living room admiring the painting she had helped him select five weeks earlier.

"I'm glad you think so. As I told you at the gallery, I've loved waterfalls since I was a kid."

She turned and surveyed the room. "You have impeccable taste."

"Kate had impeccable taste."

The sole of Elena's sandal caressed the Oriental rug. "It's a work of art."

"Let me show you the room I decorated." He started toward the foyer.

She followed him and stopped in front of a side table on which a framed eight-by-ten photograph was perched. Patrick and Kate stood arm-in-arm on a beach with ocean waves crashing behind them. Elena leaned over for a better view.

They looked so happy together. She was beautiful.

"Elena?"

"I'm coming."

She caught up to him. They walked side by side down a hallway to a pair of stained French doors framed by sidelights and a transom. She stepped back for a better view and shook her head. "That's the most elegant interior doorway I've ever seen. The beveled glass is gorgeous. Is it mahogany?"

His cheeks flushed pink. "Yes."

He pushed the doors open for her. She entered the room and stopped. Her eyes drifted from the cozy seating area nearest them to the glistening hardwood floor in the room's open center and the cherry table desk and chair in front of the far wall. The furnishings were flanked on three sides by floor-to-ceiling shelves. Along the wall to her right, the shelving scaffolded up, over, and down a pair of lanky windows. She had never seen so many books inside a home.

"Why am I not surprised that this is your library?"

A glint of pride flashed in his eyes. "We'll discuss our platonic pact in here after dinner. Speaking of which, I'm starving. Are you ready to give me my first cooking lesson?"

"Yes. Which way to the kitchen?"

"Follow me."

When they returned to the foyer, Patrick picked up the vase of fresh flowers Elena had brought from her garden. She gathered a Safran's Supermarket bag and the raspberry pie she had baked last night. He led her down a hall toward the back of the house.

"Your kitchen is amazing," she said, trying to look everywhere at once.

"Kate loved to cook."

Elena walked a lap around the granite island, saying nothing. She liked everything about the room, especially the French limestone floor, six-burner gas stove, and throng of pots and pans hanging from a copper rack. She felt Kate's presence. And her absence.

She set the pie and grocery bag on the island, pulled out a clear bag of garlic cloves, and swung it like a pendulum. "I have an idea for our platonic pact."

"What?"

"Each time we see each other—after we hug hello—one of us has to eat a half-clove of garlic."

He poured iced tea into a second glass. "One of my ideas is for us to not drink wine together."

She took the glass he offered. "Can we make an exception when we go out to dinner?"

"What about after we leave the restaurant?"

"We could drive separately."

He cocked an eyebrow at her. "To your place or mine?"

"It would depend who lived closer."

They shared a laugh. Elena unpacked a bag of shiitake mushrooms, two beefsteak tomatoes, and a yellow Williams and Sonoma apron and turned to him. "Please know that I never would have said that if we hadn't decided to start out as just friends."

"Me neither."

He cupped his hands over the tomatoes and squeezed them as if they weren't tomatoes.

"Patrick!"

His cheeks took on a tomatoey hue. "What I like is that instead of focusing our energy on ripping each other's clothes off we're focusing it on tearing our masks off and just being ourselves."

She slipped the loop of the apron over her head and reached for the ties. "How do I know your platonic pact idea isn't just a ruse to win my trust?"

He took the apron strings from her hands and tied them behind her back. "So I can have my way with you?"

"Yes."

He mimicked her half-smile, half-shrug. "Are you accusing me of practicing reverse psychiatry?"

"Yes."

"Friendship and trust are the cornerstones of a great relationship."

"I bet you say that to all the girls."

She lifted a bottle of Dawn from the cabinet under the sink, squirted a dab of it into his and her hand, and turned on the faucet.

"Okay, Mr. Budding Chef, after we wash up I'd like you to put on an apron, fill a pasta pot half full of water, and grab your two best knives and cutting boards."

He bumped her hands away from the stream of water. She

bumped his back and added, "While you're proving whether you can multitask, I'll pull the crabmeat, butter, and pasta from the refrigerator." She turned off the faucet. "Does our platonic pact permit an act as intimate as exploring each other's refrigerators?"

"Yes, but our drawers are off limits."

❦ ❦ ❦

Patrick's culinary skills were better than Elena had expected. He showed promise with a knife, took instruction well, and earned bonus points for being playful and willing to learn. After the crabmeat had swum awhile with the mushrooms and diced tomatoes in the pool of olive oil, butter, garlic, herbs, and spices, he lifted a bite to her mouth. It tasted as if she had cooked it. She took the fork from his hand, returned the favor, and resisted the urge to kiss his chin.

Moments later he carried the steaming serving dish into the dining room. She followed close behind with fresh glasses of iced tea. Tapered candles, held aloft by silverleaf holders, stood on either side of her flowers at the center of the table. The flames danced, as if to applaud the chef and his instructor. When they were seated, he looked with pride at the food and described it as the first pretty meal he had ever cooked.

The dinner tasted as good as it looked. The conversation flowed as if they were old college friends. Topics rose, fell,

232

and rose again—music, theater, homes, gardening, politics, and music. She likened the exterior of his home, with its ivy sweater covering half of its brick face, to an English cottage. He laughed when she declared slate roofs to be male for the simple reason they aged too well not to be.

The pie warmed in the oven while they cleared the dishes and brought the kitchen back to order. She breathed a sigh of relief when, after cutting two slices, the raspberries didn't run away from home. Their sweet, tart juiciness exploded on their tongues.

After dessert, Patrick blew out the candles, carried the last of the dishes to the sink, and led Elena to the seating area in his library.

The brass floor lamp's shade hovered between the blood-red leather sofa and its sister side chair, casting a soft glow. "Please make yourself comfortable while I get our platonic pact."

He started toward the desk at the far end of the room. She settled into the corner of the sofa and marveled at his use of furniture, plants, accessories, and lighting. Watching him shuffle through papers on his desk, she imagined the two of them spending a rainy afternoon curled up on the sofa together. He'd read aloud to her between naps and other more strenuous activities. A four-step wooden library ladder caught her eye. She pictured herself climbing to the top step, reaching for a book, and getting stuck.

Like a cat up a tree. Oh Patrick, please help me.

He walked toward her, his demeanor all business. She fiddled with an earring and hoped the lighting was dim enough that he wouldn't notice the flush in her cheeks.

"Here's the first draft." He handed her a stapled document and sat on the side chair, his face inscrutable.

Elena flipped to the end. "Twelve pages!" He nodded.

She skimmed the first page and groaned. "My divorce agreement is easier to read."

"It's not so bad."

"Please tell me you're kidding, Patrick."

He tried to keep a straight face and failed.

"You *rascal*." She rolled up the document and slapped it playfully against his thigh. "Where did you get this?"

"An attorney patient of mine drafted it after her divorce. She emailed the file to me, and I changed the names to ours."

He slipped a handwritten sheet of paper from underneath a magazine on the coffee table and handed it to her. "This is what I came up with last night."

"I like it better already."

"Elena, rather than my taking the lead and trying to persuade you to agree with what I've written, would you mind reading each of the items out loud and sharing your thoughts?"

"Not at all."

"I'll try to listen without interrupting you." He held his hand open, palm up, yielding the floor to her.

"It's refreshing to be with a man who values my opinion." She held the paper at reading distance and squinted. "Your handwriting is legible. Are you sure you're a doctor?"

"Some of my patients think I am."

She chuckled and read aloud:

Elena & Patrick's Platonic Pact

For 90 days from our Cirque du Soleil date, we agree:

1. To be honest with each other and ourselves.
"Great start," she said, turning to him. I know it sounds cliché, but without honesty we'll have nothing." Her eyes fell to the next item.

2. To lay the foundation for us to become best friends.
"Another good one. It's sad that so few couples are best friends. My mom and dad were."

3. To not drink wine together.
"If you continue being such a gentleman, I may be willing to relax this one." He winked assent.

4. To not whine about the lack of wine.
"I'll whine if I want to." She grabbed a pen from the coffee table and scribbled through the line of text.

5. To dress in loose clothing. (No cleavage or excessive chest hair.)
She raised a hand, covering the skin exposed by the V-neck of her blouse. "My chest hair isn't excessive." He bent over in laughter. She gave the paper a shake and continued:

6. To keep our clothes on.
"You're the first heterosexual man to tell a woman to

keep her clothes on." Elena slanted her head to what she thought was its most alluring angle. "Can we at least fantasize about each other?" His eyes said yes.

7. *To abide by a midnight curfew.*
"I feel like Cinderella." Patrick wrapped a hand around the back of her calf, lifted her foot, and slipped her sandal off and on. "Does the slipper fit, Prince Charming?" she asked. His smile told her it did.

8. *Hugs and cheek kisses are permitted.*
"Three months of nothing but hugs and cheek kisses would be torture. We'll need to renegotiate this one."

9. *To not touch erogenous zones.*
She rested a hand a few inches above his knee. "Is this an erogenous zone?" He slid his leg closer to her. She pretended not to notice and held the paper with two hands again. "I wonder what you saved for last."

10. *To perform periodic reassessments of the platonicity of our status.*

"Written by a true psychiatrist," Elena said, shaking her head. She set the paper on the table. "Platonicity. Is that even a word?"

"Yes," he said with a laugh. "And you get bonus points for pronouncing it correctly." He pointed at the pact. "What do you think?"

The leather squished as she sat back. She studied the wall of books behind his desk.

I like that he respects me. ... But I crave his touch. We have such great chemistry.

Her eyes met his. "I like it and I don't."

"Don't you think it's smart for us to walk before we run?"

"I do." Her right hand caressed the arm of the sofa. "But there's a difference between walking and crawling."

He sat forward in his chair. "Are you afraid we'll lose our spark?"

"It's not that. I just don't want us to go overboard trying to contain our chemistry." She crossed her ankles and weighed her words. "Isn't there a middle ground between too little and too much self-control?"

He reached for the pact, flipped it over, and read aloud, "Note: Items five, seven, and eight are subject to change after a twenty-four-minute cooling-off period."

She took the paper from him and reread items five, seven, and eight.

"Twenty-four *minutes*?" she asked. He grinned. She melted.

"A lot of men talk a good game, Patrick, but your actions match your words."

He scratched the back of his neck, his face grew serious. "Since I started dating four years ago, I've rushed into two relationships. The flames died out before either of the fires had a chance to build. … Crushes ended as crashes."

"I don't want that to happen to us."

"Neither do I." He looked into her eyes. "Delaying our gratification won't pour water on our fire. It'll kindle our anticipation."

He lifted the pen from the table, wrote SLOW BURN across the top of the pact, and turned to her. "If one of us starts to get carried away, the other one can say 'Slow Burn' to put a damper on things."

"But what if our tongues are tied?"

He matched her smile and ran his hands down his thighs. "Let's smolder a while, Elena. Then, when the tips of our matches finally rub together, we'll ignite a wildfire."

The hairs on her arms stood on end. She fought the impulse to kiss him. The grandfather clock chimed in the hall, startling her.

"Would you like to add or change anything?" he asked.

She thought a moment. "No. It covers all the bases."

Patrick signed the bottom of the pact and handed her the pen. She scooted to the edge of the sofa and scribbled her name beside his.

The clock continued to chime.

"What time is it?" she asked.

"Nine-thirty."

"Already? I should be going."

He stood, helped her to her feet, and handed her the pact.

When they arrived in the kitchen, he gave her the paper plate and Saran Wrap she requested. Elena cut herself a sliver of pie to take home and admired him from behind as he pulled her container of leftover pasta from the refrigerator.

They stepped into the dimly lit foyer. "Thanks for the cooking lesson," he said, turning to her.

"Thank you for a wonderful evening."

He embraced her and kissed her cheeks as if they were her lips. She reciprocated.

"I'll walk you to your car."

The porch light bled into the foyer as he opened the door.

"What's this?"

Patrick pushed the handle of the storm door, releasing a piece of yellow lined paper. He unfolded it.

"It's addressed to you."

He took the Safran's Supermarket bag from her, handed her the paper, and stepped toward the living room.

She recognized the handwriting. Her stomach fell to her knees, her handbag to the floor. She slumped her back against the wall and read:

Elena,

You cheating whore! How could you betray me like this? Now I know why you gave me back my diamond and wouldn't have sex with me during our last month together.

I Googled your boyfriend's address and found his name. I recognized his shitty grin from your father's birthday party. You couldn't take your eyes off him. (The day after you accepted my marriage proposal!) Does your shrink boyfriend know any of your secrets yet?

You'll pay for disrespecting me like this.

Michael

CHAPTER TWENTY-FIVE

I only ask to be free. The butterflies are free.
–*Charles Dickens*

Elena crumpled Michael's letter into a ball and dropped it into her handbag. A tear splashed her foot. *What if he's outside?* She pushed the door closed, pressed her forehead against the crossrail, and closed her eyes. Her knees began to buckle. She raised her arms and clung to the doorframe.

How humiliating! ... The bastard followed me here.

She heard Patrick's footsteps. He laid his hands on her shoulders.

"A nasty note from Michael," she muttered.

"Oh Elena." He turned her to him and held her close. His heart beat against her cheek, his shirt absorbed her tears.

When her breathing settled, he pulled back a half step and asked, "Can I get you anything? Water? A tissue?"

"No, I'll be fine." She wiped her face with the back of her hand.

Patrick stroked her hair. "What gives him the right to follow you here and invade your privacy? Our privacy?"

"Nothing."

He hugged her again and stepped back. "Has he done anything else like this since you broke off the engagement?"

She shook her head. "I didn't see him for a month. Then Sara and I ran into him Monday evening at a restaurant in Beaver." A chill ran down her spine. "I bet he followed me to Mario's, picked up his mother, and took her there."

Patrick glanced out the sidelight to the right of the door. "I wonder if he was watching us through the windows. Did you see or hear anything strange?"

"No."

He helped her gather her things. "I'll follow you home."

"It's late, Patrick, but thanks for offering." She adjusted the strap of her handbag. "Michael is an ass, but he's not physically violent."

"No, Elena, I insist. He's emotionally abusive. He could be waiting for you in your driveway."

Patrick opened the door, took the grocery bag in one hand and her elbow in the other, and guided her onto the porch and down the curved stone walkway. Moths, a chorus of crickets, and two lighted windows across the street were the only other signs of life. He turned on his phone's flashlight and inspected her Explorer inside and out.

"Is there any chance Michael is involved with the mafia?" he asked, holding the door open for her.

Elena climbed into her car and pictured Anthony Nardelli spilling diamonds from a red Cartier pouch onto a velvet pad. "He may know people who are, but I'm almost certain he isn't."

"Good. Lock your doors and wait here while I get my car. I'll follow you. If he's waiting outside your house, please keep driving and call the police."

"I will."

Patrick kissed her temple and closed the door.

Moments later she stopped at a red light on the Ohio River Boulevard and called Sara. After venting to her about Michael's escapade, she said, "I know it looks bad for me to be spending several hours inside a man's home."

"That's your business, Elena, not Michael's or anybody else's."

"What's funny is that my evening with Patrick was so much tamer than the ones Michael and I spent in his basement thirty years ago." She checked the speedometer and glanced at Patrick's car in the rearview mirror. "If you had been a fly on the wall, you would've laughed as I read our platonic pact aloud and commented on it."

"It's in *writing*?"

"He won't even drink wine with me. The furthest we've gone is cheek kisses."

"He may still be gay."

"No, Sara. He never was."

"Imagine if Michael had rung the doorbell and picked a fight."

"I would've strangled him." Elena turned the air conditioning vent toward her face. "Why won't he just go away?"

"Because he's loved you since high school. And just when he thought you were finally his, you slipped through his hands again. You're his unattainable quest."

"I'm a person, not a prize." She flicked her turn signal and pulled into the passing lane. "I need your help, Sara."

"What can I do?"

"I want you to call Michael."

"It's after ten."

"So what? He'll take your call."

Sara was silent for a moment. "What do you want me to tell him?"

"Two things. Say it was your idea to call him, and tell him I'm completely rattled. That's the response he wanted to provoke. He'll be thrilled." Elena braked for a red light. "Don't defend me. Try to get him to tell you what he's going to do next."

"What if he doesn't answer his phone?"

"Don't leave a message. Call him back every ten minutes between now and eleven." She stepped on the gas. "I'm passing the McDonald's in Baden. Patrick insisted on

244

following me home. I'll call you back after he leaves."

"Wow, Elena. You're so cool and collected."

"You wouldn't say that if you saw my knees shaking."

ૹ ૹ ૹ

Elena turned onto Seventh Street, slowed to a crawl, and breathed a sigh of relief. Michael's car was nowhere in sight. She turned up her driveway and parked in front of the garage.

Patrick opened her door. "Any sign of him?"

"No."

"Good." He helped her out of the car and started toward the front door. "Are all your doors locked?"

"Yes. I never gave him a key."

"Oh. Do you think there's any chance he'd break into your house?"

"No. Even a hint of trouble with the police would hurt his career."

Patrick held the screen door open for her, followed her inside, and closed the door behind him. A table lamp in the living room cast a soft glow over the foyer.

She reached for his hand. "Thank you for escorting me home."

He nodded. "I'm glad I did."

She inched closer and thought about kissing him first. *No, I'll let him take the lead.*

He gripped the knob at the base of the banister with his

free hand. His eyes crawled up and down the stairway.

"What's wrong?" she asked.

He let out a long breath. "Maybe Michael did us a favor tonight."

"A favor?"

"He reinforced why we need our platonic pact."

She looked at him, perplexed. His gaze fell to the floor. *Is this too much drama for him? Is he worried I'll get back with Michael?*

"I'll never take him back."

"That's not my fear."

He withdrew his hand, took a step back and raised his eyes to hers. "Even if Michael didn't exist, I'd still be afraid."

"Afraid of what?"

"Betraying Kate."

The hairs on the back of Elena's neck stood up.

An awkward pause filled the space between them. She watched Patrick's silhouette, his shadow. It hung on the wall, as unmoving as a painting.

Their eyes met, his asking her to be patient with him, hers answering that she'd try.

"The two times I started to get close to a woman since Kate died, the fires never got started because I felt guilty, like I was betraying her, and ran away."

"How long ago did this happen?" Elena asked, trying to sound casual, composed.

"The more recent relationship—if you want to call it that—ended almost two years ago. I'm much closer to being ready now."

The lines in his forehead eased. He took her hands in his and pulled her closer. "Elena, you're unlike any woman I've met. I don't want to run away from you."

❧ ❧ ❧

Before Patrick's taillights disappeared, Elena ran to her bedroom and called Sara.

She answered on the first ring. "I talked to Michael."

"Did you tell him he rattled me?"

"It thrilled him."

"Did he call me a cheating whore?"

"Not in those words. He kept calling Patrick your shrink boyfriend and saying he sensed a spark between you two at Dad's birthday party. He's hellbent on figuring out when you met him."

Elena sighed. "Did you tell him we met that morning?"

"I could barely get a word in."

Elena turned to pace another lap around three sides of her bed. "What else did he say?"

"He doesn't want you back."

"Good. Did he mention anything about seeing us inside the house?"

"No. He said you wouldn't have sex with him after your

engagement."

"Sara, when Michael wasn't bitching about waiting to announce our engagement, he bitched that I was using sex as a weapon. I wanted to strangle him even before he dropped the two bombs on me at his party."

"You don't have to justify yourself to me, Elena."

She sat on the edge of her bed. "Did he say what he's planning to do?"

"He's going to have a copy of the Pennsylvania Department of Health's report delivered to Patrick's office tomorrow. And unless you can prove otherwise by Monday, he's going to tell everyone you cheated on him."

"I've never cheated on anyone."

"I know." Sara paused. "I'm not taking Michael's side. But I can understand why he's angry."

"He had no right to follow me."

"Put yourself in his shoes, Elena. If he had broken off the engagement and broken your heart—and you found out he had spent an evening in the home of an attractive widow he had introduced to you the day after your engagement— wouldn't you be pissed?"

"Not if I knew they'd just met and their relationship was platonic." Elena kicked off her sandals and let out another sigh. "I just learned that Patrick may be less emotionally available than I am."

"Why?"

"He's afraid of betraying his late wife."

"I thought she died five years ago?"

"Six."

"That's a long time. All the more reason to be careful."

Elena shifted the phone to her other ear. "What do you suggest I do about Michael?"

"I'd send him an email telling him you met Patrick at Kretchmar's and that your relationship with him is strictly platonic. Say that he's helping you deal with your broken engagement."

"Home therapy?"

"I know, Elena. It doesn't look good. Tell him that, as a psychiatrist, Patrick knows better than to get involved with a woman so soon after a breakup. And hint that you may take him back."

"Why raise his hopes?"

"It'll support your claim that you and Patrick aren't seeing each other. And give Michael a reason to behave."

A pregnant pause filled the line. Elena lay back on the bed and contemplated what to do.

"Elena? Are you still there?"

"I'm here."

"Did you hear what I just said?"

"I heard."

"I'll call Michael first thing in the morning to let him know to expect your email. I'll try to talk him out of delivering the report to Patrick."

"No, Sara."

"Why not?"

"If you call him again—especially so soon—he'll smell blood and start circling. … Regardless of what Michael says, I think he still wants me back. And even if he doesn't, his ego is too fragile for him to tell anyone I left him for another man. Especially a Sewickley psychiatrist."

"What if you're wrong?"

Elena sat up. "I'll hedge my bets by calling Maria tomorrow. She'll never stop hoping we get back together. She'll help me again."

"That worked once. What if she takes his side this time?"

"She'll always take his side. Don't all mothers? … But that won't stop her from getting him to behave again."

"Wow, Elena. Where did you get your nerve?"

"Growing up as your little sister."

CHAPTER TWENTY-SIX

If pregnancy were a book
they would cut the last two chapters.

–Nora Ephron

An emotional roulette wheel spun in Elena's head later that night. Her thoughts alternated between Michael and Patrick—black ones outnumbered red ones two to one. She blinked in sync with the clock radio's fourth digit.

12:13 … Quit obsessing and get some sleep.

She rolled onto her back, kicked her feet free of the sheet, and hoped the ceiling fan's whir and click would lull her to sleep.

It didn't.

Hugging the spare pillow to her body, she wondered whether Patrick slept on his back or his side. She imagined him sleeping on his back, naked above a sheet that covered him to his waist.

What if he gets scared and runs away from me? ... Then we weren't meant to be. But I want us to be. How can I help him overcome his fear of betraying Kate? ... Be patient.

She rolled away from the clock. *Enough is enough. You've done a month's worth of thinking tonight. Give your brain a rest. You need sleep. Think only pleasant thoughts. Recapture the magic of your first hours together this evening.*

Elena's mind drifted back to the moment she'd laid eyes on Patrick's house. Her first impression of his home mirrored her first impression of him. Classy. She considered it strange—but a good omen—that they both lived in black-shuttered white brick colonials. She replayed their tour, cooking lesson, and dinner conversation, fast-forwarded to him sliding her sandal off and on, and fell off to sleep.

❧ ❧ ❧

Elena awoke with a shiver in the dead of night. She bolted upright and ran a hand through her hair. Cold sweat on the back of her neck compelled her to rub her stomach.

Thank God! She lay back down. *It seemed so real.*

She'd dreamed she was nine-months pregnant to Michael. Her water broke in late October, on the eve of her fiftieth birthday. A carved and candled jack-o'-lantern glowed from every porch they passed as he drove her to the hospital on a Harley Davidson he'd borrowed from a neighbor—he didn't want to foul his Audi's interior. She spent the majority of the dream staring helplessly at Michael and the obstetrician who had nearly killed Baby Alexa. The men groped between her stirrupped legs. Arrogant fear had been written on their faces.

"You were only dreaming," she muttered under her breath. "It was only a dream." She rubbed her stomach again. "Only a dream."

Elena pulled the comforter to her chin and stirred a while before falling back to sleep.

The clock radio sprang to life at six o'clock with the Beatles singing *Here Comes the Sun*. She straggled into the bathroom, pulled the shower knob, and sat on the toilet. An image of Michael kick-starting a Harley flashed in her mind.

Don't go there.

She stripped off her T-shirt and panties, stepped under the hot water, and let it relax her muscles. Her thoughts shifted to the day ahead. The first item on her mental to-do list was to warn Patrick to expect a delivery.

Moments later, after slipping into a pair of scrubs, she hurried to the kitchen, packed a lunch, and sliced a banana into a bowl of Honey Bunches of Oats.

How should I word it?

She carried the cereal to the island and began to type:

Hi Patrick,

Thanks again for your hospitality last night. With the exception of Michael's intrusion, everything about our time together was spectacular.

My sister Sara learned that Michael plans to have a package delivered to your office today. It's a report from the PA Department of Health about an investigation of a baby delivery that went awry. Fortunately, the baby survived. You'll see in the report that I was cleared of any wrongdoing. I'll tell you about it the next time we speak.

Elena

P.S. I'm a modern woman, but old-fashioned enough to prefer that you call me.

She pressed Send, slipped into her nursing clogs, and blew a kiss at her mom's photo.

Eleven minutes later she passed the two nurses' stations and greeted the night crew. The fragrance of Friday filled the air. She squeezed her lunch in the door of the refrigerator, stepped into the office she shared with the other shift supervisors, and exchanged greetings with Nancy Thompson.

Nancy informed her that today's star mother-to-be was Jen Fenwick, who, after nineteen years of marriage and almost as many years of trying to conceive, was on the verge of delivering her first baby.

Elena leaned over the desk and tapped the Fenwick chart on the computer screen. "Cervix fully dilated," she mumbled.

She read on and discovered that the forty-one-year-old patient had been admitted while she herself had been giving Patrick a cooking lesson.

She grabbed a pad of paper and a pen from the desk and walked with Nancy to the "Mother" nurses' station. After the change-of-shift report, they hustled to the "Baby" nurses' station.

The next two hours flew by.

Elena sat at her desk and called Michael's mother.

"I need your help again, Maria," she said after a moment of small talk. "Is there any chance we could get together today for coffee?"

"Sure, honey. Would you like to meet in the hospital coffee shop during your lunch break?"

"Hold on a second, please."

Elena muted her phone and considered Maria's offer. Meeting at the hospital would limit the amount of time they'd have to spend together. But was it too public a venue? Prying eyes and ears. … *No, word will spread that we're on friendly terms. It'll be perfect.*

"Maria?"

"Yes?"

"Sorry for the interruption. The hospital coffee shop sounds great. Eleven-thirty?"

❧ ❧ ❧

A few hours later Elena and one of her nurses helped Jen and Joe Fenwick celebrate the delivery of a healthy baby boy. Weighing in at a hair over nine pounds, Jacob Alan Fenwick had greeted the world with more hair than his father. Oblivious to the after-party his arrival had induced, Baby Jacob split his time between suckling his mother's breast and wailing.

Elena returned to the office and reviewed a few charts before lifting her purse out of the file cabinet and telling the unit secretary that she was going to lunch. When she passed Jen Fenwick's mother in the hall, the proud grandmother paused from broadcasting her news to someone on the phone, clutched Elena's arm, and mouthed the words, "Thank you."

"You're welcome," she mouthed back with a smile.

She stepped off the elevator on the first floor and mentally rehearsed what she planned to tell Maria. Rounding the bend in the hallway, she saw Michael's mother sitting at the coffee shop's crowded counter, her purse perched on the empty stool to her right.

They greeted each other with a hug and a double-cheek kiss and settled into their seats. A waitress topped off Maria's coffee, filled a mug for Elena, and shuffled off.

"I ate a late breakfast," Maria said, handing her a menu. "Please eat. Put some meat on your bones."

"I packed a big lunch today." She stabbed the menu into the metal holder, scanned the room, and recognized two people, neither of whom sat within earshot.

Maria patted her arm. "You look sad, honey. Did Michael do something?"

Elena nodded and reached for her coffee. "First I'll tell you what I think he did Monday evening," she said just above a whisper. "I'm almost certain he followed me to Mario's before he took you there."

"No, Elena," Maria said, surprise in her eyes. "Monday was the fourth anniversary of Al's death. Michael picked me up after work and took me to the cemetery. We went straight to Mario's afterwards."

Elena swallowed a gulp of coffee and guided the mug to the counter with both hands. "I'm sorry, Maria. I was mistaken. I must be paranoid after what Michael did last night."

Maria's eyes widened. "What did he do last night?"

"He followed me to a friend's house in Sewickley and left a nasty note for me in the door."

"Was it your psychiatrist friend's house?"

Elena tried not to flinch. "Yes."

"Michael told me all about your new friend," Maria said, her eyes hurling daggers. "Or is Dr. Jameson an *old* friend?"

"It's not what you think, Maria." The words came out louder than Elena had intended. Two sixtyish women seated across the horseshoe counter looked at her as if she had belched in church.

Maria shook her head and tsk-tsked. "I'm very disappointed in you, Elena. Your poor mother must be rolling in her grave."

"Leave my mother out of this."

"At first I didn't believe Michael when he told me about your psychiatrist friend. But now that you've admitted it's true, I'll tell him he'd be crazy to take you back."

"Please do."

Maria cocked her head. "You're a fool, Elena. My Michael is the most eligible bachelor in Beaver County."

"Your Michael is an ass. You're the only woman he respects."

Elena grabbed her wallet, flung a five-dollar bill on the counter, and stormed out.

CHAPTER TWENTY-SEVEN

Live mindful of how brief your life is.
–Horace

Late that afternoon Patrick stood at the wall of windows in his office and studied the parking lot three stories below. He recognized the black Audi parked near the building's rear entrance, but not the one three spaces to the left of his car. It appeared to be empty.

Jilted lovers are irrational. Keep your guard up.

He walked to his desk, slid the latest edition of *The American Journal of Psychiatry* into his briefcase, and turned out the lights before stepping into the empty hallway. After taking the stairs to the first floor, he wished Roxie the cleaning lady a nice weekend, stepped outside, and dashed to his car as if he were late for an appointment.

He locked the doors and scanned the parking lot.

Nothing unusual. Don't be paranoid. Damn, it's hot. Keep the windows up.

Patrick started the engine and pressed the air conditioner knob until "Max Cool" flashed on the dashboard screen. He leaned toward the rearview mirror. The back of his shirt peeled like duct tape off the leather seat. Shifting from reverse to drive, he turned onto the Ohio River Boulevard, checked his mirrors, and breathed a sigh of relief.

I wonder if Sigmund Freud ever had a day at the office as bizarre as this one.

His thoughts turned back to that morning when he'd read Elena's email informing him to expect a delivery from Michael. Things had spiraled downward from there. His first patient, Beverly Taylor, surprised him by neither showing nor calling. Another patient, Sharon Olson, admitted to cutting herself a week ago. And for most of the afternoon, he was fixated on shiny objects. He caught himself staring at Elizabeth Brown's purse and shoes, Jack Nolan's bald head, and Ellen Swearingen's necklace.

I hope she didn't think I was ogling her breasts.

Patrick stopped at a traffic light and wished again that Renee had picked a different Friday to begin her ten-day vacation. She would've known how to calm his ruffled feathers.

He turned up Walnut Street and made a mental grocery list. After parking in the lot behind Safran's Supermarket, he pulled his phone from his pocket and typed:

Today 6:04 PM
Hi Elena. No deliveries from Michael today.
I'll call you tonight at 9:00.

He pressed Send, searched for black Audis, and hurried
into the store.

᠀᠀᠀ ᠀᠀᠀ ᠀᠀᠀

About an hour later he savored his last bite of dinner. The
leftover angel hair pasta with crabmeat tasted almost as
delicious as it had the previous evening when it was spiced
by Elena's presence. He washed the dishes by hand,
double-checked the security system, and worked in the
library on paperwork for his mother's estate.

Ninety minutes passed.

He stacked files on a corner of the desk and passed dusky
shadows on his way to the living room. By the time he
finished his fifth lap around the Persian rug, three women
vied for his attention.

He stopped in front of his favorite photograph of his
mother. The silver-framed picture had been taken at the
celebration of her brother's twenty-fifth anniversary as a
priest, when Patrick had been ten or eleven. Irene's black hair
and white dress framed her blue eyes. Her head, tilted back
in laughter, captured her essence.

Thanks for forging me into the man I am, Mom. I'm glad you're not suffering any more. Keep dancing.

He resumed pacing. Passing an end table, he glanced at a photo of Kate and him that had been taken ten years ago on the beach at the Outer Banks. It stirred a hundred memories.

He recalled one of their long walks on the beach that week when Kate had complimented him on his graying temples and lamented that she was aging. Wrinkles mostly. She kissed him when he told her that she was sexier at thirty-six than she'd been at twenty-six.

His mind jumped ahead four years and painted a picture of Kate wearing a pregnant glow. Gray hairs sprouted like weeds from her scalp. Months earlier she had announced a ban on hair coloring. The chemicals could hurt the baby. He visualized her standing naked in the bathroom, laughing as she rubbed lotion on her stomach with one hand and pointed at her "prego" breasts with the other.

The movie in his mind faded and was replaced by an image from a few weeks later. Kate lay still, looking happy. The afternoon sun cast its light on her face. A sea of white lilies surrounded her casket.

Patrick wiped his eyes and was surprised to discover they were dry. He picked up his pace, saw Elena in his mind, and wondered whether she could be the third great woman in his life.

Is that asking too much?

He stopped in front of his new painting. His eyes floated down the stream above the waterfall, paused at the precipice, tumbled into the frothy pool, and drifted downstream to the black boulder. He admired the orange tiger lilies nature had planted in the rock's crevices and turned his gaze back to the falls.

The water flows and falls, evaporates into clouds, and falls and flows again. If it can live again, why can't I?

He studied the smattering of trees along the shoreline of the painting. *That's me. A spectator. Dry and safe. ... I offer shade to my patients and guide them through life's rapids. Saving them from drowning saves me from drowning.*

Patrick began another lap and remembered winning a trophy for third prize in a Fourth of July swimming race as a kid. *I wish I weren't afraid to get wet.* He slowed his pace and imagined Elena and him sitting on the boulder and enjoying the splendor of the falls. *She's as beautiful and as alive as any waterfall. But our timing is all wrong. She was engaged six weeks ago.*

Fear and longing pulsed in his veins. He stopped at the entrance to the foyer and recalled the pained look on her face last night when she'd read Michael's note.

It wouldn't surprise me if he's in the mob. Things could get ugly with a guy like him. ... But she's stunning inside and out.

Our conversations are incredible. … What if I end up hurting her? He sighed heavily. *I should level with her and explain the psychological underpinnings of emotional availability. We could have dinner together once a month and reassess things in six months or a year. It would give both of us time.*

He debated whether to call Renee at the Jersey Shore and decided not to bother her. She'd ask how he would advise a patient with the same dilemma and know his answer before he would—to be careful but to err on the side of boldness rather than timidity. She'd tell him to practice what he preached and stop reneging on his promise to Kate.

Patrick strode across the foyer, down the hall, and into his library, pulled a journal from the bottom drawer of his desk, and opened its leather cover. The book shook as he read his handwriting:

Memories of Kate

He opened it to a dog-eared page and began to read the list of their top ten moments together, beginning with number 10 at the top of the page.

His smile grew more wistful.

While reading about their seventh best moment—going skydiving on their first wedding anniversary—a greeting card sailed from the back of the journal to the floor. He bent over, picked up the last card Kate had given him, and opened it.

Patrick,

Happy Father's Day!

Four months from now our baby girl will be born with an outstanding Father. Thank you for loving me and "Little Irene" as she grows and kicks inside me. We're both so lucky to have you.

Savor this, your first Father's Day, and remember what Emily Dickinson said: "Forever is composed of nows."

With All My Love,
Your Kate

He held the card up to his nose, wishing it bore her scent, and slipped it back in the journal.

"It's five after nine. I'm late."

He pulled his phone from his pocket and tapped on Elena's name.

CHAPTER TWENTY-EIGHT

To be fond of dancing was a certain step
towards falling in love.
–*Jane Austen*

Five evenings later, on Franciscan Manor's oversized front porch, Patrick and Elena danced with her father and Dorothy to the Benny Goodman Orchestra's "Moonglow." Eight other dancers, four of them perched in wheelchairs, shared the slate-tiled dance floor with them. Hovering overhead, the green canvas awning tried to hold the July air hostage, but the dancers, like blades of a fan, refused to let it.

While swinging and swaying her former kindergarten teacher, Elena etched the joy written on her father and Patrick's face into her memory. The song ended, but the circular fountain continued to dance and sing on the lawn below.

The activities coordinator announced a refreshment break. Patrick and Fred started toward the men's room, Dorothy struck up a conversation with a friend at the refreshment table, and Elena approached Sara, who stood at the porch railing dabbing her neck with a napkin.

"I'm dying to know what you think of Patrick."

"He seems like a great guy, but I'm glad he doesn't live across the street from me."

"Why?"

A devilish grin spread across Sara's face. "Because I'd spend way too much time watching him mow his lawn and hang his Christmas lights."

"Sara!"

The sisters laughed.

"I'm glad you like him. Can you imagine Michael dancing with Dad like that?"

"Never. I just saw on Facebook that he subscribed to Match dot com."

"Thank God!" A wave of relief washed over Elena.

"He posted a picture of himself standing in front of his car without a shirt. More than sixty women emailed him in the first two days."

"Good for him. *Great* for me."

"Have you heard from him?"

Elena shook her head. "Six days and counting." She took a long sip of her lemonade. "If things stay calm for another week or so, Sara, would you mind talking to him about returning Mom's wedding ring."

"Not at all. Just let me know when."

※ ※ ※

Later that night Patrick sat alone on Elena's deck watching the crescent moon rise and the stars come out. The lack of a breeze didn't prevent a bouquet of aromas from escaping her garden.

The sound of her sandals on the kitchen tile grew louder. She pushed the screen door open with her hip and carried a candlelit serving tray toward him. The hourglass formed by her eyes, nose, and lips captivated him. As did the one shaped by her breasts, waist, and hips.

She handed him an Amstel Light, set the candle and a fresh bowl of salsa on the table, and sat down.

He took a swig. "What will we do if our second beers don't quench our thirst?"

"Whine."

"Wine?" he asked, puzzled.

"With an *h*, Patrick."

"You're so clever."

Her eyes narrowed playfully. "You're the clever one, suggesting we add a two-beer limit to our pact."

"Just trying to be flexible."

"Flexible in your platonic rigidity?"

He cocked his head at what he thought was an alluring angle. "Only a brave woman—or an aroused one—would raise the subject of a man's rigidity."

"Behave yourself, buster."

His tortilla chip broke in the salsa. "That's getting harder," he said, fishing the smaller piece out with the larger.

She finished ironing a wrinkle out of her bottle's label. "What's getting harder?"

The chip crunched in his mouth. He waggled his eyebrows until her cheeks were rose red. "What's getting harder is behaving myself, especially after our marathon phone conversations these past five nights."

She met his gaze. "I haven't talked so much on the phone since I was a teenager."

"I never have."

"Talking on the phone for hours may be old-fashioned, but it's still a great way to get to know someone."

He scooted his chair a few inches closer to her. "We never seem to run out of things to talk about, do we?"

Elena kicked her sandals under the table and slid the bowl of cherries toward her. "You ask more intelligent questions in an hour than most men ask in a month. Music, movies, theater, books, food, family, relationships, nature, travel, spirituality, the meaning of life. Is there an important subject we haven't discussed?"

"There's three." He sipped his beer. "The Steelers and organized religion."

"That's only two."

He slid his naked foot slowly down the slope of hers, paused toe-to-toe, and slipped it back into his sandal. "Our platonic pact is too restrictive."

She plucked another cherry from the bowl. Her eyes invited him to elaborate.

"I feel like I hammered a sign in the ground that says 'Keep Off the Grass.'"

"I could have a *field* day with that one, Patrick."

He narrowed his eyes at her. "You're quicker than usual with the one-liners tonight."

Elena swallowed the cherry and laid the pit on her napkin. "A woman needs to be on her toes when a man is trying to steal a base on her."

He looked through the screen door, intent on scouring his brain for a snappy comeback. Instead, he imagined her standing on her toes reaching into the cabinet above her refrigerator, her white summer skirt climbing up the backs of her thighs.

She lured his foot out of his sandal. He turned to her and tried again to think of a witty retort, but his mind was mush and his time was up.

"Elena?"

"*Yes?*"

"When you drag the word yes out like that, you sound like an umpire."

She slanted her eyes at him. "That's the best you could come up with?"

He raised his hands in defense. "Your beauty distracts me."

"Puhleeze!" she teased, nudging his foot. "Stop throwing curve balls at me."

Patrick tilted his head back and searched the sky. His brain brimmed with potential zingers. He discarded them one by one as soft balls that she'd hurl back at him.

I can't keep up with her tonight.

He met her gaze. "Can we please renegotiate our pact?"

"I wondered how long you'd last."

Does she have any idea how hot she looks when she tucks her hair behind her ear like that? Should I undress her with my eyes and see how she responds? … Practice what you preach, Dr. Slow Burn.

He slid the candle closer. The reflection of the flame flickered in her eyes.

"I still want us to have a long fuse, Elena. A slow burn. Do you?"

"I do."

He stretched his legs to where his feet were beyond her reach and crossed his ankles. "Most of my single patients—male and female, young and middle-aged—rush into having sex with a new partner, usually no later than their third or fourth date. Then, when the relationship fizzles soon afterwards, as it often does, they regret their decision and vow to take things slower the next time. But they don't." He uncrossed his ankles. "They're stuck in a behavioral revolving door in which they confuse physical intimacy with emotional intimacy."

She nodded understanding, her silver teardrop earrings dancing, shimmering.

"I made Michael wait six months."

Patrick wondered if his face, the expressionless mask he used every day in his practice, disguised his surprise.

"Six months is rare. Your waiting that long makes me suspect you had doubts about your compatibility with him. Either that or you had lost your libido."

"My libido was fine."

"Can we renegotiate our pact?" he asked, ditching his therapist's voice.

"What do you have in mind?"

"I'd like us to establish physical boundaries and a timeline for their expansion."

"Is that how a psychiatrist tells a girl he wants to spell out first, second, and third base and how soon he can go there with her?"

He smiled, embarrassed. "Sorry for sounding clinically unromantic."

She waved off his apology. The flame of the candle danced.

"It's getting late," he said. "We can work out the details this weekend."

The look on her face told him he'd struck a sour note.

"Patrick, would you mind if we didn't put anything in writing? The best jazz is improvised."

He nodded agreement. "Speaking of music, I heard a song earlier today that made me think of you. Would you like to hear it?"

"Sure."

He lifted his phone from his pocket. "I'll pull it up on Spotify." He swiped and tapped the screen. "The audio won't be great, but that won't matter. … Here it is."

"I know this song," she said, three or four notes into the instrumental opening. "It's by Sade. What's it called?"

"Kiss of Life."

He stood, helped her to her feet, and rested his hands just above her hips. Pulling her to him, he pressed his face against the hair above her ear and inhaled her scent. She followed his lead and their bodies glided across the deck in the delicious space between fast and slow dancing.

When the song ended, they danced to the music of the night. Moonlight guided their lips together.

CHAPTER TWENTY-NINE

It was not my lips you kissed, but my soul.

–*Judy Garland*

The next two days passed in a whirl. Elena never tired of replaying their time together on the deck. Even when she wasn't thinking about Patrick, she felt lighter, freer. She discovered previously unheard sounds and unsmelled scents at home and work and saw things with binocular eyes, but in softer hues. When she remembered to eat, flavors seemed to penetrate a wider, deeper palette of taste buds.

Thursday after work she purchased "Kiss of Life" on iTunes and memorized the lyrics while singing duets with Sade. Friday afternoon at work, when Jill Signore teasingly accused her of either buying a new sex toy or putting fresh batteries in an old favorite, she laughed and pleaded innocent to both counts.

Now, a few hours later, she scanned her closet for something to wear to the Pirates game that evening. It hadn't taken Patrick long to convince her that a baseball game would be the perfect venue to discuss first, second, and third base. She looked forward to an evening of laughter leading to whispers, and whispers leading to kisses.

Elena walked to her bed, laid three sundresses side by side on the comforter, and did the math: the three-month anniversary of their meeting was only a few weeks away. It seemed like three years ago; it seemed like three days ago.

The doorbell rang, startling her. She carried the orange sundress she'd worn the day they met to the window, and pulled the sheer back. A UPS truck was parked at the curb.

I'm not expecting any deliveries. Could it be a present from Patrick?

She hurried downstairs, greeted the driver, signed her name on the electronic clipboard, and winced at the sight of Michael's name on the screen. After thanking the driver, she dashed toward the kitchen holding a small box that was heavy enough to be empty. She shook it beside her ear and heard nothing.

"Please let it be Mom's ring."

Elena slit the packing tape with a pair of scissors. Her heart leapt at the sight of her mother's black jewel box. She popped the clamshell lid open, slipped the ring onto her finger, and examined it from every angle. Other than being diamondless, it looked the same as when her mother had worn it.

She kept the ring on her finger and unfolded the piece of yellow-lined paper Michael had taped to the bottom of the velvet box. His handwriting covered both sides of the page. She resisted the impulse to toss it in the trash unread, took a deep breath, and raised it to eye level.

Elena,

Once again, you've left me for a doctor. Once again, the boy from Bridgewater wasn't good enough for the girl from Beaver. Once again, you've wasted years of my life.

You'll be happy to learn that being dumped by you at fifty hurt far worse than it did at nineteen. Just when I thought I had finally won your heart, you stabbed a knife into mine. I ate like a glutton and barely slept for the first month. My family and friends were worried about me. Maximo recommended therapy. Imagine if I had unknowingly made an appointment to see your shrink?

I'm not surprised that your next prey is a wealthy psychiatrist from Sewickley. On second thought, I am surprised. As soon as he discovers all the demons inside your head, he'll run like hell. Don't come crying to me when that happens.

Seeing you greet your shrink at his front door shocked me to my senses. I was prepared to wait as long as it took for you to come back to me. But not now. I don't want you back. No man wants to be with a woman who wants to be with someone else.

Every trace of you went up in flames in my fire pit last Friday night. I used your photos and cards as kindling for your Georgetown sweatshirt, toothbrush, and every gift you've ever given me. I wish you could have seen and smelled the Ferragamo loafers and Burberry cashmere sweater burn. I saved the shoebox full of your love letters from high school for last.

It's one thing for you to treat me like shit, but for you to treat my mother that way in public was disgraceful. In case you've forgotten, she tried to fill your mother's shoes and loved you like a daughter. Now she hates you almost as much as I do.

You need to be punished for betraying and disrespecting me. Everyone, including your family, needs to know the truth about you. Imagine everyone's surprise when they discover you're not the perfect woman they thought you were and learn instead that you're a cheating whore and an incompetent nurse? Imagine everyone's shock when they hear your BIG secret? Your family will be ashamed of you. Your co-workers and friends will shun you. Your shrink will dump you.

I haven't decided when to seek my revenge. I may leak your secrets one at a time or all at once. I may strike during the next few days or let you sweat awhile. You'd be a fool not to take your punishment in silence. Fighting back by exposing my secret will only piss off some very powerful people and embroil you in another scandal.

Good riddance!

Michael

CHAPTER THIRTY

A woman is like a tea bag; you never know
how strong it is until it's in hot water.
–Eleanor Roosevelt

Elena's phone rang twenty minutes later. Patrick apologized for needing to cancel their date. He had just gotten off the phone with the distraught mother of a patient who informed him that her eighteen-year-old daughter was on the verge of committing suicide. He was rushing to Western Psych to meet them and would call her back as soon as he could.

Having been married to a physician, Elena knew that plans were subject to change. She empathized with the plight of Patrick's patient and her mother and tempered her disappointment at not seeing him by telling herself she wouldn't have been good company anyway. She called Emma and was relieved to hear her voice.

"Mom, I was just about to call you to ask what I should wear tonight."

For every word spoken about her date, a blue-eyed Carnegie Mellon student she'd met last weekend at a party, fifty were spilled about what Emma would wear, including shoes, jewelry, and makeup. Fifteen minutes into their conversation Elena resisted the urge to shout, *Quit obsessing and decide!* Instead, she listened with one ear and considered whether she'd want to be nineteen again.

No way. Too much drama.

"You'll figure out what to wear, Emma. Where is ..." She racked her brain and came up empty. "Did you tell me his name?"

"No. It's Peter Birkman."

"Where is Peter taking you to dinner?"

"To a Thai restaurant in Lawrenceville. Pusadee's Garden."

While Emma prattled on about her date, Steely Dan's "Hey Nineteen" played as background music in Elena's head. The talk of food awakened her appetite. She cradled the phone between her ear and shoulder and cooked a mushroom and Swiss omelet. After sliding it onto a plate, she scooped half an avocado on top, buttered a sesame bagel half, and carried her dinner and a glass of orange juice to the island.

When Emma paused to catch her breath, Elena asked her if she'd heard from Jack and was surprised to learn that he was madly in love. The past few times she had inquired about his girlfriend, including last Sunday after dinner, he responded by saying, "Maggie's fine." She wondered how her daughter could tell her everything and her son almost nothing.

After hanging up with Emma, she loaded the dishwasher and recalled their parting words before saying goodbye:

By the way, Mom, how are you?

I'm fine, Emma. Have fun tonight, but be a good girl.

Her phone rang. Kathleen Riggs' name flashed on the screen. Elena remembered that a couple had looked at her home earlier that afternoon.

"Hi Kathleen."

"Elena, they loved the house and made an offer."

A dull ache rose in her chest. She plopped onto a stool at the island. Her realtor mentioned the dollar amount and squealed, "Three percent below asking price is unheard of in this market. They're pre-approved for financing and their only condition is a home inspection. The wife is a gardener."

"An avid gardener or a hobbyist?"

"I'm not sure. She went on and on about your flowers."

After discussing a counteroffer, Elena asked Kathleen to speak with James and call her back. Before ending the call, she scheduled an appointment to take a second look at two condos in Beaver.

A little over an hour later the temperature had cooled from sweltering to hot in Elena's garden. She knelt in a bed of bearded irises, pulling weeds with a hand cultivator. Sweat burned her eyes and soaked her T-shirt and gloves. Her thoughts vacillated between Michael's threatening letter and the harsh reality that she'd soon be forced to leave her home and garden.

She predicted that James would insist on making a counteroffer and then lobby her to accept the buyers' second offer, regardless of whether they had budged on the price. His emotional connection to the house was as negative as hers was positive. He was eager to reap his portion of the profit and tie up the final loose end of their divorce.

It amazed her to think that three years had passed since she'd asked him to leave. It seemed like three months ago that Jack wore his high school cap and gown and Emma's face was sprinkled with acne. Elena had long known the house would eventually sell—just as she had known her kids would one day leave the nest—but, until recently, she'd buried this reality in the back of her mind as an unpleasant event that loomed in the distant future.

Echoes of thunder rumbled from the west. She rose to her feet, gazed at the sky, and rolled a kink out of her neck. Her thoughts turned back to Michael. She closed her eyes and imagined him tossing her things into his fire pit. After the flames consumed her old letters, his elation gave way to tears. He hung his head and bawled like a baby. Her mind raced back thirty years to the day she'd last seen him cry. She pictured him at nineteen, an Adonis, his hair parted in the middle, a gold Italian horn charm hanging from his neck to protect him from what he called "the evil eye." Weeping, he begged, *Don't destroy my life!*

Elena opened her eyes and felt as if she were waking from a nightmare. The yellow shaft of her spade shovel caught her attention. All but the shoulder of the blade was buried in dirt.

"If the bastard wants revenge," she whispered, her heart screaming, "I'll give him revenge."

She tugged the shovel's D-handle with one hand, gripped its shaft with the other, and lifted its shiny steel spade to eye level. "One for his feet so he can't run."

She stabbed the blade into the edge of the flowerbed. After yanking it loose, she took two steps to her left and raised it again. "One for his tongue so he can't talk."

She plunged the spade into the ground, pulled it free, took a step to her right, and held it aloft. "And one for his dick so he'll stop fucking with me."

The blade severed Michael's imaginary penis.

Elena hunched over the shovel and laughed hysterically until she sobbed.

She collapsed to the ground, tumbled into a sitting position, and wrapped her arms around her knees. Her shoulders heaved, her stomach shook. Tears and mucus dripped from her chin. She pulled her T-shirt over her bra and pressed it to her face.

"Help me, God."

A wave of remorse swept over her. *I should have known Michael would seek revenge. It's in his Sicilian blood. I inflicted this on myself when I took him back.* She remembered how horrible she'd felt when he told Sara about Baby Alexa. *That was one secret to one person.* She shuddered at the thought of his airing all of her dirty linen in public.

When the worst of her inner storm passed, Elena blew her nose into her T-shirt, lowered the wet cotton over her bra and stomach, and reflected on the personal attacks contained in his letter. It didn't take her long to conclude that all but one of them were either misguided or false. Her only offense had been to break his and Maria's hearts again. Michael's mother had received the treatment she deserved at the hospital coffee shop.

Elena climbed to her feet and gathered the garden tools. While pulling the cart toward the garage, she thought about the last paragraph of Michael's letter and wondered why he had referred directly to his own secret.

Is he trying to bully and scare me? Or is he afraid I'll retaliate? … He wouldn't have brought it up if he wasn't worried.

She recalled the evening the previous September when Michael had informed her that instead of spending a week's vacation in her garden she'd be spending it with him in California. He'd given her two days' notice and told her nothing else about the trip. She remembered her surprise when they boarded their first-class seats on the plane. And when their private driver whisked them in a limo to the Four Seasons Hotel in downtown San Francisco and on daily excursions to such places as Big Sur, the Napa Valley, and Muir Woods. They dined in the Bay Area's finest restaurants. She'd felt like Julia Roberts in *Pretty Woman*.

Her memory skipped forward a month to the night after her forty-ninth birthday when they sat on her deck and he admitted that one of the Pennsylvania Department of Transportation's contractors had paid for their trip. He boasted that even the theater tickets, massages, and flowers had been free. He'd made the disclosure to repay her for entrusting him with her Baby Alexa secret earlier that night.

Elena parked the cart in the garage and walked toward the deck. The word "repay" bounced around in her head. If she divulged the information to the right person in the government or media, Michael could lose his job. She stopped her mind from imagining the forces more sinister than he who could seek retribution.

Stepping inside the kitchen, she grabbed the Brita pitcher out of the refrigerator, filled a glass, and asked herself whether he would stoop so low as to reveal her biggest secret.

He's afraid that if he crosses the line, I will too. He won't risk losing his career. His identity. His ego won't allow him to say that I left him for another man. She emptied the glass and set it in the sink. *The Department of Health investigation and the lawsuit against the hospital are as far as he'll go.*

"Who else will he tell?"

CHAPTER THIRTY-ONE

I've been through it all, baby, I'm mother courage.
–Elizabeth Taylor

Fifteen days passed without Michael acting on his threat. Elena awoke on the second Sunday of August and did what she'd done each morning since receiving his letter. She wrote an *X* in black marker across the previous day on the kitchen calendar and warned herself that this could be the day he sought revenge. After peaking last weekend, her fear had begun to subside. Yesterday morning she downgraded Hurricane Michael to a tropical storm.

She spooned coffee into a filter, scribbled "Flowers for Sara" on a sticky note, and held the coffee pot under the running faucet. Today's Sunday bouquet of fresh cut flowers would be the third in three weeks that her sister would receive as a token of Elena's appreciation.

The day after Michael's package arrived, Sara had called and thanked him for returning their mother's wedding ring. Since then the two of them had struck up a texting relationship. Without either of them broaching the subject of his letter or the threat contained in it, she had become a pacifier and dating coach of sorts.

Elena turned on the coffee maker, unplugged her phone from the charger, and reread a text from Michael that Sara had forwarded to her last night.

Saturday 5:22 PM
Heather just informed me that her kids will
be spending the night at her mother's.

Elena fixed a bowl of Honey Bunches of Oats and gave herself a mental pat on the back for having resisted Michael's pressure to have sex during their final month together. She hoped last night's date with the thirty-seven-year-old blonde from Hopewell was carrying over into this morning. A sexual conquest would do wonders for his damaged ego and hibernating penis. She knew that her best chance of escaping his wrath lay in his finding a different outlet for his passion.

She sat at the island with her cereal and read an online article about midlife romance. The writer argued that the more two people have in common, short of sharing the same DNA, the more compatible they're likely to be. This made perfect sense to Elena. After reading that the theory of opposites attracting opposites is rooted in biology to balance and fill gaps in the gene pool—not to promote a couple's happiness—she muttered to herself, "No wonder the divorce rate is so high."

A nagging voice in the back of her head told her to get busy and scolded her for agreeing to move up the closing date on her home to the day before school started. It loomed twenty-two days away. She glanced at the six to-do lists strewn across the kitchen table and sighed. Yesterday, for every item she'd crossed off the lists she had added two or three new ones.

Her mind spun. She reminded herself that the $7,600 it would cost to fix the termite problem was a bargain compared to the $16,000 she had originally feared. She wondered how her furniture would fit and look in her new condo. Her dad would be moving back home from Franciscan Manor this week. Jack and Emma would be heading back to college in two weeks. And she was completely smitten with Patrick.

❧ ❧ ❧

That evening the sun painted reds, yellows, and oranges across the canvas of the western sky as Patrick and Elena climbed the hillside to the grass parking lot at Hartwood Acres Park. She smiled inside. The sound of Chris Botti's trumpet echoed in her mind's ear. A smorgasbord of remnant flavors—cheese, grapes, fried chicken, chocolate, and wine—clung to her tongue, reminding her how much her picnic dinner had pleased Patrick. Their conversation had reached new heights. They'd woven threads of lacy banter around strands of intellectual silk.

They loaded their things into his trunk and beat most of the traffic. Five minutes later he turned onto Route 8 and finished explaining how the double bass creates the groove and swing that underpins most jazz. "I'll play a song to show you what I mean," he said, plugging his phone into the stereo. "A song is worth a thous—"

"Wait a minute, buster."

He turned to her, his eyebrows raised.

"Double bass?" she asked.

"Yes."

"Didn't you get your fill of second base last night in your library?"

He matched her smile and returned his eyes to the road. "My sofa insisted that I invite you back."

"Tell him—" Her eyes narrowed. "What's his name?"

"… Henry." He said the name as if he were referring to a former British king.

"Tell Hank I accept his invitation."

"I'll call him now," Patrick said with an almost straight face. He lifted his phone and swiped his thumb across the screen.

Elena took the phone from him and held it hostage on her lap. "Who knew that fooling around with our clothes on could be so steamy?"

"Are you trying to seduce me?"

"Maybe," she said in a come-hither voice.

He jiggled the steering wheel, making the back end of the car dance. "How do you expect me to drive?"

"Carefully."

He rescued his phone from her lap. "Wasn't I going to play a song for you?"

"Yes. Double bass."

He slowed down and scrolled through his music library between peeks at the road. "You'll win three bonus kisses if you can name this musician in five notes or fewer. Don't look."

She covered her eyes with her hand.

"Here goes. ..."

"Charlie Brown!" she squealed like a game-show contestant.

"It only took you three notes. Impressive. But you'll need to be more specific."

She tapped her toes to the beat. "Pig-Pen is kicking up a cloud of dust on the bass."

"Who else?"

Elena touched a finger to her lips and imagined the *Peanuts* characters performing on a stage. "Schroeder plays the piano beautifully. And doesn't Snoopy play the guitar?"

"Yes, but who recorded the CD?"

"The Vince Guaraldi Trio. Why didn't you ask?"

"I did."

She exaggerated a sigh and pointed at an empty Citizens Bank parking lot up ahead. "You can pull over and give me my bonus kisses now."

"You can wait until we get home," he said, mischief in his eyes. "Last night I discovered the wonderful effect waiting has on you."

"And I *you*."

Their eyes kissed.

They listened a while to the music. Patrick said, "Focus your attention on Pig-Pen's bassline."

Fifteen or twenty seconds passed and he added, "Can you hear how the double bass outlines the harmony and anchors everything?"

"Yes."

"Good. Now feast your ears on Schroeder's piano. Listen to how his notes surf on top of Pig-Pen's."

Elena closed her eyes and let the music take her away.

Her thoughts drifted back to yesterday evening. After telling her he wanted to show her a book, Patrick had led her to the sofa in his library and asked, "How about an appetizer before dinner?"

More than their appetites were whetted.

They sat up, rearranged their clothing, and debated the merits of dining in. When she reminded him that it was his turn to make sure they behaved, he insisted on dining out. On the way to the restaurant, she teased him that he'd hidden the book he wanted to show her down his pants. She called it "The Hardback."

They skipped a salad, passed on dessert, and raced home at dusk for another appetizer.

The red leather sofa—*Henry*—applauded their every move. The hundreds of books surrounding them felt to her like an amphitheater of speechless authors. The presence of an imaginary audience heightened her arousal.

When she had asked Patrick if he thought they were straying toward third base, he zipped her skirt and told her how glad he was that all the kissing and cuddling of first base had carried over to second.

Who knew that fully-clothed foreplay could be so hot? Never has a make-out session cast a deeper spell of anticipation over me. The word "session" danced in Elena's mind.

Her thoughts shifted to how much she looked forward to touring Patrick's office later in the week. *I wonder what it would be like to have a session on his psychiatrist's sofa.* She squeezed his thigh. *Should I surprise him and wear vintage lingerie?* She pulled her hand away. *If I don't settle down, we'll end up in a ditch. The song's almost over. What's the least sexy subject I can bring up? ...*

The song ended. She turned down the stereo and said, "The music's fabulous, but downsizing sucks."

He nodded once. His eyes bounced from her face to the road and back. "Downsizing is one of life's most difficult transitions, especially when it's done alone."

"I have so much to do. I'm overwhelmed."

"That's normal."

"It's normal to feel crazy?"

"You'd be crazy if you felt normal."

He lowered the volume further and reached for her hand. "What aspects of downsizing are stressing you out the most?"

"I don't want to complain."

"Venting isn't complaining." Their eyes met again. "Remember when Jack and Emma were little and you kissed their boo-boos and encouraged them to cry?"

"Yes."

"Well, we adults bleed, too, but mostly on the inside. And when we do, it feels good to talk to someone who cares about us. Afterwards our wounds are still there, but they don't hurt as much."

Elena tugged at the hem of her shorts. "I dread the thought of leaving my home and garden. I know they're not people, but I feel like I'm about to lose two members of my family."

"A double death," he said. "I understand."

"A triple death. I'll be fifty in October." Her eyes welled up. "I feel like I'm stepping off life's up escalator and onto the down one."

"Welcome aboard."

"What? You're two years younger than I am."

"Yes, but men tend to age faster and die younger." He looked at her with mock surprise. "I thought all women knew that."

Her hint of a smile persuaded him to continue. "The down escalator's not so bad. You see the mistakes people on the up escalator are making."

"I never thought of it like that."

He withdrew his hand from hers, brushed the tips of his fingers across her cheek, and tucked her hair behind her ear. "What will you miss most about your home and garden?"

For the next fifteen or twenty minutes, Elena poured her heart out to him about the frustrations of downsizing from her 3,600-square-foot home on two acres to a 1,600-square-foot condominium with no yard of her own and a balcony the size of her former kitchen pantry. Patrick's touch and his words soothed her.

When she finished, he looked her in the eye and said, "Thanks for sharing that with me."

"Thank you for listening."

They drove in silence. Darkness set in.

"Elena, would you like to hear a story about a butterfly?"

"Sure."

He scratched his temple and began: "Once upon a time there lived a butterfly named Bella whose babies were no longer caterpillars. Bella spent her nights alone under a leaf in an oak tree. One evening, after a long day of sipping nectar and fertilizing flowers, she returned home and discovered that her giant oak had disappeared. Bella flew in frantic circles until darkness and exhaustion rendered her search impossible. She spent a sleepless night in a magnolia tree across the street from her old home.

"The next morning a yellow Caterpillar bulldozer dug a basement under what a day earlier had been the canopy of her tree. Bella recognized the houses on either side of the hole and realized she hadn't been dreaming. Her home was gone forever. She glared at the Caterpillar and cried all day.

"As the sun rose the following morning, it dawned on Bella that her new leaf lay under the eave of a porch roof. A voice inside her cerebral ganglion said, 'Your new home will keep you dryer during storms. It's shadier and not as drafty as your old one. Think of all the energy you'll save. And besides all that, it's cozier.'"

Patrick hesitated long enough to catch Elena's eye again and return his gaze to the road. "Bella flew off to her favorite garden that day, celebrated with her family and friends, and lived happily ever after."

"Aw, what a beautiful story."

"Sweetheart, just as everything worked out for Bella, everything will work out for you in this new chapter of your life."

Did he just call me sweetheart? She pinched her arm. *He did!*

"You've done it again, Patrick."

She paused, letting out a long breath. The expression on his face asked what he'd done.

"You've helped me to see the light at the end of another dark tunnel. I need to embrace change and focus on the upside of downsizing."

"Wanting to change is half the battle." He scanned the mirrors and crossed into the passing lane. "What was the other dark tunnel?"

"I'll never forget how relieved I was when, after you read the report on the Department of Health's investigation, you shared your two horror stories about malpractice attorneys. You helped me to put my nightmare into perspective."

He stopped at a red light and turned to her. "You were the hero, Elena, not the villain."

He leaned across the console. One kiss led to a second. The driver behind them tapped his horn. Patrick sprang up like a jack-in-the-box and stepped on the gas pedal.

A comfortable silence filled the car.

Elena's phone rang. She pulled it from her pocket. "Why would Emma be calling me? We talked for over an hour this afternoon." She swiped her thumb across the screen and lifted the phone to her ear. "Hey Emma."

"Are you back from the concert yet, Mom?"

"We're on our way home now." Elena heard a sniffle.

"What's wrong, honey?"

"I'm late, Mom."

"Late for what?"

"My period."

CHAPTER THIRTY-TWO

You never understand life
until it grows inside of you.
–Sandra Chami Kassis

Two weeks later a family of early birds awakened Elena before dawn. She opened her eyes long enough to read 5:49 on the clock, snuggled under the covers, and reminded herself that this would be her final Sunday at home.

Only six more days till moving day. The finish line is in sight. You'll get through this. Focus your energy. Be strong.

Her thoughts turned back to the sense of accomplishment she'd felt just after midnight when she finished consolidating her six to-do lists down to three: "URGENT," "Important but Not Urgent," and "Later." She thought of a few items to add to a fourth list, "Garden Care," which she planned to compile and give to the home's new owners at the closing a week from tomorrow.

I wonder how much the new owner knows about irises. Maybe she'll offer to let me visit them. If she doesn't, should I offer to help her next spring?

Elena bounced out of bed and hurried into the bathroom. Denesting was stirring waves of energy and stamina in her that were akin to the ones her nesting instinct had kindled before Jack and Emma were born. Like then, she was working like a maniac to get her house in order. Unlike then, she wasn't thirty. Her lower back ached, but her years in the trenches as a mother and nurse were paying mental dividends.

Stepping into the shower, she applauded herself for surviving the challenge of deciding which of her furniture and other possessions she would be taking with her to the condo. "Stay or Go" had become her mantra twelve evenings ago when she started working her way through the house separating the "Go" items into three groups: Dad's basement, consignment, and Goodwill. She identified them by writing a giant D, C, or G on packing boxes and attaching sticky notes to unboxable items such as floor lamps.

Thank God I didn't let Sara talk me into having a garage sale. It would have been too painful to watch strangers—and worse, people I know—sift through my stuff like vultures.

Elena squirted body wash onto a sponge and reviewed what she, Patrick, Sara, Dan, and her father had accomplished yesterday. By mid-morning, her dad's basement had been stuffed with furniture, kitchenware, linens, and other items

Jack and Emma could use in their first apartments. By mid-afternoon, two consignment shops had taken possession of everything too valuable to donate to Goodwill, including the teak deck furniture that wouldn't fit on her balcony and forty-seven articles of her clothing. And by mid-evening, the Goodwill loading dock had overflowed with everything else. Her house looked bare, but she felt lighter, freer. Patrick and Sara were more confident than she that what remained would fit into the condo.

I hope they're right.

She lathered her leg and reached for the razor.

Dad was in rare form yesterday.

Snapshots of her father floated through her head. Perched in a folding chair in front of the garage, he directed traffic, cracked jokes, supervised the collection of garbage, and cheered everyone on. After their pizza dinner, he looked like a schoolboy when he asked for permission to leave early to visit Dorothy at Franciscan Manor. His eyes twinkled when he said, *We're planning her escape.*

Elena's thoughts shifted to the present and what she wanted to accomplish before Patrick and Sara arrived. She dried herself with one of the two bath towels she hadn't packed, slipped into a pair of old shorts and a T-shirt, and started toward the kitchen.

Passing Emma's bedroom door, she felt an inexplicable urge to step inside the room. The early morning light cast shadows on packing boxes that lay scattered across the bare mattress. She reached for the light switch.

Her eyes were drawn to a stack of photographs from a disassembled wall collage. The photos lay on an uncovered pillow, leaning like the Tower of Pisa. She moved a box of books to the floor to make room for her, pressed down on the pictures to keep them from avalanching, sat down, and began to sort through them. A kaleidoscope of memories and emotions flooded her mind.

"*Aw.*" She lifted a snapshot of Emma swaddled in a pink blanket and nestled in the arms of her then thirty-year-old mother. "The day we came home from the hospital," she whispered. "Look how chubby we both were. She was such a good baby."

Elena pulled a school picture from the pile and gazed in wonderment at her daughter's missing front teeth. *Still the same Emma smile. And her mother's mop of red hair.* She turned the photograph over and read her handwriting:

Emma – Second Grade

She dug through the stack and found another of her favorites. It featured Emma wearing lip gloss, braces, and a training bra. Elena's memory took her back to the early January afternoon when Emma had informed her that most of the girls in her class had returned from Christmas break wearing bras. After dinner that evening, they drove through a snowstorm to the mall and bought a three-pack at Macy's. Emma had cried all the way home because her breasts weren't developing according to schedule. *Look at them now!* Elena thought, shaking her head.

Her eyes were drawn to two photos, one from Emma's senior prom, the other a group shot of her and her girlfriends trying to look sophisticated in their graduation caps and gowns. *So beautiful and innocent.* She shifted her weight on the mattress and heard something hit the hardwood floor. A box of Playtex tampons lay on its side.

She closed her eyes and visualized Emma, her face fraught with anguish.

Motherhood is wonderful, but not at nineteen.

Elena's rendition of *Every Mother's Worst Nightmare* began to play on the stage of her imagination. In the opening scene Emma dropped out of college and worked a dead-end job until six weeks before her due date. The theater curtain closed and opened with Elena guiding her first grandchild down her daughter's birth canal. The third scene showed glimpses of a day in the life of three generations living in a cramped condo. When the curtain opened a final time, Elena stood alone, muttering, *I warned her a thousand times to make good decisions. ... I fail when my kids fail. I'm a terrible mother.*

"Stop reliving your nightmare!"

Elena opened her eyes. Her mental theater went dark.

She recalled Emma's response two Sunday nights ago to her question, *Who's the father?*

Christopher, she had answered. *A few weeks after I broke up with him, he showed up at a party I was at. I drank too much. He invited me back to his apartment to talk. I didn't resist his advances. I cried in his arms afterwards. I haven't talked to him since that night. I went off the pill because I didn't think I'd need it. I'm so sorry, Mom. I'm scared to death. What should I do?*

Elena replayed her reaction to Emma's revelation: *How could you do this to yourself? I knew I never should have let you live at Katie's house this summer. ... Adoption is an option. Abortion isn't. What are you going to tell your grandfather and Aunt Sara? You'll always be my daughter, Emma. I'll love you no matter what. ... Did you take a pregnancy test?*

Elena felt the raw fear that had boiled in the pit of her stomach while Emma drove to Walgreens, returned to Katie's house, and peed in a cup.

She relived the joy and relief she'd felt when Emma screamed over the phone, *I'm not pregnant!*

CHAPTER THIRTY-THREE

The body is meant to be seen, not all covered up.
–Marilyn Monroe

Two Fridays later, Elena arrived early for her appointment at Esthetics Salon and Spa in Sewickley. After checking in, she sat alone in the small waiting area and flipped through the latest edition of *Shape* magazine. Few of the photographs and none of the words registered in her mind. Her knee bobbed like a sewing machine needle. She tamed it with her hand and set the magazine down.

Sitting back, she closed her eyes and basked in the anticipation of tonight's sixty-day anniversary celebration with Patrick. After dinner at Andora Restaurant, they planned to drive to his home and run to third base together. *Eyes on skin. Skin on skin. ... Finally.*

The festivities would begin with a tour of his office, which the busyness of moving had forced her to delay. She tried again to imagine what it looked like. His unwillingness to show her a photograph of it only added to the mystery. All he would tell her was that the sofa was covered in nautical blue leather and long enough for him to nap on. Given their encounters on the red leather sofa in his library, this aroused more than idle curiosity.

Elena turned her thoughts to Renee Ballard, whom she was excited and nervous to meet. She debated what questions to ask her if she got the chance. *His quirks and faults? Yes. ... Kate? No. Wait until you know her better. Remember, everything you say will get back to him.*

She walked down the hall to the bathroom, locked the door, and studied herself in the mirror. As always, her little black dress set off her auburn hair and green eyes. She pictured Michael scoffing at her last September when she'd splurged on it at a boutique in San Francisco. The Ana Karina corset dress, one of two little black dresses in her closet, was worth every penny. Men and women, young and old, raved about it. She couldn't wait to see the look on Patrick's face when he saw her in it.

Elena's smile widened when she turned sideways. She looked slender yet curvy. The dress showed just enough skin. Glancing down at her backless black high heels, she liked what they did for her legs and chuckled under her breath.

When was the last time I shaved my legs twice in one day?

She faced the mirror again and inspected her quartet of jewelry. The dangly pearl earrings he'd never seen, the chunky pearl bracelet on her left wrist, and the pearl ring on her right hand all passed muster. She nodded at the reflection of her unadorned neck, reaffirming that less was more—she didn't want any obstacles in Patrick's path when he undressed her.

Elena reached inside the neck of the dress, adjusted her black chantelle bra, and recalled standing in front of her bathroom mirror an hour ago thinking her nipples looked like blushing spiders beneath the twin webs of embroidered lace. She imagined herself modeling the bra and matching thong for Patrick in his library. *I'll be too nervous. Maybe a month from now on our three-month anniversary. ... I may as well pee while I'm in here.*

Sitting down, she made a mental note to promote the mood-enhancing benefits of candlelight to Patrick on their way home from dinner. She told herself to refrain from mentioning dim lighting's other advantage and marveled at how two women lived inside her. The first was confident in herself and the body she had worked hard to maintain. The second worried about her future and was sensitive to the havoc two pregnancies had wrought on her breasts and stomach.

Elena washed her hands, returned to the reception area, and pulled her phone out of her clutch to check the time. She'd rather be late than forgo her manicure and bikini wax. If necessary, she'd skip the pedicure. Her phone swished, announcing a text. Her heart thumped.

Today 3:55 PM
Two more sessions. I'm ready to burst.

Today 3:56 PM
Wait for me.

She pressed Send and scrolled back through their texts until she found the first one he'd sent that morning.

Today 6:17 AM
Good morning, Elena. Happy Anniversary!

Today 6:21 AM
Happy Anniversary, Patrick! I'm glad we decided to wait until tonight to celebrate.

Today 6:22 AM
Me too. I can't wait to see you in your little black dress.

Today 6:25 AM
I can't wait to see you in your black and white houndstooth sport coat.

Today 6:28 AM
The crystal ball in my head just informed me that you'll be wearing something black and lacy beneath your dress.

Today 6:30 AM
Are you a mind reader?

Today 6:43 AM
This morning I am, but tonight I'll be a body reader. Seeing, touching, dancing. Skin on skin.

Today 6:45 AM
You made me blush. ... Off to work I go. Have a super day.

Today 6:47 AM
You too. I'll be fantasizing about you.

Elena paused from reading long enough to remember arriving at work and resisting the urge to ask Patrick about his fantasies.

Today 7:49 AM
Today is a slow baby day. Only two women are in labor.

Today 7:52 AM
A patient canceled her 10:00 session. Normally I'd be a little irked, but not today. You'd smile if you knew what I was just thinking.

Today 8:11 AM
I've been smiling since I woke up. What were you just thinking?

Today 8:54 AM
I imagined myself sitting at my desk in the library and voilá, you slipped into the room dressed as a French maid. I pretended to be engrossed in a book while you pranced around with your feather duster.

Today 9:51 AM
The drool dripping from your chin inspired me to approach you and ask in a French accent, "Sir, do you prefer sheer or fishnet stockings?"

Today 9:55 AM
"Mademoiselle, I'd give my right arm to be caught in your fishnets."

Today 10:03 AM
What would you do if I sashayed to the wall of books, climbed to the top step of the ladder, stretched for a book, and...

Today 10:04 AM
And what? (He asks, his eyes burning a hole through her skirt.)

Today 10:06 AM
And got stuck like a cat up a tree. What would you do?

Today 10:07 AM
I'd rush to your side and tell you to fall into my arms.

Today 10:09 AM
Hold me tight, gallant knight.

Today 10:14 AM
Elena, I long for us to paint our masterpiece:
Our bodies the canvas.
Our passion the paint.
Our hands and tongues the brushes.

Today 10:15 AM
Bravo to my poet painter!

"Elena." A hand shook her shoulder.

She flinched, the phone fell onto the floor at her feet. Looking up, she saw a familiar, smiling face.

"Stephanie." Blood rushed to her cheeks. "Hi."

"I was just about to call a hypnotist to snap you out of your trance."

"I'm sorry," she said, reaching for her phone. "The smell of hair coloring must have gone to my head."

Stephanie laughed. "Come on back."

Elena followed her esthetician friend to her alcove station at the end of the hall and sat in the chair. Stephanie dipped a cotton swab into nail polish remover and asked in a conspiratorial tone, "Were you reading one of the *Fifty Shades of Grey* books on your phone?"

"No," Elena chuckled. "Do you remember last month when I told you about my new friend?"

Stephanie took hold of Elena's left hand. "The Sewickley psychiatrist?"

"Yes, his name is Patrick Jameson. We're celebrating our two-month anniversary tonight."

"How exciting. Tell me more about him."

"Okay, but first, can we finish a mani, pedi, and bikini wax by 5:45?"

Stephanie looked at the clock. "We'll make it happen. What color would you like?"

"Let's stay with California raspberry."

"Where did you get your dress? It's gorgeous."

Elena shared the story behind the dress and brought Stephanie up to date on her relationship with Patrick, including how Emma and Jack had met him last weekend and really liked him. While their conversation occupied the front of her mind, her reflections on the platonic pact absorbed the back of it.

As she had expected, establishing and abiding by physical boundaries had helped Patrick and her to cultivate their friendship and not be obsessed with sex, at least not to the extent other new couples seemed to be. She liked that he respected her—and himself—enough to wait. His actions showed the depth of his character and his feelings for her. She knew how rare it was to find a man who needed to feel emotionally bonded with a woman before having sex with her. And she had no doubt they would be compatible as lovers. Their fully clothed makeout sessions had satiated her desire better than all but the best naked sex with James or Michael ever had. But she yearned for more.

James waited three weeks.

Michael waited six months.

Patrick is making me wait.

CHAPTER THIRTY-FOUR

The most precious possession that ever comes
to a man in this world is a woman's heart.
–Josiah Gilbert Holland

Patrick glanced at his phone and gave Renee a knowing look.
"It's Martin Gillespie. I'll try to be brief." He excused himself,
started toward the wall of windows, and greeted his caller.
Elena followed Renee into her office.

Talking his patient out of attending happy hour took
longer than he had expected. When the call ended, a burst of
laughter rose from the other room. Thinking he was the butt
of their joke, Patrick hurried to the door and overheard Renee
say, "And he snores like a goat during his no-show naps."

He swung the door open, strutted to the kitchen-island
desk as if he'd just been announced as a guest on *The Tonight
Show*, and bleated, "*Maah, maah.*"

"No wonder my ears were burning," he said above the women's laughter.

"We were just getting acquainted. Elena is everything you said and more."

Elena nodded her appreciation and said, "I can see why your patients all love Renee. She's so easy to talk to."

"I'm glad you two spent some time together." He topped off their champagne glasses and turned to Renee. "Did you tell her all of my faults?"

"I'd need a week."

He rolled his eyes. "How about my most embarrassing psychiatric moments? Did you—"

"You mean like the afternoon you were gassy and begged me to run home to get a bottle of perfume?"

He slouched his shoulders and pretended to sigh.

"Elena told me her side of the story of how you two met. I couldn't get over how dashing you were."

"You call forgetting where I was going dashing?"

Renee stood and lifted her handbag from the back of her chair. "Flustering a man who appears to be unflusterable is one of the greatest joys in life for a woman over forty."

"I was beyond flustered." Patrick held his phone out to her. "Would you mind taking a few pictures of us before you go?"

"Not at all."

Elena spent a moment in front of the wall mirror adjusting her black straw hat, the one she'd worn the day she met Patrick. She had waited until arriving at the parking lot of his office building to put it on.

Renee arranged them in a pose, made them laugh, snapped three photos, and hugged them both before saying goodbye.

When the door clicked shut, Elena tugged on his hand and started toward his office. "She has a terrific personality. I feel like I know her already."

"You two really hit it off. A minute ago, when you weren't looking, she nodded at you and gave me a two-thumbs-up sign."

Elena led the way through the swinging white door. "We should have her and her husband over for dinner soon. I'm dying to ask her more about you."

"She's dying to try our chicken marsala."

Elena stopped in front of the sofa, turned Patrick's back to it, and pressed down on his shoulders. The blue leather squished. She smiled provocatively. "How would you like to make a wish of mine come true?"

"I'd love to. How?"

"Pull me onto your lap and kiss me like you mean it."

❧ ❧ ❧

They dined alfresco in Andora's courtyard. The Indian summer evening was perfect. The jumbo lump crab cakes, served with a red onion caper sauce, rice pilaf, and a vegetable medley, were delectable. They skipped coffee and dessert, but lingered long enough to watch the stars rise, finish their bottle of wine, and play footsie under the table. The stakes of their game rose with their feet. They jumped like startled cats when the waiter delivered the check.

The temperature fell three degrees during their ten-minute drive back to Patrick's house. Before he turned into his driveway, Elena glanced in the sideview mirror and was relieved to not see any trailing headlights. He parked in the garage and led her past the laundry room into the kitchen. The dim lighting cast intimate shadows on the limestone floor. He set his phone and keys on the island. She converted the back of one of the barstools into a hat rack.

He reached for her hand and started down the hallway. The clatter of heels on hardwood filled the gap in their conversation. She wondered if, beneath his smooth exterior, he was feeling the same blend of anticipation and angst that she was.

The open library doors invited them inside. The harvest moon shone through the tall windows, guiding their path to the seating area.

Patrick clicked on the lamp.

Elena gasped. "What's all this?"

"The roses are for you. The chocolate-covered strawberries are for us. ... And the candles are for me."

"Thank you for the roses." She kissed his lips, laid her clutch on the coffee table, and dipped her nose into the velvety red petals. Their feminine fragrance complemented the room's masculine aromas of leather and books.

She rose to full height and narrowed her eyes at him. "Why are the candles for you?"

"They'll help me to cast a spell on you."

"A spell?"

The words hung in the air.

Elena slipped her shoes off and settled into a corner of the sofa, Patrick lit the candles, turned off the lamp, laid his houndstooth jacket over the arm of the side chair, and started toward the wet bar.

"I'll pour us a nightcap."

She pulled his sport coat onto her lap, slid a hand down one of the silky, still-warm sleeves, and hugged the fabric to her chest. The scent of his cologne—the scent of him—leaked from the collar, sending shivers down her spine. Her nipples hardened.

It's about time our physical intimacy catches up to our emotional intimacy. ... Remember, he doesn't expect perfection.

He finished pouring a finger of Hennessy Cognac into the second brandy snifter and felt her eyes on him as he carried their drinks to the desk and navigated the iTunes library on his laptop.

"I created a special playlist for us," he said, loud enough for her to hear.

"How thoughtful of you."

How romantic of him.

He aimed a remote at the windowed wall of books. The sound of Al Green's "Love and Happiness" filled the room.

Patrick stepped toward her and watched her watching him.

Damn, she's hot. ... Relax. Take your time. What if we get carried away?

He handed her drink to her, sat beside her, and tinked their glasses together.

She joined him in taking a sip. "Delicious."

After setting his glass on the table, he lifted a chocolate-covered strawberry from the plate and held it up to her mouth.

Elena bit off the tip. "Yum."

She plucked a strawberry from the dish. Grins, lip smacks, and moans sufficed for language as they took turns feeding each other. She chewed her last bite and felt a stray morsel of dark chocolate hanging precariously from her upper lip. His eyes followed her tongue as it toyed with and captured the chocolate.

Sting's rendition of "Someone to Watch Over Me" began to play.

Patrick helped her off the sofa and led her to the open center of the room. A few steps into their dance, he started to sing softly in her ear. His heart beat against her cheek.

He knows all the words. He even sounds like Sting—longing, vulnerable, as if he wants me to watch over him. I will if he'll let me.

He timed their arrival at the sofa with the end of the song. Their feet stopped, but they held their embrace. The heat in his eyes ignited a fire in her loins. The opening notes of Frank Sinatra's "Summer Wind" blew in from across the room.

Elena tipped her head back and met his lips. Their tongues danced on both sides of the floor. She debated whether to undo the top button of his shirt and decided to let him take the lead. *We're in his house. ... Once things heat up, what can I do to drive him mad with passion?* The library ladder flashed in her mind.

Patrick traced the tip of his tongue around her lips and weighed whether to pick up the pace of his seduction. *The longer the wait, the sweeter the reward. But don't take all night. Should I tell her I love her? ... No, save that for a special moment when you're not about to rip her clothes off.*

He lifted his mouth from hers and feathered kisses across her jawline to the lobe of her ear. His thumb and forefinger found the tab of her zipper and slid it slowly down her back. He peeled the dress over her shoulders and down her arms. His heart galloped at the sight of her thinly veiled breasts. He knelt on one knee and guided the dress down her legs, careful to keep it from touching the floor. Standing again, he draped it over the back of the chair and took a step back.

His feasting eyes told Elena everything she needed to know. He kissed the tops of her breasts and inhaled her scent. She pulled the shirttail out of his pants, raced up the line of buttons, and dragged the sleeves down his arms. The candlelight caressed his skin. Her eyes and fingers explored him from neck to navel.

He's built like a swimmer. Just enough muscle. Just enough hair. ... "Hey, it's our song."

Shaking her body to the rhythm of Sade's "Kiss of Life" melted the last of Elena's inhibitions. Midway through the song, Patrick's pants and socks were strewn on the chair. She glanced at the exclamation point under his black boxers and saw that he too was leaking.

"You belong on the cover of next year's Sexiest Therapist calendar."

He reached his hands around her back. "You're the only woman I'm posing for."

He unfastened her bra, slid the straps down her arms with maddening slowness, and watched transfixed as her nipples and areolas reddened, swelled, and sprouted tiny buds under his touch. His tongue dabbed a warm coat of paint on her left nipple. She moaned softly while his lips and the edges of his teeth worked it into her tiny crevices. A fire raged between her legs.

She massaged his shoulders and the back of his neck and scalp. He gave her other rosy bud equal attention. The crotch of her thong was soaked.

He cradled her lower back and the bottoms of her thighs in his arms, carried her to the sofa, and nestled in beside her. They kissed passionately. His thumb caught the strap of her thong. She wiggled her hips to speed its descent and tugged his boxers down.

He caressed her inner thighs, inching higher.

I'll go as far as he'll take me. She traced a circle around his belly button and crawled lower.

He arched his hips toward her, craving friction, union. *It's been so long since a woman has touched me like that.*

"It's crowded down here, Elena," he whispered. "Would you like to go upstairs?"

"Yes."

Patrick sprang to his feet and helped her to hers. Holding a candle like a torch, he took her hand and whisked her out of the library, down the hall, up the curved stairway, and into his bedroom. He set the candle on the nightstand, pulled the comforter to the foot of the bed, and helped her up.

She lay on her side, reaching for his hand. Their knees bumped. He glanced at the framed photograph on the nightstand and stopped.

"I can't do this, Elena."

CHAPTER THIRTY-FIVE

Of all ghosts the ghosts
of our old loves are the worst.
–*Arthur Conan Doyle*

Elena crossed an arm over her breasts. *"What?"*

Patrick's knee slid off the bed, his chin fell to his chest. "I can't," he muttered.

She sat up sideways and saw the picture of Kate glowing in the candlelight.

She still haunts him!

"I can't either, Patrick." She swung her legs to the floor. "Not when there's another woman in the room."

She grabbed the candle and rushed out the door.

"I'm sorry, Elena."

Steps creaked beneath and behind her. Tears spilled from her eyes. She dashed down the hall and into the library, laid the candle beside the others, and reached for her bra on the floor.

"Please try to understand," he pleaded.

She pulled her arm away from his grasp, turned her back to him, and strung the bra around her waist. After hooking the clasp, she spun the cups into place and slipped her arms through the straps. She scrambled into her dress and zipped it as far as she could. He fastened his pants and threaded his arms through the sleeves of his shirt. She stepped into her shoes and searched the sofa for her thong.

"Here." He handed it to her, damp and fragrant.

How humiliating! She balled it into her fist, reached for her clutch, left her roses on the table, and scurried toward the French doors, her heels clacking.

"Now that we're dressed, can we please talk?"

Elena turned down the hall and walked faster. Patrick's bare feet smacked the floor behind her. An unseen lamp in the living room threw muted light into the foyer. She stepped aside to let him pass. He turned on the outside lights and opened the door.

An autumn breeze greeted her on the porch. She descended the stone steps, started down the walkway, and heard him following her.

The moon hid behind a veil of clouds. A light went out across the street. *Slow down, his neighbors may be watching. Do you want to be alone this winter? I'm so confused. And hurt. And pissed.*

She wrestled with how to leave things with him. One part

of her wanted to shake him and scream that Kate was dead. Another part of her longed to hold him, comfort him.

"Would you still like me to help you hang pictures tomorrow afternoon?"

"No." She turned down the driveway. "The pictures can wait."

Calm down. How will I explain to Sara and Dad if he's not with me at dinner tomorrow night? … I want him with me.

Elena fumbled in her purse for her keys and pressed the fob. He opened her door. She climbed into the seat and started the engine.

"Pick me up at five-thirty and we'll talk after dinner."

He kissed her cheek and closed the door.

❧ ❧ ❧

Early the next evening Elena sat at the head of a table for six at the Wooden Angel Restaurant in Beaver. The aroma of garlic flatbread spilled from a nearby table. Her guests studied their menus. She reread the description of an entrée: *Pappardelle noodles with sautéed Gulf shrimp, scallops, jumbo lump crabmeat, baby spinach, saffron cream sauce.*

She closed her menu and turned to her father, who was seated to her left. "What are you having, Dad?"

He peered at her over the rim of his black-frame glasses and his menu. "I'm trying to decide between the roasted Berkshire pork chop and the Maine lobster pot pie."

"You can grill a pork chop for dinner tomorrow. Treat yourself tonight."

He closed his menu and grinned. "Then lobster pot pie it is."

She patted his arm and stole a glance at Patrick at the other end of the table. He looked tired and ill at ease, not himself. A pang of anxiety stabbed at the pit of her stomach. Their earlier conversations in the foyer of her condo, during their five-minute drive to the restaurant, and while waiting to be seated had been stiff. Playful banter was nonexistent. Lulls predominated. Their after-dinner talk loomed like an ice-water bath.

Sara leaned toward her and whispered, "Are you and Patrick fighting?"

"No. You'll love this wine."

The waiter arrived with two bottles of Argentinian Malbec.

Elena tasted it, asked him to pour, and swept her eyes across the room. She didn't recognize any of the mostly elderly diners. The handful of unoccupied tables surprised her. It dawned on her why they were empty. She hadn't made the reservation until yesterday afternoon. An early seating was all she could get. The waiter finished pouring and agreed to return in ten minutes to take their order.

She slid her wineglass closer. "May I please have everyone's attention?" When all eyes were on her, she continued. "I'd like to propose a double toast. Since you're all thirsty, the first one will be brief." She raised her glass and paused to make eye contact with her father, Dorothy, Patrick, Dan, and Sara.

"Thanks everyone. Cheers."

She clinked glasses with her dad and Sara and sipped her wine.

"Don't worry, Sara won't let me talk too long." She cleared her throat and smiled. "I want to thank all of you again for helping me with my move. I couldn't have done it without you. At least one of you showed up every time I needed help, sometimes without even being asked. Thanks for tolerating my moods and never making me feel like a burden."

Her eyes flitted from face to face around the table. "It's hard to believe two weeks have passed since we filled Dad's basement and the Goodwill loading dock. The movers did all the heavy lifting last Saturday, but each of you was there to help me unpack and get settled in. ... I like my condo. It's nice to have half as much space to clean and no grass to mow. And unlike at my old house, everything works. So far, my new neighbors seem nice. But I miss my girls terribly."

She paused to take a breath. *You're rambling! Everyone's hungry. Stick to your plan and go around the table.*

Elena reached for her sister's hand. "Once again, Sara, you've proven how much better a sister you are to me than I am to you. Thank you from the bottom of my heart."

"Dan, thanks for being my handyman these past few years, my logistics expert during the move, and the brother I never had."

She looked at Patrick and hesitated. *Save him for last.*

She turned to her father. "Dad, thanks for sharing your basement, running errands, cracking jokes, and being my Rock of Gibraltar."

"Dorothy, you've been busy with your own move. Thank you for the beautiful crocheted placemats, for putting a spring in Dad's step, and for teaching me lessons in kindergarten that I use every day."

She turned to Patrick and searched for the right words. Sara kicked her shin under the table.

"Patrick helped me—"

Sara kicked her harder and shot her a look of alarm. Elena followed her sister's eyes and winced. The hostess was seating Michael and his date in the booth behind her father and Dorothy.

Did he follow me here?

She gripped the arms of the chair and glanced at his date long enough to doubt that she was over thirty-five and suspect that she had paid for her breasts. Michael thanked the hostess, helped his date into the booth, and turned around.

"Hi Sara and Dan," he said with a plastic smile. They waved back, awkwardly. He laid his hand on her father's shoulder. "Hello, Fred. It's nice to see you out and about. You're looking terrific."

"How nice of you to crash our party, Michael," Elena hissed in an undertone.

His smile disappeared. "Excuse me?"

She nodded across the room. "You could have requested one of the open tables."

"I reserved a booth and didn't see you until we turned the corner. Would you like us to leave?"

"No. I insist you stay."

"Are you sure?" he asked, surprised.

"Yes, but I guarantee the conversation at our table will be better than the one at yours."

He looked at his date, whose fingers were tapping her phone, and turned back to Elena. "At least I met her *after* you broke off our—"

"I see you still have a thing for redheads," Elena said with a condescending smile. "Only this one's young enough to be your daughter."

"Does your father know you cheated on me?"

"That's enough you two," Sara said, pinching Elena's arm.

Michael turned, slid into the booth beside his date, and sat directly in Elena's line of sight.

The slippery bastard!

Elena scanned the table. Sara was frowning at her, Dan and Dorothy were exchanging flabbergasted looks, Patrick was staring at the ceiling, looking miserable, and her father was shaking his head.

"I'm sorry everyone," she said, raising her wineglass. "Please give me a minute to finish my toast. Then we'll order."

She gazed across the table. "Patrick helped with the move more than I ever dreamed possible. No task was too big or too small for him. His patience and kindness are unmatched. He's the first man to ever treat me with as much respect as my father does." She tipped her glass toward him. "Thank you, Patrick, from the bottom of my heart."

Her eyes swept around the table. She resisted the impulse to sneer back at Michael. "Thanks again, everyone."

She lifted her glass higher. "Here's to family and new beginnings."

CHAPTER THIRTY-SIX

The difference between a rut
and a grave is the depth.
–*Gerald Burrill*

Shortly after Elena and her guests' entrées were served, Michael and his date slipped out of their booth unannounced, never to return. The adrenaline rush from her confrontation with him, coupled with the wine, helped Elena to feel more comfortable around Patrick. She still didn't look forward to their conversation after dinner, but she no longer dreaded it.

After dessert and saying their goodbyes, the two of them drove across town to River Road and parked a quarter mile from her father's home. They walked side by side toward a secluded bench overlooking the Ohio River, neither reaching for the other's hand, neither saying a word.

The sun had set. A September chill filled the air. Moonlight filtered through a cluster of clouds and glistened off the water, which stretched like a black snake through the wide, straight valley below.

He turned and stopped in front of the bench, took off his navy blazer, and draped it over her shoulders. "It fits you like a boxer's robe. You should wear it the next time you enter the ring with Michael."

"He'd never put the gloves on." She sat and pulled the jacket to her chest for warmth. "Bullies are cowards."

Patrick joined her on the bench. "He doesn't seem like your type."

"He never was."

A houseboat, its empty upper deck ablaze with party lights, puttered downstream looking lost and lonely.

"Your confrontation with him surprised me."

She took a slow breath and cautioned herself not to sound defensive. "My first reaction on seeing him was to suspect he had followed us there and slipped the hostess a twenty for the booth beside us." She turned to him. "But that's not what set me off."

"What did?"

"The way he acted as if he and my father were best buddies." She shook her head. "The two of them got along, but they were never close. Dad saw through his masks better than I did."

Patrick crossed an ankle over his knee and gazed at the river. "What did you think of his date?"

A train horn sounded in the distance. Elena measured her words.

"Like every woman my age, I get annoyed when I see a fifty-year-old man with a woman who's never had a gray hair or a baby wreak havoc on her body." She stifled a sigh. "Middle-aged men have it so much easier."

He nodded agreement. "We do. Except in the middle of the night when our bladders wake us from a sound sleep."

"Look." She pointed across the river at a freight train whose locomotives were rumbling onto the massive, cantilevered Pittsburgh & Lake Erie Railroad Bridge.

"Its headlights could light up an airport runway," he said in her ear. The noise grew louder, the bench shook beneath them. "I love to watch and listen to trains."

"Me too. I used to listen to them in bed at night when I was growing up." She smiled up at him. "Did you know that it's good luck for a couple to kiss while a train crosses a bridge?"

Their lips met in a tender but tentative kiss. When the locomotives rolled onto land, cutting the sound in half, he pulled his mouth away and asked, "Did you make that up about the good luck?"

"Yes, but in case you're wondering, I meant every word of my toast to you at the restaurant."

He lifted a brow. "You laid it on pretty thick."

A breeze blew up from the river. Elena pressed her legs

together, leaned forward, and inched the blazer closer to her knees. She watched the train and contemplated how to broach the subject of Kate.

"You should be glad Michael made an appearance," she said, turning to Patrick.

"Why is that?"

"Because seeing him convinced me to go a little easier on you."

"Once again, Elena, I'm sorry about last night."

The sincerity in his eyes warmed her heart. She mustered a half smile. "I accept your apology, Patrick, but I have mixed feelings. … One part of me admires you for loving Kate so much." Her lips turned down. "But another part of me is afraid you'll never be able to love again."

He uncrossed his leg and studied the grassless patch of ground at their feet. "I understand."

Her expression softened. "At least you're not the typical widower who remarries before the grass grows on his wife's grave."

"My patients who've done that are all either divorced or miserable."

She slipped a hand from under the blazer, reached for his, and watched the last train cars cross the bridge. The sound fell from an echoing clamor to a whimper.

"Every woman would be thrilled to have a man be as faithful to her memory as you've been to Kate's."

He opened his mouth to speak but didn't.

She continued, "I've been racking my brain since last night trying to figure out whether your fear of betraying her was the only reason you wanted us to wait ninety days."

"It wasn't the only reason." His eyes drifted upriver. "Remember how we wanted to be sure it wasn't just lust?"

"Yes."

"How we wanted to minimize the chances of either of us getting hurt?" She nodded, holding his gaze. His foot tapped against an exposed tree root. "And how we wanted to put the horse of friendship before the cart of intimacy?"

"Yes, and I treasure our friendship. But last night you … " Her voice trailed off.

Their eyes fell to the trio of boats passing in front of them, none in a hurry. His free hand fidgeted on his lap.

"We agreed to wait ninety days, Elena."

"Ninety is just a number." She sat up and faced him. "My head and my heart tell me we've waited long enough."

"Please be patient with me."

"I want to be patient, Patrick, but I'm scared. I'm afraid your heart is already taken. That you'll never get over her."

He exhaled a deep breath. "You're the first woman who's been in my bed since Kate."

"It's as if there's another woman—a perfect woman—in our relationship." She wrung her hands and sighed. "I can't compete with perfection."

"Kate wasn't perfect."

His words hung in the air. Elena resisted the urge to ask him about Kate's shortcomings.

The knot in his brow relaxed. He inched closer to her. "I care about you, Elena."

She wished he would lift her into his arms and carry her back to the car. Her second wish, a kiss, didn't materialize either. The moment passed.

Her eyes climbed the trunk of an oak tree. She wanted to drop the subject of Kate and bury her fear in the recesses of her mind. But she needed answers.

She turned to him. "You've been a widower for six years. I broke off my engagement three months ago. ... Don't you think it's odd that I'm more emotionally available than you?"

"Kate was the love of my life. Michael filled a gap in yours."

The truth of his words failed to quiet the voice in Elena's heart.

"May Kate's soul rest in peace," she said respectfully. "But she's never coming back. And you're not betraying her."

An awkward silence fell between them. Patrick tilted his head back and searched the sky. Elena stared at the rocky bluff across the river. Her mind raced.

Don't be timid. Tell him exactly how you feel.

"Our relationship doesn't mar or diminish what you and

Kate had together. It doesn't mean you're forgetting her."

He met her gaze, but said nothing. She could almost hear the wheels spinning in his head.

"You'll always love her, Patrick. I'd never expect or want you to stop. … I think it's great that you have pictures of her around the house. Mementos. But not in your bedroom."

"About a year ago I tried to move her picture from my nightstand into a guest bedroom. But the next day I felt guilty and put it back."

She reached for his hand. "If you had been the one to die young, wouldn't you want her to find love again?"

"I would."

The wind kicked up, rustling the leaves in the trees.

Elena clutched the lapel of his sport jacket at her throat. "As you know, I've read your book and every one of the hundred and twenty-seven reviews of it on Amazon. Your being a grief expert gives me hope, but it also unsettles me." She paused, hoping he'd grasp the implication of her words.

"Grieving has helped me to understand and empathize with grievers."

An idea flashed into her mind. "I didn't forgive my mom for dying until shortly after Jack was born, more than ten years after she had passed away. Could one of the reasons you haven't fully grieved Kate be that you need to forgive her for dying?"

He shook his head. "Kate had no say on the timing of her death." His face grew more sober. "It took me a few years to forgive myself for sleeping instead of saving her and the baby."

Elena nodded sympathetically. "Why is it easier to forgive others than ourselves?"

"It's a quirk of human nature'."

"Do you still sleep in the same bed?" she asked without thinking.

"Yes."

She pressed her back against the bench's wooden slats, making them whine.

You've interrogated him enough.

She stared at the river and reviewed what that afternoon she had decided were her two best options: she could either give him an ultimatum with a deadline or attempt to snap him out of his fear by seducing him.

… An ultimatum might push him away instead of pulling him closer. … He'll be more relaxed in my bed.

She turned to him, slid her hand out from under his blazer, and laid it on his chest, feeling through his shirt. "You're a red-blooded man," she said in a voice that straddled the line between sweet and sultry. "During our steamy moments together, I've seen the look in your eyes. I've felt your body's response to me." Her fingers traced a path across his stomach and over his hipbone to his thigh. She leaned into him, hugged his arm between her breasts, and felt his muscles relax.

"I want us to be intimate," she whispered in his ear. "I want us to be lovers. ... I want us to be one."

Their eyes met. His surrender was imminent. The moon hid behind a cloud.

He blinked twice, looked at the river, and sighed.

"It wouldn't be just sex," she said.

"I know, Elena. I need more time."

"How long?"

"... I don't know."

"I've fallen head-over-heels for you, Patrick. If you feel the same way about me—if you want us to be a couple—you'll need to make room in your heart for me."

He leaned forward, elbows on his knees.

She nudged him gently in the ribs. "Please look at me."

He did as he was asked. "But I can't abandon Kate."

"You're right. You can't abandon Kate. She's dead."

He bolted upright and riveted his eyes on the bluff across the river. Elena tried not to squirm and debated whether to apologize.

No. It's strong medicine, but it's what he needed to hear.

If you can't love a woman other than Kate, I'd rather know now."

"Tonight?"

"No, but soon. You know in your heart that we love—" she caught herself. "You know that if we made love tonight it would be much more than sex."

Another silence fell between them.

Please look at me. ... Say something. ... Please. ...

Patrick rose to his feet, stuck his hands in his pockets, and walked to the edge of the wooded hillside fifteen feet away. His back rose and fell with his breathing.

My talk of love scared him. What should I do?

Before she could decide, he started toward her. "It's getting cold. I should take you home."

She wanted to scream but didn't.

Neither of them spoke during the five-minute trip to the front door of her condo. He kissed her cheek, said goodbye, and walked away.

Elena closed the door, ran to the sofa in her living room, and lay down, covering her face with her hands.

"He's running away from me," she sobbed. "I love him. ..."

Her phone rang. *I bet that's him.*

She reached blindly to the floor and fished her phone out of her handbag. Emma's smiling face flashed on the screen. Elena sniffled, wiped the back of her hand across her nose, and took a deep breath.

"Hi Emma."

"Is it true, Mom, is it true?"

"Is *what* true?"

"That you had an abortion. Michael just posted it on Facebook."

CHAPTER THIRTY-SEVEN

Shame is a soul-eating emotion.
–Carl Jung

"Yes, Emma. It's true."

Dead silence filled the line.

Elena pulled herself off the sofa and paced from the living room to the kitchen and back. Tears rolled down her face. "I'm so sorry, honey."

"I feel sorry for you, Mom."

"Don't feel sorry for me. Feel sorry for the baby."

Emma sniffled. "I do."

Elena let out a sob and buried her face in a dishtowel. "You don't hate me?"

"No, Mom. If anything, I love you more."

"That's such a relief." Fresh tears streamed down her cheeks. "It's why I became a maternity nurse. Why I'm always telling you not to get pregnant. And preaching that abortion isn't birth control."

"Thank God I wasn't pregnant last month."

"It's haunted me for thirty years."

Silence filled the line again.

"I'll borrow Katie's car and drive home tonight. You can cry in my arms, Mom, just like I have so many times in yours."

"I'd like that, Emma. Very much." She turned around at the refrigerator and started again toward the living room. "Read what he wrote."

"Are you sure?"

"Yes." She wiped her eyes and blew her nose into the dish towel. "I need to know what he said."

"Are you sitting down?"

"I will be in a second."

Elena stepped to the corner of the sofa and sat, curling her legs under her. She took a deep breath. "Okay, I'm ready."

"Here goes." Emma read Michael's Facebook post:

> "Three months have passed since Elena broke off our engagement. Many of my friends have asked me what happened between us. Until now I've remained silent. But the time has come for me to set the record straight.
>
> "After I loved and supported her emotionally for two years following her divorce, including

while she was investigated by the Pennsylvania Department of Health in connection with a baby that almost died at the hospital, Elena decided to leave me for another man. She claims to have met her boyfriend, a psychiatrist from Sewickley, the day after she accepted my marriage proposal. But it was obvious to me when I saw them together that day that they had known each other much longer. How long, only they know.

"Clearly, Elena has a thing for doctors. Maybe her shrink boyfriend will be able to help her deal with her emotional baggage, including the guilt she feels for aborting our baby thirty years ago.

"I wish her well."

Emma sighed into the phone. "He's such an asshole."

Elena gripped the sofa cushion in her free hand. "I want to castrate the bastard."

"How old were you when you had it?"

"Your age. A second-semester freshman."

Emma's pause told Elena that she was surprised.

"Did you have it in Washington or Pittsburgh?"

"At a clinic in DC." She leaned her head back and closed her eyes. "On a frozen February morning."

"Were you alone?"

"My roommate went with me. Frances Chevalier."

"It must have been a nightmare."

Elena gulped down a sob. "It still is."

"Thirty years is a long time, Mom. It was a mistake. You're only human."

"It was a huge mistake, and I'm still paying for it." She sighed heavily. "My private hell is now public."

"The people who matter will stand by you."

Elena climbed off the sofa and stepped toward the kitchen. "Michael's full of shit about when Patrick and I met. And he didn't bother to mention that I was cleared of any wrongdoing in the state's investigation."

"What happened?"

"I'll tell you about it in person."

"I should get there around eleven-thirty. Until then, why don't you ask Aunt Sara to come over?"

"I'll call her and Jack after we hang up. I hope they haven't read it yet."

"They'll understand." Elena heard the sound of a zipper through the phone. "My bag is packed. I'll call you from the road."

"I love you, Emma."

"I love you too, Mom."

Elena said goodbye, curled into a fetal position on the sofa, and wept.

I'm so ashamed.

Should I retaliate?

Will I ever see Patrick again?

CHAPTER THIRTY-EIGHT

Can I see another's grief,
and not seek for kind relief?
—*William Blake*

Late the next afternoon, Elena walked toward the elevator in her building and debated whether to drive from the underground garage to her father's home. *It's less than a mile. The exercise and fresh air will do me good. What if I see someone I know? I could hide behind my Audrey Hepburn hat and sunglasses.*

She stepped inside the empty elevator and pressed the button for the first floor. When the door closed, she traced an "A" on her forehead with her thumb.

I deserve my scarlet letter.

She exited the elevator and hurried outside. A grasshopper buzzed past her head. She turned down Market Street, walked a few blocks, crossed Bank Street, and stopped to watch a cardinal drink from a birdbath. The breeze shook a yellow leaf out of a maple tree.

She turned onto River Road and studied the passing cars without turning her head. No one seemed to notice her until Pam Milligan, who had graduated from high school a year ahead of her, smiled and waved out the window of her yellow Volkswagen Beetle. Elena returned the greeting and breathed a sigh of relief. *At least I'm not a complete outcast. She must not be on Facebook.*

Her mind raced. *Remember, embarrassment and shame never killed anyone. Things could be so much worse. It was sweet of Emma to mother me last night and today. Jack and Sara took the news so much better than I feared. Thank God Patrick and my college friends aren't Michael's Facebook friends.*

She said hello to a young couple and stepped onto the street to make room for them and their baby stroller.

I hope Emma and Jack wait until they're thirty to have children. ... Dad has probably never even heard of Facebook. Remember, don't overwhelm him with everything. Only tell him about Baby Catherine. And don't mention the name or he'll cry about Mom. ... Remember to pick up your old diaries.

Elena turned up her father's driveway and admired the slate-roofed Tudor. Orange mums in gray urns lined the porch steps, welcoming her home. She let herself into the house and sniffed in vain for clues as to what they'd be having for dinner.

"It's me, Dad," she shouted from the foyer.

"I'm in the kitchen," he hollered back.

She walked down the hall into the kitchen and stopped in her tracks. "New appliances!"

Her father, grinning like a boy who had just caught his first fish, grabbed his cane from the back of a chair and stepped toward her. "Lanie, the look on your face is worth twice what they cost."

She returned his kiss on the cheek. "No more hideous olive green," she said, approaching the side-by-side refrigerator and freezer. She opened the doors. "And no more aluminum ice cube trays with the handles that freeze to your fingers." Shutting the doors, she admired the new stove and dishwasher, took a few steps back, and surveyed the room again. "What a dramatic difference."

"The old ones still worked, but they begged me to let them retire." He took her elbow. "I have another surprise for you. Close your eyes and don't peek."

Elena's smile widened. She covered her eyes with her hand and let him guide her to what she suspected was the family room.

"Okay, you can look."

Her nose led her eyes to the floor. "The shag carpet's gone!"

He nodded, beaming.

"I love the color." She rubbed the sole of her shoe on the new carpet. "The pile is nice and thick."

"I was surprised how simple it all was. I picked out the appliances at Sears in less than an hour. And it took half as long at the carpet store."

She patted him on the back. "I'm proud of you, Dad. What inspired you to finally leave the 1970s behind?"

He pushed his glasses up the bridge of his nose. "As you know, Dorothy is moving back home this week. I'm having her over for dinner on Friday."

Elena tried not to raise her eyebrows. "Dorothy hasn't seen the house yet?"

"We drove by a few times, but I never brought her in."

"Why not?"

His eyes fell to the floor. "I was too embarrassed."

"Aw." She squeezed his arm.

He turned and started toward the kitchen. "I hope you're hungry."

❧ ❧ ❧

After dinner on the patio, Elena swallowed her second bite of apple pie and took a deep breath. She told herself to be calm and scooted her chair closer to her father. His eyes and fork caressed his pie.

"Dad," she said, digging her nails into the palm of her hand, "I need to get something off my chest. Something from thirty years ago."

"Are you finally going to admit to putting that ding in my old Lincoln?"

"It's a thousand times worse."

He reached for her hand. "What is it, honey?"

"I did something unforgivable."

His old blue eyes begged her to unburden herself.

"When I was nineteen I—" Her eyes fell to the table and rose slowly back to his. "—I had an abortion."

He shimmied his old and new hip forward in his chair and held his arms out.

"Let me hold you, Lanie."

She leaned into him. "I'm so ashamed."

"Now, now." He brushed stray hairs away from her face and kissed her temple. She clung to him.

The courtyard fountain gurgled a lullaby.

He pulled his head back and wiped her cheeks with his thumbs. She sat back in her chair and thanked him with her eyes.

"Did Michael pressure you to have it?"

"Yes, but it was my decision."

He removed his glasses, laid them on the table, and rubbed his eyes. "Elena, I have a confession of my own to make."

He pinched the bridge of his nose and slipped his glasses back on. His Adam's apple bobbed. "I killed two men in Korea. One with a bullet. One with a bayonet."

"Oh, Dad."

They held each other close.

A moment passed.

She slid back into her seat and said, "The guilt has weighed on me for thirty years. Do you still feel guilty?"

He shook his head slowly. "Shortly after your mother died, I accepted her death as my punishment and forgave myself for killing the men." She nodded, encouraging him to continue. "I shifted from grieving them to grieving her. … I was lost without your mother. I couldn't fill even one of her shoes with you girls." Remorse glistened in his eyes. A lone tear trickled down his cheek. "I hope I'm a better father now than I was back then."

"Dad, all three of us were lost those first few years. You bear none of the blame for my mistake."

He swallowed hard. "I'll accept that, but only if you'll accept that you've paid for your mistake. A thirty-year sentence of guilt and shame is long enough. Think of all the babies you've saved."

Her eyes fell to the patio. "But I didn't save my own."

He leaned closer and took her hand in his. "Lanie, God forgave you a long time ago. I forgive you, too." He placed his hand under her chin and raised her head until their eyes met. "You need to forgive yourself."

"I know, Dad. I know."

He gave her cheek a pat and, settling back in his chair, wiggled his caterpillar eyebrows at her, coaxing a hint of a smile to her lips.

She reached for her fork. "Thanks for being so understanding. I feel twenty pounds lighter."

"I do too, honey. Please don't tell anyone what I told you. No one knows. Not even your Uncle Mick."

She nodded agreement. "Did Mom know?"

"Yes."

Elena wiped her mouth with her napkin and glanced at her watch. It struck her that two days ago at this time she had been touring Patrick's office. It seemed like a week ago.

Should I ask for his advice? ... It can't hurt.

"There's one other thing, Dad."

"Another somber look? Don't tell me you've decided to become a nun. I'll have *none* of that."

"Ha. No convent would take me."

They shared a laugh. "Is it about Michael?"

She shook her head. "I wondered if you could give me some advice about Patrick."

His eyes narrowed. "Are you two having problems?"

"Only one, but it could be a deal-breaker."

"Oh?"

"You know how his wife passed away six years ago?"

"Yes."

"Well, he's afraid of betraying her."

"I see. Tell me more."

Elena, pausing to think, separated the crust from her pie with the side of her fork and raked the pieces to the edge of her plate. It dawned on her that her father had grieved her mother and she had mourned Baby Catherine far longer than Patrick had grieved Kate.

How can I expect him to let go of his grief when I won't let go of my own?

She turned to her father. "One of the many things Patrick and I have in common is that we've both spent years caught in a tidal wave of grief."

"You two aren't alone, honey. Humanity's grief could fill an ocean."

She stared at the fountain in the center of the courtyard. "How do you suggest I deal with his fear?"

He took a slow sip of his coffee. "It's a balancing act. On the one hand, if you push him too hard, too fast, he'll spit out your hook before you reel him in."

"Dad!"

"I wasn't born yesterday, Elena. I see the way you look at him."

"What else were you going to say?"

He folded his hands over his stomach and thought a moment. "You don't want to scare him away, but you also don't want to wake up a year or two from now and realize that he's unlikely to ever get over her. I suggest you be patient with him, but only for so long."

"How long?"

He chewed and swallowed his last bite of pie. "Six months from when you started to date sounds about right to me. Who knows, his heart may be more open than you think. But don't be surprised if he takes a step back for every step or two forward."

She folded her napkin and set it beside her plate. "I wonder if Patrick's being a psychiatrist is a blessing or a curse."

"Hmm. My guess is it's a little of both. It can't hurt that his education and years of experience have given him a deep understanding of human nature." Her father crossed his ankles under the table. "But he may have been drawn to the field, at least in part, by a desire to cure himself. It's not uncommon." He tapped his temple twice. "We're all a little touched."

He glanced at his watch and reached for his cane. "It's later than I thought. Dorothy is expecting me."

"You go ahead. I'll clean up."

Elena stood, helped him to his feet, and kissed his cheek. "Thanks, Dad."

෨ ෨ ෨

A half-hour later Elena walked past the sign in front of her condominium building.

Elysium on the Park

She reminded herself to Google the word Elysium. The word asylum popped into her head. She trotted up two flights of stairs and hurried down the hall to her front door. It hit her that this would be the second Sunday night she'd be sleeping in her new home.

How can it be the middle of September already? I wonder how my girls are doing without me.

Stepping inside, she slid a box of framed art and photographs closer to the wall and regretted not having hung pictures with Patrick yesterday afternoon. She sat on a barstool at her kitchen peninsula and typed a few words on her laptop, clicked on a Wikipedia article, and scrolled down the screen.

> In Homer's *Odyssey,* Elysium is described as a paradise:
> *to the Elysian plain ... where life is easiest for men. No snow is there, nor heavy storm, nor ever rain, but ever does Ocean send up blasts of the shrill-blowing West Wind that they may give cooling to men.*
> —Homer, *Odyssey* (4.560–565)

"Where life is easiest for men," she muttered aloud.

Her thoughts turned to Michael. *Revenge is his paradise. I hope he rots in hell. ... Should I retaliate and blow the whistle on him? I can't let him get away unscathed. He needs to be held accountable. I need to defend myself to set an example for Emma and Jack. ... Okay, but don't do anything rash. Sleep on it for a night or two.*

She checked her email. Her heart leapt at the sight of Patrick's name.

Elena,

I apologize for my abrupt departure last night. Not to make excuses, but I didn't want to say or do anything I'd regret.

I hope your day has been better than mine. I hiked five miles this morning and read at least a hundred pages of *The Count of Monte Cristo* this afternoon. But my mind was elsewhere. The tug-of-war in my head rages on.

Thank you for being honest with me last night. I don't blame you for being hurt, disappointed, angry, and confused. One part of me wishes we could celebrate our sixty-day anniversary again, only this time without all the drama. Another part of me knows and accepts that our seemingly perfect fairy tale couldn't last forever.

Let's hope this is the storm before the calm. Please be patient with me.

Patrick

Elena jumped to her feet. "Our fairy tale isn't over."

CHAPTER THIRTY-NINE

It is never too late to be who you might have been.
–George Eliot

Patrick fell asleep on his library sofa later that evening. The chiming of the grandfather clock in the hall awoke him at midnight. He felt a weight on his chest, closed *The Count of Monte Cristo* on his finger, and squinted to shield his eyes from the lamp's glare. A ray of hope broke through the mist in his mind. He sprang to his feet, rushed to the desk, and tapped his laptop awake.

She wrote back!

Hello Patrick,
 Your email brightened my day.
 I accept your apology. Once again, thank you for being honest with me. Few men would be so open in admitting their fears to a woman. You've earned my trust and respect. I'm sorry for reacting

so emotionally. If nothing else, at least we know where things stand between us. Your dilemma has become our dilemma. I'll do my best to be patient with you.

You and my father are among the fortunate minority who have found true love. Unfortunately, you're also among the minority of the minority who've lost it at a young age. My fear is that, like him, you'll choose to spend decades alone.

I recommend you read a book called *MidLife Grief - The Quiet Depths* by Dr. Patrick Jameson. One of the book's Amazon reviewers, *GeorgieGirl*, described him as a brilliant therapist who is as handsome as Cary Grant. I reread the final chapter tonight and feel better prepared to tear the scab off an old wound of my own.

Besides your wit, what I missed most about you today was the warmth of your smile, the sound of your voice, and the touch of your hand on mine.

While you're weighing your choices, let's continue to grow as friends.

Elena

P.S. Not all fairy tales end tragically.

Patrick, smiling from ear to ear, resisted the urge to immediately write back to her. He stepped across the room and turned off the lamp. The moon shone through the front windows, guiding a path to his bedroom. He brushed his teeth and climbed into bed.

His body lay still. His mind tossed and turned. Thirty-five minutes passed. He turned on the lamp, picked up a book he had stumbled across in his library before dinner, and, once his eyes adjusted to the light, studied the front of the dust jacket.

THE PSYCHOTHERAPY
OF C. G. JUNG

Wolfgang Hochheimer

The title was framed above and below by artwork, hand-drawn to resemble thornlike, alternating black and red brainwaves.

It looks like a horror movie poster from the 1960s.

He flipped to the copyright page.

1969. Good guess.

He skimmed the inside flap and backtracked to reread two sentences: *Jung's researches began in pathology but one of his primary contributions to the science was his use of therapy as an educational instrument and as a technique for the discovery of the deeper motivations behind man's rational and irrational activities. As Dr. Hochheimer writes, the so-called illness of many people is often only their thirst to understand a meaning of life.*

The sun was rising when Patrick finished the book.

⁂ ⁂ ⁂

"Elena is a real catch," Renee said a few hours later.

"You made quite an impression on her, too. I'm glad you two hit it off."

"How was your anniversary celebration Friday night?"

"Terrific." Patrick yawned, covering his mouth.

"I see you had better things to do than sleep this weekend."

He matched her grin. "A gentleman doesn't kiss and tell."

"Chris Andresky will be here any minute. Go splash some cold water on your face."

"Good idea." He started toward his office.

※ ※ ※

Four hours later Patrick sat at his desk chewing his first bite of a pear. Renee swung and held his door open. "I have a few errands to run. Do you need anything while I'm out?"

He shook his head and swallowed. "I'll be napping."

"Enjoy your snooze." She turned and stepped away. "I'll be back in time to wake you for your one-o'clock."

"Thanks," he said through the swinging door.

He bit the pear and looked at the framed photograph on his desk, a candid shot of Kate and him at the wedding of Andy Bedrossian, his best friend from Notre Dame. The outer office door clicked shut. He swiveled his chair and gazed at the corner of the sofa where he had kissed Elena Friday evening.

Patrick's feet followed his eyes across the room. The leather squished and hugged his backside as it had when Elena had pressed down on his shoulders. He closed his eyes and replayed her asking him if he'd like to make one of her wishes come true. He pulled her onto his lap. She tipped her head back to meet his lips. Her look of love had thrilled and terrified him.

It still did.

He opened his eyes and stepped to the wall of windows. The Ohio River flowed confidently toward Beaver. A tugboat without barges motored toward Pittsburgh.

She adds color to my black and white world. If I break things off with her, I'll go back to hiding inside my comfort zone. I'll surround myself with my patients, books, and memories. I'll be safe but sterile. Alone. … I'll survive, but I won't thrive. Do I want that? He imagined the two of them sipping wine together on a boat at sunset. *Elena is my second chance. Our love could blossom into a lush garden. … Or die on the vine if I don't stop living in the past.*

Patrick took the last bite of his pear and squeezed the core in his hand. Drops dripped.

If I dither for weeks and months, another man will snatch her up. Then we won't even be friends. No man would tolerate that. I wouldn't either.

The cars of a stopped freight train, as if frightened awake by the release of their brakes, jerked backwards in a thunderous chain reaction. The office floor trembled for an instant. The train crawled forward.

I need to quit torturing myself and decide. Who can I talk to? Renee? … No, she'd strangle me. I haven't seen my poker buddies in over two months. They're all married. … What about Fred Shaughnessy? He's been a widower for decades. I wonder if he has any regrets. … Opening up to him would be risky.

Patrick hurried to the bathroom in his office, rinsed and dried his hands, and pulled his phone from his pocket.

That same Monday afternoon, Elena walked toward her office and was stopped in the hall by Janet Doyle, an RN with whom she had worked for more than a decade.

"I'm sorry to hear about your loss, Elena," she said in a consoling tone. "You were so young. I meant to tell you this morning, but never got the chance."

"Thanks, Janet."

"A few months ago we all thought you were crazy for breaking off your engagement with Michael. Now everyone thinks you were smart to dump him. No one believes you cheated on him. And personally, I hope you give him a taste of his own medicine."

"I'm thinking about it." Elena stepped forward and said over her shoulder, "Great job with the Gallagher delivery this morning."

"Thanks."

Moments later she closed her office door and typed a text to Sara:

12:48 PM
My day is going much better than expected. Everyone is sympathetic and pissed as hell at Michael. They've taken to calling him "The Dick!"

After pressing Send, she sat at the desk, took a bite of her turkey sandwich, peeled the lid off her yogurt container, and asked herself for the hundredth time when and how she should tell Patrick about Michael's Facebook rant. She decided to play it by ear and see where their relationship went from here.

She checked her email on her phone and smiled.

It's about time he wrote back.

Hi Elena,

Thanks for accepting my apology and agreeing to try to be patient with me. I hope the iceberg of fear in my head melts before another man sweeps you off your feet.

Our romance may be on hold, but our friendship isn't. Rarely a day passes in my practice without a patient, usually a woman, expressing a wish that she and her partner were better friends.

Would you like to go for a hike on Saturday at McConnell's Mill?

Patrick

PS. Your laughter, your mind, and your feisty spirit are what I miss most about you.

Elena dipped the spoon in her yogurt and chuckled. *My feistiness would be at the top of the list of things that Michael and James miss least about me. ... Who says our romance is on hold?*

CHAPTER FORTY

Punishment is justice for the unjust.
  –Saint Augustine

That evening Elena sat at her balcony table and unfolded a paper napkin on her lap. The steam rising from her dinner plate failed to mar her view of the parking lot. The leftovers from the Wooden Angel two nights ago smelled even better than they looked. Her mouth watered. She bowed her head and closed her eyes.

Thank you, God, for family, friends, flowers, and food. She reached for her fork. *Please give me fortitude.*

She chewed her first bite and wrinkled her nose. The pappardelle noodle and baby spinach leaf lay limp on her tongue. The shrimp and scallop tasted tired. She pondered the mystery of where the saffron cream sauce's flavor had gone.

An image of Michael's face crept into her mind. *The bastard needs to be held accountable. He underestimated me.* Elena took another bite and slid a legal pad and pen toward her. *Is there a better alternative, something I haven't considered?* She doodled a quartet of hangman's nooses and thought of six or seven ways to retaliate against him, each of which she had already rejected since Saturday night.

Her thoughts turned to the first of what she regarded to be her two best options, lashing back at him on Facebook by revealing the details of his Italian shoe collection, his foot fetish, and his struggles with erectile dysfunction. She liked that the punishment would match the crime and be social rather than professional. She disliked the idea of stooping to his level and wondered how she'd be able to avoid sounding like a teenage girl hellbent on revenge.

Elena shifted mental gears and began to mull over the other finalist among her payback options, reporting Michael to the state for accepting the trip to San Francisco as a gift from a contractor. She scribbled notes with her right hand and ate with her left.

Ten minutes later she dropped the pen on the table, pushed her half-eaten dinner aside, and read what she had written:

<u>*Advantages of Whistleblowing*</u>
1. It's private, not an ugly Facebook fight.
2. Compared to Facebook or doing nothing, I'll be setting a better example for Emma and Jack.

3. *Stronger medicine. He'll be more likely to stop attacking me.*
4. *He'll be less likely to bully other women in the future.*

Disadvantages of Whistleblowing
1. *He'll probably only get his wrist slapped, but if they discover he accepted other gifts (bribes), he could lose his job.*
2. *Instead of disarming him, it could provoke him. (Don't underestimate him. He could pay someone to do his dirty work.)*
3. *The contractor who paid for the trip could seek retribution. (But wouldn't that only add to his troubles?)*
4. *Maria would be devastated if Michael lost his job.*

Elena tossed the tablet on the table and sighed. "What should I do?" she whispered aloud. "Should I wait a few more days to decide? ... No, the longer I wait, the less likely I am to do anything. I need to decide tonight."

She stood and gripped the balcony railing.

Which choice will I be less likely to regret a year from now?

¤¤ ¤¤ ¤¤

A few hours later Elena took a long, slow breath and tried to ignore the whiz and whir of the printer in Emma's bedroom. The machine spit out two pieces of paper. She grabbed them, sat on the bed, and read:

Elena Shaughnessy
295 Market Street #324
Beaver, PA 15009

<u>VIA CERTIFIED MAIL, RETURN RECEIPT REQUESTED</u>

Mr. Eugene DePasquale, Auditor General
Pennsylvania Department of the Auditor General
613 North Street, Room 229
Harrisburg, PA 17120-0018

Dear Mr. DePasquale,

My name is Elena Shaughnessy. I am the former fiancée of Michael Marino, the Assistant District Engineer for Maintenance of District 11 of the Pennsylvania Department of Transportation.

I am writing to inform you that Michael received an all-expenses-paid vacation to San Francisco last September from the owner of Santelli Paving in Pittsburgh. When I accepted Michael's invitation to accompany him to California, I was under the impression he would be paying for the trip. After flying first class and having a private driver take us to the Four Seasons Hotel, I grew suspicious. The same driver was at our disposal the entire week. He took us on daily excursions to such places as Big Sur along the Pacific Coast Highway and the Napa Valley. He waited in the car while we dined at the Bay Area's finest restaurants.

Michael spared no expense (i.e. flowers, massages, concerts, theater), but it wasn't his cash he was throwing around. A month after the trip, he confessed to me that Johnny Santelli had given him the vacation as, in Michael's words, "An expression of gratitude."

I wouldn't be surprised if the amount of work contracted to Santelli Paving has increased significantly since Michael became the Assistant District Engineer four years ago.

Please correspond in writing if you have any questions and to inform me of the findings of your investigation.

Sincerely,

Elena Shaughnessy

cc: Michael Marino via Certified Mail

"That'll give the bastard a taste of his own medicine."

Elena printed two more copies of the letter and cursed until she solved the mystery of how to print envelopes. After returning to the dining room table, she signed and folded two of the letters, licked the envelopes, and tucked them into her purse.

She picked up her phone and typed a text to Patrick:

Today 9:09 PM
Hiking at McConnell's Mill on Saturday sounds like fun. I'll pack us a picnic lunch.

CHAPTER FORTY-ONE

How unhappy is he who cannot forgive himself.
  –Publilius Syrus

Three hours later, Elena lay in bed and finished reading what she had written long ago but until now had never read, her diary entries from a week before she discovered she was pregnant until a month or so after her abortion. Crumpled white tissues dotted the blue comforter, giving her bed the appearance of a limousine idling outside a 1970s wedding ceremony.

She closed her eyes and, looking less like a bride than a passenger in the back of a hearse, took herself back to the frigid February morning of the abortion procedure. Her mind's eye saw Frances Chevalier trying to comfort her during their ride on the Metro. The façade of the clinic, a nondescript low-rise at the edge of downtown Washington,

D.C., popped into her head. She remembered completing a mound of paperwork and being struck by the mixture of anxiety and relief written on the faces of the other young women who shared her fate. Huddled beside their escorts, they reminded her of shell-shocked soldiers awaiting treatment, happy to be off the battlefield but uncertain of what lay ahead. No men were present.

The nurse called out my name. Hospital art hung on the walls of the treatment room. Antiseptic smells couldn't mask the odor of fresh blood. The counselor sounded as if she were reading from a script. I signed another document and changed into a patient's gown. ... More new faces. The sound of suction haunts me still. ... The cramps afterwards were horrible. The worst I've ever had. The procedure took less than ten minutes, but we were there for close to five hours. I sobbed on the Metro. I bled for days.

Elena sat up, wiped her face with a fresh tissue, and fixed her pillows. She nestled her head back down and closed her eyes again.

Don't forget why you did it. ... You avoided a shotgun wedding. You got to stay at Georgetown. You didn't disappoint Dad. ... Everything worked out. You switched majors and found your calling. It gave you an excuse to break up with Michael. Can you imagine life without Jack and Emma? ... Remember, a third of women your age have had an abortion.

Her eyes opened wide. "Quit rationalizing. You could

have kept Baby Catherine or given her up for adoption. You chose to terminate her."

Elena grabbed her lap desk from its perch between the bed and the nightstand and leaned it against her upraised thighs. She picked up her journal and pen and began to write where she had left off a few hours earlier:

> *Yes, it was my decision. But it takes two to make a baby. I hated Michael for getting me pregnant and pressuring me to have the abortion.*
>
> *I was scared to death. I never dreamed the emotional scars would cut so deep or linger for decades. Unlike Dad in Korea, I killed a living part of me. No wonder I still grieve and feel guilty. Will the war inside my soul ever end?*
>
> *Did my guilt lead me back to Michael? (Unconsciously) Was I trying to shift half my load of guilt onto him? Had I planned all along to hurt him again? Or BOTH?!*

A chill swept through her. She noticed two silver-dollar-sized tear spots on her nightshirt and weighed whether to stop writing and try to sleep.

"No. I have more to say."

My Punishment
1. *Never getting to hold, love, and be a mother to Baby Catherine.*
2. *Being publicly humiliated by Michael.*
3. *Letting everyone down. (God, others, and myself.)*

4. *James and Michael. And never finding true love.*
5. *Will I burn in hell? Or be punished enough*
   before I die?

Elena rolled her wrist a few times and flipped the page. An image of her father flashed in her mind. She continued writing:

- Dad has grieved Mom for 35 years.
- Does extreme grief run in my Shaughnessy blood?
- Or is it an Irish thing? (Patrick is Irish.)
- Will I ever stop grieving?
- Is that asking too much?

She closed the journal on the pen, turned off the lamp, and cried herself to sleep.

❧ ❧ ❧

Elena awoke in the middle of the night, her chest heaving like a bellows. She sat up, turned on the lamp, and squinted. *You'll remember how it ended. Begin at the beginning, the people mover.* She arranged the lap desk, opened her journal, and wrote furiously:

I was walking on the people mover at the Charlotte airport and saw a young mother sitting on a white rocking chair cradling an infant in her arms. I knew immediately that it was Baby Catherine. (A thirty-

year-old version of me. Same green eyes, post-pregnancy flab, and wavy hair, only chestnut brown and a few inches longer.)

I hopped over the railing of the people mover, rushed up to her, and said, Is that you, Catherine? I saw recognition in her eyes. She said, Hi Mom.

We hugged and kissed and cried. Our conversation went something like this ...

You're thirty now and a Mom. I need to stop thinking of you as an infant. Your baby is adorable. What's her name?

We named her after you. Her father and I call her Lanie. Here, would you like to hold her?

I held her in my arms. Hello, little Lanie. I'm your grandmother. She had that baby smell and cooed as I cuddled her. Her hair was red.

A flight was announced over the public address system. It dawned on me that my connecting flight would be departing soon. I handed the baby back to Catherine and said, Your little brother Jack is getting married tomorrow. I need to get going or I'll miss my flight. Is there any chance you two could come with me to Dallas?

She explained that the baby was only __ weeks old (I can't remember how many) and couldn't travel that far. She invited me to visit her in Atlanta.

The next thing I remember is crying and saying, I'm so sorry I wasn't there for you, Catherine. I'll understand if you hate me. Will you please forgive me?

I forgave you a long time ago, Mom.

We hugged and cried, exchanged phone numbers, and kissed goodbye. I ran toward my gate and woke up.

Elena laid the journal on the nightstand and turned off the lamp. "It was so real. So wonderful." She snuggled under the covers and replayed the dream forwards, backwards, and forwards again.

Her thoughts drifted back to her conversation with her father yesterday evening. *I kept my secret from Dad for thirty years, but God knew it all along. ... Dad loves me unconditionally. Does God?*

She closed her eyes. With each breath she felt as if a stone had been removed from her heart, replaced by a pebble of gratitude.

"He gave Jack and Emma to me," she whispered aloud. "He gave us all good health. He helps me to deliver, care for, and save babies."

She wiped her eyes with the back of her hands. "God never stopped loving me. He forgave me long ago. I was just too blind to see it. Accept it."

A sense of peace washed over her. She reached for the lamp, opened the journal to a clean page, and wrote:

I forgive myself.
But I'll never forget.

CHAPTER FORTY-TWO

To know the road ahead, ask those coming back.
−Chinese Proverb

Elena dropped her wallet into her purse without looking. "Either tomorrow or Thursday," the postal clerk said, scratching his gray beard. "You can track and verify proof of delivery at USPS dot com."

"I'll do that." Her phone swished, announcing a text. "Thanks."

She stepped away from the counter, frisked the bowels of her purse, and lifted the phone to reading distance.

Finally!

She parked herself beside the exit and read:

Today 12:17 PM
A picnic lunch on Saturday sounds good, but please don't go to any trouble. I'll pick you up at 11:00.

Elena pushed the door open with her hip and sighed. *I waited fifteen hours for that?*

🐾 🐾 🐾

"Dinner was delicious, Patrick," Fred said, his chair scraping against the concrete patio. "Thanks for bringing it."

"I'm glad you liked it."

"The fortune cookie didn't satisfy my sweet tooth." He scooted to the edge of his seat and reached for his cane. "Will you have a slice of apple pie with me?"

"Sure."

"Coffee?"

"No thanks. Can I help?"

"I can handle it." Fred pushed off the arm of his chair and toddled toward the kitchen.

Patrick's eyes swept around the courtyard's ivy wall and followed the cross-shaped path of brick pavers that divided the garden into quadrants. He spent a moment admiring the moss-lipped fountain burbling at the center of the cross, then turned his attention to the shrubs and flowers.

I bet the rhododendrons are older than I am. The flowerbeds remind me of children in need of a mother. I wonder how they looked when Elena's mom was alive.

The screen door slid open.

"The Pirates are winning two nothing," Fred said, walking

across the patio carrying a serving tray in one hand. After setting the tray on the table, he hung his cane over the back of his chair, sat down, and served Patrick a paper napkin and a plate of pie topped with vanilla ice cream. "Do you mind if we use our dinner forks?"

"Not at all." He reached for the fork on his dinner plate. "I can count on one hand the number of times I've used my dishwasher over the past six years."

"Me too. It would take me a week to fill it."

Patrick smoothed the napkin on his lap. "Elena told me she inherited her sweet tooth from you."

"That, along with a few of my other vices. She got her color from her mother. Her red hair. Her mint green eyes." Fred stretched a hand toward the courtyard. "And her green thumb."

Patrick pictured the eight-by-ten photo of Elena and her mother that had hung beside the kitchen door of her home. He'd seen the facial resemblance, but the color of her mother's hair and eyes was hidden behind the black and white film.

"It's beautiful back here," he said, dipping his fork into the ice cream and pie. "Have you ever participated in a garden tour?"

"Not since Jimmy Carter was president. Elena told me Sunday evening that she plans to take care of my garden next spring. It'll be just like old times."

"She really misses her flowers."

The men chewed their first bite of pie. An image of Elena's *Peace, Love, Garden* bumper sticker flashed in Patrick's mind. He swallowed and summoned the courage to broach the subject that had prompted his visit.

"As I mentioned to you on the phone yesterday, Fred, I'd like your advice on something."

"What's on your mind?"

"You've been a widower much longer than I have." He hesitated a moment. The warmth in Fred's eyes invited him to continue. "I was wondering if you've ever regretted remaining single?"

Fred set his fork on his plate and lifted his napkin to his mouth.

"Three months ago I would have answered your question differently."

"Before you met Dorothy?"

"Yes. Before Dorothy, I hadn't been on a date in more than twenty-five years."

"Oh." Patrick paused, his fork midair. "Did you date much during your early years as a widower?"

"Not at all until Elena went away to college. Then, over the next three or four years, I went out with a handful of women. But I never told my girls." He sipped his water. "I didn't want them to think I'd forgotten their mother."

"I understand. Were any of the relationships serious?"

He shook his head. "I dated one woman for six weeks or

so. The others I never took out more than two or three times. My heart was locked and the key was buried."

The word buried reverberated in Patrick's head. Fred's openness emboldened him to say, "Since Kate's death, I've been more of a spectator than a participant in life. I've woven a blanket of memories and wrapped myself in it to keep her alive."

"I did the same thing," Fred said, his eyes full of compassion and understanding.

"I haven't been a happy widower."

"There's no such thing as a happy widower."

Patrick's eyes paced a lap around the courtyard wall. Fred's words sank into his mind.

"You seemed happy before you met Dorothy."

"When you're in your eighties, it's easier to be happy. ... Fewer wants." The side of his fork clanked against his plate. "But something was missing."

They exchanged knowing looks and chewed their pie.

"Thanks to Dorothy, I'm like a tree that's flowering again after decades of dormancy."

"I'm happy for you, Fred."

"Dorothy lost her husband nineteen years ago. We lived less than a mile from each other all those years." His eyes drifted to the courtyard and back. "Regardless of whether you and Elena end up together—which I hope you will—please don't follow my example and grieve for thirty-five years."

"It's hard to let go."

"It gets harder with time."

"It does?"

Fred nodded. "We're already awash in metaphors, Patrick, but I'll throw in one more." He pointed west toward the Ohio River. "You're a fish in the prime of life. You've swum a thousand miles of grief, from here to New Orleans. The banks of the Mississippi are in sight. … You have to decide whether to come ashore or keep swimming into the gulf. … The gulf of grief."

He paused, smiling a paternal smile. "Nothing in life compares to the love of a good woman. A woman who looks after you and lets you look after her. A best friend and partner on life's journey." He patted Patrick's arm. "Kate will understand."

Patrick acknowledged Fred with a nod and turned his gaze to the fountain. Images of Elena and Kate alternated in his mind. The shadows of dusk crept closer.

He let out a deep breath and turned to his host. "Thanks, Fred."

"I hope I helped."

"You did. You've given me a lot to think about."

"That reminds me, Patrick. I have one other suggestion."

"Yes?"

Fred tapped his temple. "Try not to overthink matters of the heart."

"I know." He wiped a hand across his brow. "I'm analytical to a fault."

"It's a sure sign of your intelligence. It helps you to untangle the knots in your patients' heads. But when it comes to love, I suggest you quiet your mind and listen to your heart."

Patrick smiled. "You should have been a therapist."

Fred grinned. "I should have been a lot of things." He pushed his plate away. "By the way, I kept my promise and didn't tell Elena about our dinner plans. I'll let you decide if and when to let her know."

"I don't want to keep secrets from her, but I also don't want to confuse her any more than I already have."

"All she needs is the truth."

Fred grasped and shook the hand Patrick offered him.

Moments later, after clearing the table, the two of them stepped into the foyer. Fred's eyes grew wide. "I just remembered something. I'll be right back."

He soon returned, holding a small book.

"I stumbled across this about six months ago. As you can see, it's called *On the Shortness of Life*. Seneca wrote it. Are you familiar with him?"

"Wasn't he a Roman philosopher?"

"Yes. He lived during the time of Christ. The book helped me find the courage to stop living in the past."

Fred flipped to a bookmarked page. "Listen to this."

"If each of us could have the tally of his future years set before him, as we can of our past years, how alarmed would be those who saw only a few years ahead, and how carefully would they use them!"

He closed the book and handed it to Patrick. "I'd like you to have it."

CHAPTER FORTY-THREE

Nothing is to be preferred before justice.
 –Socrates

That Wednesday after work Elena beat the crowd to the employee parking lot and opened her Explorer's sunroof. The Indian summer weather convinced her to ignore the speed limit as she wound down Dutch Ridge Road's steep curves. The canopy of yellowing leaves blew kisses in her wake. She cruised into the flats of Beaver, breathed a sigh of relief at the lack of flashing lights in her rearview mirror, and drifted to a red light at 4th Street.

Don't forget to get gas and stop at the library. The front cover of Abel Keogh's Dating a Widower appeared in her mind, the oversized "O" in widower doing double duty as a gold wedding band. She'd discovered the book on Amazon during her lunch break. *Does Patrick ever think of me? ... Will I hear from him before Saturday?*

The light turned green. She stepped on the gas and her phone rang. She pulled it out of her scrubs pocket. The blood drained from her face. *Michael got the letter. Be calm.* She took a deep breath and swiped her thumb across the screen.

"Hello Maria."

"Elena, Michael needs to see you."

"Why?" she asked, trying to sound surprised.

"To talk about your letter."

"What did he say about it?"

"That it was personal. He sounded worried. Please meet with him."

Elena paused. *Feel her out. She'll tell you what he's thinking.*

"Do it for me, Elena, not for him."

"Did you know that Michael attacked me on Facebook?"

"He just told me. I—"

"Doesn't he know that character assassination is mental abuse?"

"He does now. He's very sorry and wants to make it up to you. Please meet with him."

Seconds passed in silence. Maria exhaled a mouthful of smoke and wheezed. "Please!"

"I'll do it for you, Maria. But I have two conditions."

"Conditions?"

"Yes. I want you to be there as a buffer. I'll leave immediately if he acts up."

"He won't act up. When can we meet?"

Elena parked across the street from the library and glanced at the dashboard clock.

3:44. Make him sweat.

"The soonest I'm available is six o'clock. And I have a second condition."

"What?"

"That you forgive me for storming out on you at the hospital coffee shop a few months ago."

"You're family, Elena. You're forgiven. Let's meet in my kitchen."

"No. We'll meet at Starbucks."

❧ ❧ ❧

"You two should settle this on your own," Maria said, lifting her purse from the patio table around the corner from Starbucks. "Elena, Michael knows what I'll do to him if he acts up. Do you mind if I go home?"

Elena raised her caramel frappuccino to her lips and turned her gaze from Maria's pleading eyes to the teenage girls giggling at the table beside them. *Should I let her go and give her my copy of the letter? Or should I make her stay and watch him squirm some more? ...*

"No, Maria, I don't mind."

"Good."

Maria stood and kissed four cheeks. "Behave yourself, Michael."

She hurried to the street corner, lit a cigarette, and started across College Avenue.

Elena glared across the table at Michael and reminded herself to be silent and make him grovel.

His shoulders sagged. His eyes shifted back and forth between her and the black iron stairway attached to the side of the building. He wiped the back of his hand across the puddle of sweat between his lower lip and chin.

"Once again, Elena, I'm sorry for attacking you publicly. It was cruel of me. I never dreamed you'd threaten my livelihood."

She bit her tongue to muzzle herself.

"The letter was post-marked yesterday," he continued. "I called Joe Lombardi and told him I sent a certified letter to Harrisburg. He said there's a ninety-five percent chance it'll arrive tomorrow."

Elena held her glare. Michael studied the stairway a while and turned to her. "I learned more than I ever wanted to know about certified mail this afternoon. You may be able to stop the letter before it's delivered. Can I show you what I found out?"

She counted under her breath. *One, two, three, four—*

"Do I have to beg?"

She finished counting to ten and shook her head.

"Can I show you what I learned?"

She nodded. He leaned over the arm of his chair, pulled his laptop out of his leather bag, and opened it on the table.

"It'll take me a second to connect to their Wi-Fi."

Elena bit her tongue harder. The stab of pain strengthened her resolve.

"Here it is," he said, his voice and hand shaking. "It's from the U.S. Postal Service's website." His eyes met hers. "It'd be easier if I read it out loud to you. Do you mind?"

She gave her head a quick shake. He leaned toward her and read in a low voice:

"Items are intercepted at the initial destination delivery unit and redirected at the request of the mailer. USPS Package Intercept service is not a guaranteed service. USPS does not refund the Package Intercept fee, as it is not charged until the package is successfully intercepted. When customers submit a Package Intercept request on-line, they will be provided with an estimated total (intercept fee plus estimated Priority Mail postage). The Postal Service will attempt to intercept and redirect the shipment, but does not guarantee that it will be able to do so."

"I wish they'd quit saying it's not guaranteed," Michael said, his eyes fixed on the laptop. "It costs $11.50 plus the cost of Priority Mail to return it. There's a link where customers can check the delivery status of a package or letter."

He peered at her over the screen, his eyes pleading. "Do you have the receipt in your purse?"

"No."

He sighed. His mouth drooped with boyish contrition. "What I did to you was wrong and immature, Elena. I'm very sorry."

Keep your guard up, she warned herself. *He'll say or do anything to get what he wants.*

She counted to ten again and watched him squirm. "Saying you're sorry does nothing to repair the damage you've done to my reputation."

"I know."

"You got only one of your facts straight. The deadliest one."

He gripped the edge of the table. "I know."

She crossed her arms and scowled at him. "Why should I save your ass?"

"Because you'll ruin me if you don't," he said, his voice trembling. "I'll lose my job. No one will hire me."

"Why didn't you think of that Saturday night?"

"I was too pissed to think."

"Too pissed to think?" she scoffed, rising to her feet. "That's how I felt when I wrote and mailed *this*." She reached into her handbag, lifted her copy of the certified letter, unfolded it, and smoothed it on the table in front of him. He handed the letter back to her, a look of defeat on his face.

"You've shot all your bullets, Michael, and I'm still standing." She refolded the letter, slipped it into her bag, and sat back down. "Who has all the leverage now?"

He slumped further in his chair. "I'll make it up to you, Elena. Anything you want."

She resisted the urge to gloat, pretended to study her nails, and reviewed her mental list of demands.

"You can start by posting an apology on Facebook."

A glimmer of hope sprang into his eyes. "I'll write it tonight."

She wrinkled her brow. "It better be good. None of your phony bullshit."

"Do you want me to say that you saved the baby who almost died?"

"No."

"Should I say you'd never be unfaithful, especially after James cheated on you?"

"Leave James out of it."

"What about the abortion?" he whispered, looking away. "Should I mention it?"

"No. It's true."

His eyes met hers.

"It was your abortion, too, Michael."

Regret lined his face. "I know."

He held her gaze a moment longer, then turned away. Elena reached for her drink and stared at the passing traffic. For the first time in thirty years, the two of them had broached the subject of the abortion. One part of her wanted to weep. Another part of her wanted to shout for joy that Michael had acknowledged their shared culpability.

He cleared his throat and faced her again. "I'll delete my post from Saturday night. And I promise to never bother you again."

"Regardless of what happens with the letter?"

"Yes."

His look of remorse faded, but his intensity remained. "How soon can you go online and submit the intercept request form?"

"I won't be home until nine or so."

"That late?"

"It'll be the deadline for your apology." She lifted her handbag from the back of her chair and set it on her lap. "If it's acceptable to me, I'll submit the request form tonight. If it's not, you should expect a call from the Auditor General's office."

"If the letter gets through, will you call Harrisburg and deny your claim?"

She shook her head twice. "I won't lie."

"Who else knows about the letter?"

"No one."

"Keep it that way. Please."

"That'll depend on whether you leave me alone." The metal legs of her chair scraped against the brick pavers. "Your mother would be devastated to learn that you accepted a bribe."

He pulled his money clip from his pocket, stripped off a twenty-dollar bill, and laid it on the table in front of her. "For the post office."

She pushed the money back to him. "Buy your mother some flowers."

Elena stood and swung her bag over her shoulder. "Send Sara a text after you post your apology. She'll let me know."

"How will you let me know whether the post office intercepts the letter?"

"I'll email you as soon as I find out. Between now and then, don't pester me."

જી જી જી

It was dark when Elena arrived at Sara's home. Within minutes they were sitting on the deck with an open bottle of wine. The mid-September air felt like summer but smelled like fall.

"Here's the letter."

Sara slid the candle closer, held the paper in its light, and squinted. "It's so official looking, like something a lawyer would write. Dear Mr. DePasquale."

Elena basked in her sister's body language.

"I like the introduction. San Francisco … Spared no expense. … Ouch! Throwing cash around. … Inform me of the findings."

She set the letter on the table. "No wonder Michael is scared shitless."

"It took me over two hours to write it."

"I couldn't have written it in two days." Sara reached for her wineglass. "While we're waiting for his text, tell me again what happened at Starbucks. Start at the beginning."

"Maria arrived first. They probably arranged it that way to try to soften me up."

While Elena recounted the story, Sara peppered her with questions and checked her phone every few minutes.

She glanced at it again when Elena finished. "It looks like he's going to make us wait until nine. Maybe that means his ego isn't getting in the way of his apology."

"Or the opposite."

Sara refilled her wineglass. "How are things with you and Patrick?"

"I don't know."

"What do you mean you don't know?"

Elena crossed her arms and sighed. "I haven't heard from him since early yesterday afternoon."

"Are you two still going hiking on Saturday?"

"Yes."

Sara's eyes narrowed. "Would playing hard to get help?"

"Help who, him or me?"

"Give it time, Elena, give it time. You told him you'd be patient. You'll know soon enough if you two are meant—"

The wrought iron table rattled. Sara grabbed her phone and read aloud: "Please tell Elena I've held up my end of our bargain."

She slid her iPad to the edge of the table and awakened it.

"What did he say?"

Sara tapped and scrolled. "Here it is."

She read aloud:

"I'd like to apologize to Elena Shaughnessy for what I wrote about her here on Saturday night.

"In my rush to hurt and embarrass her, I failed to mention that she was cleared of any wrongdoing in the Department of Health's investigation of the near fatal baby delivery. Everyone who knows Elena knows that she's an outstanding nurse. Doctors and nurses have shared firsthand accounts to me of how she saved babies' lives.

"After seeing her and her new friend at the Wooden Angel on Saturday night, my jealousy got the best of me. Elena would never be unfaithful.

"I wish her well."

Sara looked up from the screen. "Wow! You couldn't have written it better yourself."

"I know." Elena breathed another sigh of relief. "Make sure he deleted the post from Saturday night."

Sara tapped and scrolled and set her iPad in front of Elena. "It's gone. Do you think the Harrisburg post office will be able to intercept the letter?"

"No."

"Why not?"

"Because I never mailed it."

CHAPTER FORTY-FOUR

Life shrinks or expands
in proportion to our courage.
–Anaïs Nin

The following afternoon Elena turned out of the hospital parking lot and called Sara.

"Elena, Michael's freaking out. We've exchanged at least thirty texts since your lunch break."

"Good. He deserves to suffer."

"I got swept up in the drama and wove a tale."

Elena chuckled. "This ought to be good. What did you tell him?"

"He thinks you've talked your way through five layers of postal bureaucracy and got the postmaster, Robert Varano, involved in chasing down the letter."

"*What?*"

"I found his name online. Michael thinks the main Harrisburg post office received your letter yesterday afternoon and loaded it onto a delivery vehicle this morning. It remains undelivered—at least there's no record of delivery—but they can't seem to lay their hands on it. I've alternated between raising and dashing his hopes. He's shitting bricks as we speak."

Elena laughed. "You're a character."

"I feel like I'm in a movie."

"Well, the movie is about to end. I'll email him as soon as I get home. Thanks for all your help, Sara."

"Thank *you*. I've had more excitement in one afternoon than most married women have in a month."

They shared another laugh and said goodbye.

Moments later Elena stood at her kitchen peninsula and typed on her laptop:

Michael,
    You dodged a bullet this time. The Harrisburg post office was able to intercept the letter. It's on its way back to me.
    Be well and let there be peace.
    Elena

She pressed Send and happy-danced around the kitchen.

❧ ❧ ❧

That evening after dinner Elena crossed River Road and walked along the curb toward oncoming traffic. She reflected on the middle course she'd struck in defending herself.

Instead of sending the letter or backing down, I outwitted Michael and held him accountable. He'll never underestimate me again. ... Forgiving myself for the abortion freed me from thinking I needed to tear him down to build me up. ... Thank God this chapter of my life is over.

She gazed downriver. Ten miles away, above the Shippingport Nuclear Power Plant, veils of steam painted the cloudless sky a white shade of gray. The nearest stream of vapor resembled a question mark, backwards and dotless, as if a second-grader had painted it.

Images flashed in her head. *Jack, Emma, and Dad are healthy, happy, and independent. ... The condo feels like an empty nest now, but it'll eventually feel like home. ... I hope my girls are okay. Dad's flower beds need me. ... My gray roots need a touch-up. Is my hair appointment next Tuesday or the week after? ... No wonder I can't remember, I'll be fifty next month. Fifty sounds SO old. ... What will my life be like ten years from now? What if my kids and grandkids live far away? I don't want to grow old alone and become a cat lady. Maybe I'll get an Australian Shepherd puppy with a black eye-patch. I'll name him Patch.*

She pictured herself walking with Patrick and Patch along River Road, attracting a crowd. *I don't need a man in my life, but I want one. ... It's been more than two days since I've heard from him. What if he can't let go of Kate?*

Elena walked faster and wondered if she'd end up subscribing to one of the online dating websites. A slideshow of first dates whirled through her mind: Gloomy Glen ... Suave Sam ... Pretentious Pete ... Dumb Dave ... Philandering Phil ... Uncle Albert ... Musclebound Max ... Neurotic Nick ... Rich Dick.

A squirrel chased another squirrel up the trunk of an oak tree and down a branch.

I wish Patrick would chase me. ... We make a great couple. We'll be best friends. Passionate lovers. Happily married. ... I'm not Kate, but I can love him just as much as she did.

She turned down the tree-lined gravel road toward the railroad tracks and river.

My strategy to get rid of Michael worked. Now I need to think of a way to keep Patrick from slipping away. ... He's worth it. I'm worth it. We're worth it. She kicked a rock the size of a tennis ball to the side of the road. *Being patient for six months may work, but it's passive. Better to err on the side of boldness. The sooner I know whether he can love me, the sooner we can move forward. Together or apart. ... But what if I say or do something foolish and scare him away? ... Trust yourself.*

She looked both ways for trains and hurried across the tracks.

You've thought it to death for nearly a week. Be a brave eagle, not a scared crow. Be honest with him. Tell him about Baby Catherine. Tell him how you finally overcame your grief. Tell him you've fallen in love with him. Do it now.

She pulled her phone from the pocket of her jeans, swiped and tapped the screen, and held it to her ear.

What should I say?

It rang four times.

Should I hang up or leave a message?

"Hello Elena."

"Patrick. I expected to get your voicemail."

"I hope you prefer me."

"I do. I'm—" She felt her courage melt. "I'm calling to invite you to dinner tomorrow evening. Are you available?"

"Yes. What time?"

"Six-thirty?"

"What can I bring?"

Wine will relax me. Loosen my tongue.

"How about a bottle of wine?"

"Red or white?"

"Either. I haven't decided what to cook. I have a few things to tell you, Patrick."

He hesitated. "Should I be worried?"

"No. I look forward to—to seeing you."

Chapter Forty-Five

True love never dies; it is only when we let go
that we can truly say goodbye.
–Ruth Jane Lajoie

Patrick worked a half-day that Friday and arrived home at noon. He changed into a pair of old shorts and a T-shirt, made a turkey sandwich, and wrapped it in a paper towel. After laying a shovel and a gallon of water in the trunk of his car, he backed out of the driveway and called Elena, hoping that she'd be on her lunch break.

She picked up after the second ring. "Hi Patrick."

"Hello Elena."

"You don't sound like yourself. Is something wrong?"

"Today would have been my mother's eighty-second birthday."

"I'm sorry."

"Thanks. Renee insisted on rescheduling my afternoon

appointments. I'm heading to the cemetery now and plan to stop at a nursery on the way. Do you have any flower recommendations?"

Elena thought a moment. "Is her tombstone flat or raised?"

"Raised."

"Mums are colorful and hardy."

"Mums for Mom. How fitting. Elena, the other reason I called." He hesitated. "I don't think I'd be a good dinner companion this evening."

"I understand."

"I'll be fine tomorrow. Can I still pick you up at eleven for our hike?"

❧ ❧ ❧

An hour later Patrick knelt in front of his mother's tombstone at Sylvania Hills Cemetery. Aboveground he had the place to himself. The earthy smells of grass clippings and chrysanthemums clung to his nostrils. He removed the third mum from its nursery container and lowered it into the remaining hole. After sprinkling and tamping potting soil, he brushed his hands against his shorts and lifted the plastic jug.

The water sounded happy to be free. The dirt drank lustily.

He dropped the empty container behind him, picked up a wax paper bag, and gazed at his mother's memorial photograph.

"Happy birthday, Mom," he whispered. "You would have turned eighty-two today. In keeping with tradition, I brought you two Kretchmar's lady locks."

Patrick opened the bag, laid the cream-filled pastries on the ground between the tombstone and the mums, and shook the remnants of powdered sugar from the bag.

"They'll sweeten your soil."

Soil, soul—soul, soil. The words echoed in his head.

He crumpled the bag, tossed it into a nursery container, and sat on the grass with his arms swung back like a double kickstand. Three cumulus clouds lulled overhead.

"You're in a better place now, Mom. I hope heaven is everything you expected and that you and your old dance partners jitterbug every night."

He looked at her photo again. "I have some big news to share with you. I've been dating a woman named Elena. You met her a few times, back when your memory wasn't so great. You said we looked good together. I'll never forget when you told us the story about your wedding cake hat. Speaking of which, it's now Elena's hat. She was honored and thrilled when I gave it to her. I donated all your other hats to Friendship Ridge."

He shifted his weight, reached forward, and slid the fingers of his right hand across the letters etched into the granite.

IRENE A. JAMESON

"I'm surprised by how good it feels to visit you here, Mom."

Mum blossoms tickled the underside of his arm as he pulled it away from the tombstone. He tipped his head back and tried to solve the mystery of how he could be so comfortable grieving his mother and the opposite when it came to Kate.

She was half Mom's age when she died. They both died suddenly. … Kate's been gone so much longer.

It dawned on him that the clouds were no longer a trio. One of them continued to hover overhead. The other two were drifting eastward, side-by-side.

"I need to fly again," he said under his breath.

※ ※ ※

A little over an hour later, Patrick carried three orange mums across the lawn to Kate's tombstone at the Sewickley Cemetery. He set the flowers on the grass, laid his hands on the slab of granite, and whispered, "Hi Kate. I miss you."

He returned to his car for the shovel, potting soil, and refilled water jug. While walking back, he marveled at how weathered Kate's tombstone was compared to his mother's.

He unearthed the remains of the petunias he'd planted in May and dug holes for the mums. Tossing the shovel onto the ground, he pulled a piece of red paper from his back pocket and knelt in the grass.

"I wrote you a letter on the back of a nursery flyer."

Patrick unfolded the paper and read aloud:

Dear Kate,

Since you've been gone, I've nearly drowned in a sea of grief. I know you wouldn't have wanted that for me. I'm sorry for letting you down. If I had died instead of you, you would have grieved twice as much as me, but for half as long. You would've found the courage to move forward sooner and find love again, without forgetting me.

I've fallen in love. Her name is Elena. You'd like her. She's a maternity nurse from Beaver with a son and daughter in college. Like you, she has a personality and style all her own and treats me like a prince.

Finding Elena doesn't mean I'm losing you, Kate.

Forever in Love,
Your Patrick

He tore the letter into three pieces, folded them in half, and dropped one into each hole.

Chapter Forty-Six

Absence diminishes mediocre passions and increases
great ones, as the wind extinguishes candles and fans fires.
—*François de La Rochefoucauld*

That evening Elena dined on her balcony with Abel Keogh's
Dating a Widower. Ninety minutes passed in a blur. Dusk's
gray veil was descending. She read the closing paragraph of
the chapter "How to Talk to a Widower" and turned the page.

Chapter 6: Sex and Intimacy with Widowers

"This ought to be good," she said under her breath. Her
eyes raced. She licked her finger and started to flip the page
before she finished reading it.

*This book was written for me. Too bad I didn't discover it a
few months ago.*

Her phone swished, announcing a text. She lifted it off the table and smiled.

Today 7:42 PM
The orange mums look terrific. My day turned out to be much better than I had expected. How was yours?

Good. His visit to the cemetery went well. She marked her page and typed:

Today 7:44 PM
I'm glad your day got better. Did you know that it's going to be sunny tomorrow with a high near 80?

Today 7:45 PM
Yes. Do you have any plans on Sunday?

Today 7:45 PM
Not yet. Why?

Today 7:46 PM
Would you like to go to the Pirates game with me?

Elena typed, erased, and typed some more. *Take a risk. See how he responds.*

Today 7:49 PM
Yes, but only if you promise to chase me to first base after the game.

Today 7:50 PM
If you run fast, I may not be able to catch you until second base. Or third.

Today 7:51 PM
I'll wear my running shoes.

Today 8:02 PM
And I'll wear sandals. ... (Sorry, I was on the phone.) Would you mind if we got an earlier start tomorrow?

Today 8:03 PM
Not at all. What time?

Today 8:03 PM
Seven

Today 8:04 PM
Yikes! Why so early?

Today 8:07 PM
I have a hot date tomorrow night. I need to get a haircut and make myself presentable. Unfortunately, this takes longer than it did 20 years ago.

Today 8:08 PM
Who's the lucky girl?

Today 8:09 PM

It's a secret. I couldn't get her out of my mind all week.

Today 8:10 PM

I'm excited for you. Where are you taking her?

Today 8:12 PM

To a special place. I'm going to surprise her. I want to show her how much I care about her and thank her for being patient with me.

Today 8:15 PM

How romantic. Women love surprises. You'll score bonus points if you let her know how to dress for the occasion.

Today 8:19 PM

I'll be sure to let her know. Speaking of how to dress, in case you slip and fall into the creek tomorrow or someone challenges you to a splash battle, I suggest you bring a change of clothes, an extra pair of shoes, and a bikini.

Today 8:20 PM

My bikini retired a few years ago.

Today 8:21 PM

That's too bad. It would have increased your chances of winning the splash battle, from none to slim.

Today 8:22 PM
I don't need a bikini. I have other weapons in my arsenal.

Today 8:23 PM
Should I wear a wetsuit and scuba fins?

Today 8:24 PM
YOU in a snug wetsuit? You wouldn't need to splash me to get me _ _ _.

Today 8:26 PM
Then I'd better hurry to the scuba shop before it closes. Be sure to get lots of rest tonight.

Today 8:28 PM
You too. Instead of six days, it feels more like six weeks since I've seen you.

Today 8:29 PM
It does. I'm excited to see you, Elena. XO

Today 8:29 PM
And I you, Patrick. OX

Elena pressed Send. "That's the Patrick I know and love. I wonder what got into him."

She went inside, washed her dinner dishes, and debated whether to borrow Emma's white bikini.

My 36-C's could be just the medicine he needs. Especially if he splashes me. ... Where is he taking me tomorrow night?

Chapter Forty-Seven

Romance is everything.
–Gertrude Stein

"Portersville. Isn't this our exit?" Elena asked Patrick, wondering if the excitement of their being together again had distracted him.

"It would be if we were going to McConnell's Mill."

"Where are you taking me?"

"I'm kidnapping you."

She returned his wink. "Being abducted by a certain Sewickley psychiatrist is high on my bucket list."

"Guess where I'll be holding you hostage?"

"Hmm? ... Presque Isle on Lake Erie?"

"No. Guess again."

"Niagara Falls?"

"You're getting closer, but not geographically."

She scrunched her brow. "A waterfall?"

"Waterfalls. It's the best place in Pennsylvania for a splash battle."

"Did you bring your wetsuit?"

"It's in the trunk."

She rolled her eyes.

"You don't believe me?"

"No."

He pointed out the windshield. "There's a pull-off up ahead. Would you like me to show you?"

"Yes."

They drove in silence for a moment. Patrick veered off the interstate, parked, and scrambled to the back of the car as if a bathroom emergency had arisen. He smacked the corner of the trunk to get her attention, waved at her, and pointed to his right.

Elena pivoted in her seat and watched him stroll into a meadow where the sun was kissing frostlike beads of light through the thick September dew. He bent over and gathered a cluster of yellow daisies. "Aw, how sweet of him." He meandered to a patch of Queen Anne's lace, helped himself, and started back to the car. After vaulting over the guardrail, he tucked the flowers behind his back, stepped to her door, opened it wide, and swung his arm around.

"For you, sweetheart."

"I love wildflowers!" She held them to her nose. "Thank you, Patrick."

"I knew we'd stumble across wildflowers at some point today, so I brought you a vase from home." He closed her door, opened the one behind her, and reached to the floor.

The rumble of a passing truck faded. "I've never heard of a kidnapper being so thoughtful," she said over her shoulder.

"I've never heard of a kidnappee being so beautiful."

He returned to the driver's seat and poured water from an Aquafina bottle into a Mason jar unlike any she'd ever seen. Tall, slope-shouldered, and blue-tinted, it looked like a container royal gardeners in England would have used for canning during the lean days of World War II.

He set the vase on the leather console. "I'll hold it here while you perform your floral magic."

Elena laid the flowers on her lap, twirled a few sprigs of Queen Anne's lace, and dropped them into the jar. "Guess what two things wildflowers remind me of?"

"Your girls?"

"That's the easier one," she said, nodding. "What else?"

He gazed at the meadow a moment and turned to her. "Tie-dyed hippies who just bathed at a Macy's fragrance counter?"

"Ha! Excellent guess."

She dipped her head toward him and combed her fingers through her wavy bob.

"Your hair?"

She sat upright again. "It's wild and colorful."

"I see a connection to much more than your hair."

Patrick wedged the jar between his legs and ran his fingers up her thigh and along the skin above her elbow, leaving a trail of goose bumps in their wake. "Your legs are the roots, your arms the stems."

He brushed his fingertips down her cheek and across her lower lip, making her smile widen, her pulse leap. "Your cheeks and lips are the petals."

He raked his fingers through her hair and kissed her forehead. "You're my wildflower."

Her heart swelled in her chest. She tipped her head back and met his eyes. He kissed her lips, rubbed the tip of his nose against hers, and slid back into his seat.

She remembered to breathe. "Please don't send a ransom note to my family."

"I won't, provided you agree to pay the ransom yourself."

"With what?"

He tried not to smile. "We'll start with kisses."

They exchanged longing looks.

"I missed you this week, Elena."

"I missed you, too."

She slipped three daisy stems into the vase, like arrows into a quiver, and wrapped her hand around the mouth of the jar. "Do you mind keeping this here?"

Before Patrick could reply, she gave the vase a quarter turn and pressed it against his crotch.

His mouth gaped open. "What's gotten into you?"

"Me? What's gotten into *you*?"

"You."

"Good answer."

She lifted two daisies from her lap and snapped an inch or so off each of their stems. "Did something happen this week?"

"A couple of things." He started the engine. "I'll tell you once we get back on the road."

Elena tingled with curiosity. She stole glances at him as he drove toward the white line, waited for two trucks to pass, and pulled onto the highway.

"Tuesday evening your father and I ate Chinese takeout on his patio."

A hundred questions raced through her mind. "He never said anything to me."

Patrick set the cruise control and met her gaze. "We agreed that I would tell you."

"What did you two talk about?" she asked, trying to sound casual.

"Mostly about how hard it is to let go of the past." He checked his mirrors and crossed into the passing lane. "I don't think he'd mind my telling you that he regrets not being more open to meeting Dorothy twenty years ago."

Elena read between the lines and smiled. "I'm glad you two had a talk."

She lowered the last of the Queen Anne's lace into the vase, put the finishing touches on the arrangement, and hugged the jar between her thighs. "What was the other thing that happened to you this week?"

His eyes bounced from hers to the road and back. "After visiting my mother's grave yesterday, I stopped at the nursery again and planted mums at Kate's grave. I wrote and read a letter to her."

"Are you comfortable talking about it?"

He nodded. "I apologized for letting her down."

"You let her down?"

"She wouldn't have wanted me to grieve for as long as I have. She would've found the courage to move forward sooner."

"I see." Elena stared at a pasture dotted with bales of hay.

Listen. Let him talk.

"I told her about you."

"Oh?" She turned to him.

"Besides telling her you're a Mom and a maternity nurse, I told her she'd like you and that the two of you have a lot in common."

"We've never really talked about what Kate and I have in common, besides you. Did you mention anything specific?"

"I told her you have a style and personality all your own." He turned his eyes back to the road. "That you treat me like a prince. And ..."

"And?"

His smile widened into a grin. "And that you have perfect breasts."

"You didn't say *that*." She punched his arm playfully and buried her nose in the flowers.

He tickled her ribs. Laughing, she captured his hand and pinned it against her thigh. The mischief on his face gave way to a look of contented resignation. The sparkle in his eyes remained.

"How did you feel after you read the letter to her?"

"After reading it, I tore the paper into three pieces, dropped one into each hole, and planted the mums. Since then I've felt a sense of peace. Closure."

She bit her lip to contain her smile and waited for him to say more.

"If Kate had known you and known she was going to die young, she would've wanted us to get together."

Elena opened her mouth to speak but didn't.

Patrick exited onto I-80 east. She clutched the neck of the vase and looked at the rural landscape without seeing it. *How wonderful that he sought Dad's advice and wrote a goodbye letter to Kate.* The meaning of his words seeped from her mind into the nooks and crannies of her heart. *He wants us to be a couple. We're meant to be together. … Tell him about Michael.*

She turned to him. "Michael attacked me on Facebook last Saturday night."

Patrick's brow wrinkled. "I'm sorry to hear that."

"In a way, he did me a favor."

"A favor?"

"I'll spare you the details for now, but without retaliating publicly, I gave him a taste of his own medicine. He apologized on Facebook, and I'm certain he'll never bother me again."

"Good for you."

Elena reminded herself of the other two things she wanted to share with Patrick. *Now isn't the time to tell him about Baby Catherine. Or that I'm in love with him. Besides, I want him to say it first.*

She glanced at the dashboard clock. "Where are you taking me?"

"To my favorite place in Pennsylvania. A waterfall lover's paradise called Ricketts Glen State Park."

"Where is it?"

"On the western edge of the Pocono Mountains."

Her mouth fell open. "The Poconos are all the way across the state."

"It's a four-and-a-half-hour drive. That's why I wanted us to get an early start." He lifted a book from the pocket of his door and handed it to her.

She read the cover aloud: "*Pennsylvania Waterfalls: A Guide for Hikers and Photographers* by Scott E. Brown."

"Open to my bookmark and you'll see photos of waterfalls on the Falls Trail."

She flipped through glossy pages puckered by dried water and marked up with a pen and folded corners. "They're beautiful."

"They're much better in person. A few miles from the park there's a secluded stream that the author regards as the prettiest in the state."

"I can't wait to see it all with you."

"When we arrive, we'll spread a blanket in a field and eat the picnic lunch you packed for us."

He grabbed a pillow from the backseat and handed it to her. "Put your seat back and I'll treat you to a playlist of my favorite Miles Davis ballads. Take a nap if you'd like."

She reclined the seat and arranged the pillow behind her head. *There's no way I'll be able to sleep.* She closed her eyes and hummed the melody of "When I Fall in Love."

His fingers stroked the underside of her wrist. "Listen to Miles blow his trumpet as if he's making love to his woman."

For the next thirty or forty minutes, they spoke without words as Patrick caressed Elena's scalp, her cheek and jaw line, her lips, her ear and neck, her arm and hand, her knee, her thigh.

Lava stirred inside her volcano.

CHAPTER FORTY-EIGHT

Love is the poetry of the senses.
–Honoré de Balzac

Midafternoon Patrick and Elena stood at the edge of the Falls Trail watching Kitchen Creek tumble over a ledge and roar downstream like a sheet of nervous ice. Aromas of dampness, ancient and newborn, filled the air. The chatter of young male voices grew louder until two preteens passed behind them.

"Be careful," shouted a woman in a maternal New York accent.

Patrick pulled *Pennsylvania Waterfalls* from the pocket of his daypack, opened it to a marked page, and finger-counted blue dots on a map.

"Twenty-one. Isn't it amazing that a three-mile hike could have that many falls?"

Elena nodded and joined him in exchanging greetings with a fortyish couple who appeared to be the boys' parents.

Patrick aimed his phone at the waterfall. A shaft of sunlight leaked through the forest canopy, casting a spotlight on his face. Gold starbursts surrounded the rims of his pupils. Narrow blue rings, which looked as if they had been painted by hand, stopped the whites of his eyes from spilling into the pools of green. Elena searched them and thought she saw love.

"Your eyes are kaleidoscopes," she said, smiling.

He slipped the phone into his pocket and turned to her, the corners of his eyes crinkling. "What do you see in them?"

"Mostly contentment."

He tucked a stray lock of hair behind her ear and tipped her chin up. "Your eyes are emeralds. … Is that joy I see in their depths?"

She nodded. He kissed her forehead and took a half-step back. His dilated pupils rolled like marbles down her face and paused at her neck before bouncing from her breasts to her eyes.

He wanted you to catch him looking. Flirt back.

"Guess what I haven't stopped thinking about since you picked wildflowers for me this morning?"

His eyebrows arched. "Please don't tell me you're thinking about reporting me to the Council for the Conservation of Roadside Wildflowers."

"No, you silly man." She made eyes at him. "Guess again."

"Have you been working up the courage to ask me to go skinny-dipping?"

"No," she whispered. "But an image of you in a tight wetsuit keeps popping into my head."

A lusty smirk spread across his face. "What keeps popping into mine is a picture of you wearing nothing but creek water."

Before she could respond, he pulled on her hand and started up the trail. "I can't wait to show you the prettiest stream in Pennsylvania."

"Won't that make you late for your big date tonight?"

He turned back to her and smiled. "My big date's not till late."

※ ※ ※

Virgin hemlocks and firs towered overhead. The slopes rising from either side of the streambed were too steep and rocky for trails. Patrick and Elena blazed their own path up Sullivan Run, splitting their time between wading through the creek up to their knees and dodging puddles, boulders, and sunbathing grasshoppers. They hadn't seen a soul since turning onto Sullivan Falls Road. More than fifteen minutes had passed since the mountain water had sent a wave of goose bumps up her legs.

The sound of an unseen fall beckoned them upstream. They hiked around a bend and stopped. Water gushed and foamed like a torrent of champagne over a tangle of boulders.

He tugged on her hand, pulling her closer. "Welcome to our private waterfall."

"It's gorgeous!"

He led her to a boulder below the falls. Centuries of water had carved the slab of gray sandstone into a slanted perch, perfect for viewing the falls. He climbed onto the rock and sat. Elena declined his offer of help and shimmied and twirled, her backside landing between his parted thighs, her feet dangling with his over the edge of the boulder. She leaned her back against his chest and nestled her head in the crook of his shoulder. He wrapped his arms around her and held her tight.

The dancing water and its music captivated them. His breath warmed her ear and neck. His heart beat against her back. He felt like home.

"Elena?"

She turned her head and tilted it back until their eyes met. "Yes?"

"I love you."

"I love you too, Patrick."

He kissed her lips.

She rested her head on his shoulder. A tear trickled down her cheek.

"Look, sweetheart," he whispered. Her eyes followed his finger to two hawks soaring high above them. "Aren't they majestic?"

Her mouth fell open. "Yes."

The pair of birds spent the next few minutes hunting from treetops, hovering for prey, and chasing each other—or so it seemed.

"*Kee-eeeee-ar,*" the smaller one squawked, and they flew out of sight.

Patrick sat up, lifting Elena with him. "Did you know that red-tailed hawks mate for life?"

"No."

They climbed off the rock and stepped toward the waterfall.

"Look again," he said, pointing above.

She tipped her head back and saw only sky. Cold water splashed her neck and the front of her T-shirt.

"Hey!"

She bounded a few steps forward, spun around, and kicked a sheet of water that landed on target. "Take *that.*"

"You kick like a girl," he yelled above the roar of the falls.

She dodged all but the tail of his kick-splash. "So do you."

The next flurry of splashes disturbed as much water as if two elephants had bathed.

"Catch me if you can," she shouted, fleeing for cover behind the boulder. He chased her and launched another attack. After ducking and escaping the worst of it, she stood and propped her hands on her hips in an "I dare you" pose.

"You've met your match, mister."

"Tell me something I don't already know."

They stared each other down. With each breath, the expression on Patrick's face evolved from that of a warrior to that of a lover.

"You look incredibly sexy, Elena."

"Men will say anything when they're chasing their prey." She dashed to the side of the creek.

He followed her to the edge of her splashing range and held his fire. "Why didn't you tell me you look this hot in a wet T-shirt?"

She kept her eyes on him and turned, giving him a profile view. "You never asked."

He took two steps toward her and stopped. "You have the body of a woman half your age."

"You haven't seen me naked in broad daylight."

"I haven't." He rubbed his hands together and grinned. "But I'm about to."

"In your dreams, buddy."

She kick-splashed him, darted upstream, and turned back a few feet below where the falling water sprayed the creek.

He threw his T-shirt onto the rocky shore and strode toward her. A hunger for something other than food rose like fumes from his body. He stopped five feet away and undressed her with his eyes.

A wave of anticipation washed over her. She widened her stance, securing her feet in tiny cracks in the bedrock. *Should I surrender?*

Patrick held his hands out, palms up, and stepped closer.

"Do you surrender?" she asked.

He wrapped his hands around her wrists and pinned them behind her back, firmly but not too firmly. "Do *you* surrender?"

She tugged against his hold.

He tightened his grip and pressed his lips to her ear. "If you don't, you'll leave me no choice."

Elena jerked her wrists again.

He kissed her hard on the mouth. She gasped, turned her face away, and pretended to put up a fight. He backed her toward the falls, his groans and moans parrying hers like clattering swords. Water lapped over her shoulders and down their bodies.

He pulled her to him and kissed her again. She broke her hands free and clung to his neck, the waterfall's inexhaustible force thrusting her softness against his hardness. Their tongues explored, teased, caressed—hungrily, tenderly. She longed to feel his naked body pressed against hers.

Patrick tore his mouth away, peeled her soaked T-shirt up and over her head, and hurled it to the side of the stream. His stubbled cheeks and chin brushed against her cleavage, pouring fuel on the fire in her loins. He took a half-step back, unhooked her bra's front clasp, and opened the lace gates to her breasts.

His eyes lusted. Elena leaned back and let the water push the strap over her left shoulder, then her right. He guided them down her arms, past her hands, and stuffed most of the fabric into the pocket of his shorts.

The tips of his thumbs grazed the tight buds of her nipples, making her breath catch, her knees weak. She held his shoulders and bent over as he knelt in the stream, removed her shorts and panties as one, and flung them to the shore. He kissed a line from hipbone to hipbone. His fingers glided down her triangle of hair and opened the folds of her sex.

Her body ached with need, her heart with love.

He rose to his feet and kissed her neck. Her hands trailed down his chest and torso. She unbuttoned and unzipped his shorts. His manhood pulsed, straining to escape its cotton prison. She hooked her thumbs inside the waistband and crouched, pulling his shorts and boxers down his legs and under his feet.

Patrick helped her up, led her to the side of the falls, sat down in a few inches of water, and leaned his back against the dripping, mossy wall of rock.

Their eyes locked. Elena tossed his shorts onto the shore, laced her fingers through his, and lowered herself onto him.

Their bodies melted into one.

Chapter Forty-Nine

You know you're in love when you don't want to fall asleep
because reality is finally better than your dreams.
–Dr. Seuss

When they arrived back at the car, Patrick built a makeshift dressing room by opening the passenger doors and draping their picnic blanket over the windows. No cars passed as they changed into dry clothes and settled into their seats.

He started the engine. "I'm starving. Are you hungry?"

"Famished."

Elena flipped the sun visor down and opened the vanity mirror.

He pulled a slip of paper out of his wallet. "Here's the address of a local restaurant with good online reviews. It's called the Brass Pelican. The food will probably be better than anything we'll find along the interstate. What do you think?"

"Sounds good to me." She bent her head toward him. "Look what the creek did."

He buried his free hand in her mop of damp curls and tilted her head back until her eyes were level with his. "I thought I did that."

She matched his grin and returned her gaze to the mirror. While she tamed her curls into waves, he typed the restaurant's address into the GPS and started up the road. Gravel rattled against the wheel wells. She felt his eyes on her.

"Imagine yourself a year from now, sweetheart," he said. "What one thing about today do you think you'll remember most—besides our lovemaking?"

She closed the visor and turned to him. He winked at her. "Sorry for sounding like a therapist."

"I like your questions, Patrick. They make me think." Elena reached for his hand. "Hmm, a year from now ..."

She scanned the forest landscape through his side of the windshield. Images from their day flitted across her mind's eye, some as still photos, others as movie clips. His early morning bear hug and kiss. The look on his face when he told her they were going on a day trip. Wildflowers. Her sleepless nap and their long talk afterwards. His understanding and empathy when she told him about Baby Catherine. Their picnic in the meadow. Hiking. Waterfalls. Hawks. Their splash battle. His muscled chest. Feeling adored. Feeling sexy. Their shared ecstasy.

"It'll take me a week to narrow my list to one thing."

"Then how about your three favorites? In no particular order."

"Three I can do."

She closed her eyes and sifted through her memory again, eliminating items one by one. When three finalists remained, she turned to him. "I'll never forget how surprised and thrilled I was to learn that you were whisking me away for the day."

His eyes filled with mischief. "I remember telling you that I was kidnapping you."

"Kidnapping is a form of whisking. They both take planning. Initiative."

"Okay, that's one." He turned back to the road.

"The Falls Trail hike was spectacular. I never dreamed such a place existed. And it's practically in our own backyard."

"Rickett's Glen is a well-kept secret. I only discovered it a few years ago."

"And the third thing—" She waited until his eyes met hers. "This one's my favorite, hands down."

"What?"

Her lips curled into a smug smile. "Winning our splash battle."

Patrick's eyes grew wide. "I thought we agreed it was a tie?"

"The physical battle was a tie. Both of us were drenched. But I won the psychological battle."

"How?"

"You couldn't take your eyes off me."

Elena inhaled, arching her back, luring him.

"Eyes on the road, buster." She took his chin in her hand and gave it a quarter turn to the left.

The navigation system's female voice instructed him to turn right and travel for one-point-three miles.

"All kidding aside, Patrick, I know what I liked best about today. Besides you-know-what."

"What?"

"The way you treated me with such a blend of tenderness and passion. I've waited my whole life for that." She leaned closer and kissed his cheek.

"What's your favorite memory?" she asked, settling back in her seat.

"Our waterfall kiss, after you surrendered."

"*You* surrendered first."

He nodded agreement. "It was a small price to pay to …"

"To what?"

His smirk widened. "Have my way with you."

"That was my plan all along."

"I know."

She jabbed him with her elbow. "No you didn't."

The navigation guide announced a right turn and directed him to proceed for six-tenths of a mile.

They drove in silence. Two chestnut horses grazed in a pasture. Patrick's restless eyes and hands told Elena that he doubted a restaurant could be located in such a remote area.

"*You have arrived at your destination.*"

He started up a winding, tree-lined driveway. A log home at the crest of the hill appeared, disappeared, and reappeared.

"That doesn't look like a restaurant," he said in a puzzled voice.

"It doesn't. And there aren't any cars."

He braked to a stop at the top of the driveway and reached for the slip of paper and his phone. "I must have the wrong address."

She pointed out the windshield. "Don't you love the green metal roof?"

He turned to her and took her hand in his. "Do you remember when I told you we were going someplace special tonight, Elena?"

"Yes?"

This is that someplace special."

❧ ❧ ❧

Elena awoke the next morning to the sound of soft snoring and curtains flapping in the breeze. The crisp mountain air smelled of pine and love. Lying naked on her back, her eyes closed, she basked in Patrick's breath tickling her hair, his arm resting below her breasts, his leg crossing hers in a crooked X.

She opened her eyes and, with catlike grace, lifted his arm, rolled toward him, scissored his leg between hers, and laid his hand on her hip. Watching him sleep, she reflected on their night of passion. She purred with contentment. Anticipation.

She nestled her cheek against his chest and closed her eyes. The rhythmic motion and sound of his heartbeat nearly lulled her back to sleep. The sun peeked through the curtains.

Today is the last day of summer. A summer I'll never forget. … If we hadn't met, both of us would still be trapped inside our emotional straitjackets. Grief. Guilt. Living in the past. … Each of us fought and won our own wars. Patrick is my reward. And I'm his. … I'm going to shower him with love. Not to try to make him forget Kate, but to pick up where she left off. I'll—

He kissed her forehead. "Good morning, darling."

"Good morning, love."

CHAPTER FIFTY

My love is deep; the more I give to thee,
The more I have, for both are infinite.
— *William Shakespeare*

Six weeks later Patrick and Elena joined ten or twelve other couples at Sara and Dan's annual Halloween party. The hosts, dressed and hatted as Bonnie and Clyde, greeted their guests by waving snub-nosed revolvers and escorting them like hostages to the wet bar off the kitchen.

Emma and her date came dressed as Olive Oyl and Popeye. Jack and his girlfriend Maggie strutted into the party looking groovy, he in his grandfather's green leisure suit and she in an orange pantsuit she'd found on a Goodwill mannequin. Fred and Dorothy disguised themselves as the old man and his spinster daughter from the *American Gothic* painting, their pitchforks doing double duty as props and canes.

When the party was in full swing, Sara turned down the music, stepped to the open area between her kitchen and family room, and cleared her throat.

"May I have everyone's attention, please? … It's time to announce this year's winners for best costume." She lifted a bottle of wine to eye level. "The prize is a bottle of Ghost Pines Cabernet Sauvignon. For the first time I can remember, only two couples received votes. And the winners are …" Her eyes swept back and forth across the crowd. "Batman and Batgirl."

Everyone clapped and cheered as Patrick and Elena stepped forward hand in hand, wearing wide grins below their masks. Their capes waved behind them as if to cool the path their boots had blazed.

Sara hugged them both, handed the prize to Patrick, and said, "Stay up here you two."

Elena half-smiled, half-frowned. "But you promised."

Sara, slipping back into character as Bonnie, slid her pistol from the waistband of her skirt, waved it at Elena, and winked at Clyde, who pulled the trigger of his gun and aimed its flame at a "50" candle perched atop a Kretchmar's Bakery chocolate mousse cake.

"As most of you know and none of you can believe," Sara said, "my little sister turned fifty a few days ago. Elena wouldn't let me throw a party for her, so Clyde and I decided to piggyback a little celebration onto tonight's festivities."

Bonnie, Clyde, and Batman led the singing.

Batgirl blushed.